A cold reception for a cold fish . . .

"Look, Mr. Turnbull—*Phil*," Talia said, mimicking the familiar manner in which he'd addressed her, "Bea and Howie opened this restaurant in 1992. They're fully aware of the original concept, as you call it, but times have changed. This is the twenty-first century. We all have to grow—evolve, you might say."

Turnbull's smile faded. For a man who'd been blessed with stunning good looks—wide-set blue eyes, perfectly sculpted nose, full lips—he had all the natural charm of a scorpion. "Are you implying, Ms. Marby, that I'm some sort of Neanderthal?"

"No, not at all." Although, now that she thought about it—Talia blew out an exasperated breath. "Honestly, Mr. Turnbull, I don't understand your objection to the comic book store. They're all the rage these days. Think of it this way—it could bring a lot of new business to the arcade."

"Business for *this* place, maybe." His lips twisted in contempt. "But do you really think the kinds of people who shop at a comic book store are going to be interested in vintage lighting?"

Talia's patience had reached the end of its tether. "I don't know the answer to that, but right now Bea has a business to run, and it's my job to help her. So unless you're going to order some fish and chips, I'll have to ask you to leave."

Turnbull shook his clipboard at her. "This is not over, Ms. Marby, not by a long shot."

FILLET
OF
MURDER

LINDA REILLY

BERKLEY PRIME CRIME, NEW YORK

THE BERKLEY PUBLISHING GROUP
Published by the Penguin Group
Penguin Group (USA) LLC
375 Hudson Street, New York, New York 10014

USA • Canada • UK • Ireland • Australia • New Zealand • India • South Africa • China

penguin.com

A Penguin Random House Company

FILLET OF MURDER

A Berkley Prime Crime Book / published by arrangement with the author

Berkley Prime Crime Books are published by The Berkley Publishing Group.
BERKLEY® PRIME CRIME and the PRIME CRIME logo are trademarks of Penguin Group (USA) LLC.

For information, address: The Berkley Publishing Group,
a division of Penguin Group (USA) LLC,
375 Hudson Street, New York, New York 10014.

ISBN: 978-0-425-27413-2

PUBLISHING HISTORY
Berkley Prime Crime mass-market edition / May 2015

PRINTED IN THE UNITED STATES OF AMERICA

10 9 8 7 6 5 4 3 2 1

Cover illustration by Dan Craig.
Interior text design by Laura K. Corless.

To my husband, Bernie, whose faith in my success has been my guiding light. I can't count the times you performed culinary magic in the kitchen while I was busy trying to create it on the page. I am truly blessed.

ACKNOWLEDGMENTS

I want to express my deepest gratitude to my agent, Jessica Faust, who cheered me on from the beginning of this quest and never let me doubt myself. A big thank-you goes to Ellery Adams for taking a chance on me and introducing me to Jessica. Without the two of you, this book would not have been written.

A huge thank-you to my editor, Michelle Vega. Michelle, you are such a joy to work with, and I'm thrilled that you "get" my characters!

A shout-out to all the talented people at Berkley Prime Crime for their various contributions, and for such a fabulous cover.

A tip of the hat to Sophia Annas and Kelsey Dakoulas for willingly slogging through my first draft. Your insightful comments inspired me to make this a better mystery. And to Diane Rene, who supplied me with helpful tips on cooking when I needed them most!

I can't imagine having written this book without the support of the Guppies—an extraordinary online community of writers.

Last of all, hugs to Mom and Dad. You bestowed me with a lifetime of unconditional love and encouragement, and from that flowed my passion for books. A girl couldn't ask for two better parents.

ACKNOWLEDGMENTS

1

"Don't do it, Bea. He's not worth it." Talia Marby clamped her hand firmly around her employer's wrist, preventing Bea from pitching a chunk of fresh haddock at the man on the opposite side of the counter.

"But that wanker won't leave us alone, Talia!" Bea spoke as if the man weren't standing six feet away, glowering at them. "He comes in here nearly every day to harangue me, and he's gone to the hospital twice to bother Howie. I won't have it!"

"I know, and I agree," Talia soothed, her fingers still locked around Bea's slender wrist. Bea was in such a state that she was afraid to let go. Afraid that the man with the reddish-gold hair and ice-cool glare brandishing a clipboard at them would end up with a fish in the face. "But you know we can't solve anything this way, right?"

Cheeks flushed, raven-tinted curls springing out from her petite head, Bea Lambert let out a noisy sigh. "Right," she grumbled. She lowered her hand and yielded to Talia's grasp, letting the haddock dangle from her fingers.

Talia rescued the fish with one hand and squeezed Bea's shoulder with the other. "Let me handle this," she said, propelling Bea toward the opening next to the counter that separated the dining area from the kitchen of Lambert's Fish & Chips. "Whitnee should be here any minute. She can help you get the mushy peas ready. It's after eleven, so the lunch orders are going to start coming in."

Bea turned and cast one last look at the man, her leaf green eyes shooting darts at him. "Bother Howie again and you'll be sorry, Turnbull." She paused for effect and then tromped into the kitchen, vanishing into the small alcove that was hidden from view from the dining area.

Phil Turnbull, the man with the clipboard, pointed a finger at Talia. "You tell her I'm not finished with her. I just got in some new information about that comic book store and she needs to hear it whether she likes it or not!"

Standing as tall as her five-foot-two frame would allow, Talia speared Turnbull with the most threatening look she could muster. With her blond, pixie-style hair and small-boned physique—and wearing a blue apron with a grinning fish emblazoned across the front—she probably looked about as intimidating as her mom's cairn terrier. She was fed up, however, with Turnbull popping in almost daily to harass Bea, and would do whatever was necessary to defend her.

"You have nothing more to say, Mr. Turnbull. Bea and Howie have no objection to the comic book store coming to the arcade. Either you stop hounding them or they'll have to get a restraining order against you." Talia was fairly sure Bea would never go for such a thing, but it was all she could think of at the moment to get rid of the pest.

Turnbull's demeanor did an abrupt one-eighty. He flashed a toothy grin that put Talia in mind of a hammerhead shark, and then spoke his next words in a lilting tone, as if trying to pacify a crazy person. "Ms. Marby—Talia—legal action will surely not be necessary. I'm simply trying to remind Bea and Howie of the original concept of the Wrensdale Arcade, and why a comic book store would be totally out of place in this charming, old-world environment. If we all apply pressure by signing this petition, the landlord will be forced to give in. He can't fight us all, can he?" The smile stayed pasted on, but his gaze took on a predatory gleam.

Talia stopped short of rolling her eyes at his sudden change in attitude. The man was such a phony!

Turnbull was the proprietor of Classic Radiance, the vintage lighting store that sat at the far end of the shopping plaza known as the Wrensdale Arcade, in the Berkshires. Designed to resemble an old English village, the arcade boasted six other shops, three on each side, with Lambert's Fish & Chips located on the southern side, between Sage & Seaweed and Jepson's Pottery.

The aroma of hot oil wafting from the kitchen reminded Talia that the eatery would soon be bustling with customers. Standing here, having this argument with Turnbull, was a nuisance she didn't have time for.

"Look, Mr. Turnbull—*Phil*," Talia said, mimicking the familiar manner in which he'd addressed her, "Bea and Howie opened this restaurant in 1992. They're fully aware of the original concept, as you call it, but times have changed. This is the twenty-first century. We all have to grow—evolve, you might say." She tilted her chin slightly to one side, a habit she'd adopted as a stubborn toddler.

Turnbull's smile faded. For a man who'd been blessed with

stunning good looks—wide-set blue eyes, perfectly sculpted nose, full lips—he had all the natural charm of a scorpion. "Are you implying, Ms. Marby, that I'm some sort of Neanderthal?"

"No, not at all." Although, now that she thought about it—Talia blew out an exasperated breath. "Honestly, Mr. Turnbull, I don't understand your objection to the comic book store. They're all the rage these days. Think of it this way—it could bring a lot of new business to the arcade."

"Business for *this* place, maybe." His lips twisted in contempt. "But do you really think the kinds of people who shop at a comic book store are going to be interested in vintage lighting?"

Talia's patience had reached the end of its tether. "I don't know the answer to that, but right now Bea has a business to run, and it's my job to help her. So unless you're going to order some fish and chips, I'll have to ask you to leave."

Turnbull shook his clipboard at her. "This is not over, Ms. Marby, not by a long shot. I'm not going to abandon this fight, not when I'm so close. A comic book store will ruin the arcade, and I don't intend to let that happen. That hippie at the pottery shop is the only other holdout, and he's about to cave. Your precious Lamberts will, too. Mark my words." He pointed a manicured finger at her nose.

"Is that a threat, Mr. Turnbull?" Talia felt her temper rising, even as she kept her tone mild.

Turnbull's face reddened. "No, I didn't mean it that way. I just—"

"You'd best leave now," Talia told him. Feeling a bit like the Ghost of Christmas Future, she raised her arm and pointed ominously at the door. "Today is Wednesday, and on Wednesdays, at approximately ten to twelve, the chief of police picks up his order of fish and chips. I'm sure he'll be quite interested to hear about your campaign of harassment against Bea and Howie."

"Fine," he said, in a low growl, "but you tell your *boss* she hasn't heard the last of me." Turning on his heel, he stomped toward the door and whipped it open. Before he could step out onto the cobblestone plaza, Bea's young employee, Whitnee Parker, rushed past him at only slightly under the speed of sound. The force sent Turnbull tottering backward. He managed to keep his balance, but his clipboard clattered to the blue-and-white tile floor.

"Oh my gosh, I'm so sorry! Are you all right?" Whitnee bent down to retrieve the clipboard. As she did so, two of the textbooks jammed into her shoulder tote slipped out and tumbled to the floor. Turnbull kicked one of the books aside and snatched up his clipboard before she could get to it.

"What's the matter with you?" His upper lip curled into a snarl. "Don't you ever look where you're going?"

"I . . . I'm so sorry. I was running late and I didn't—"

"Why are you always such a ditz, anyway?"

Whitnee's face crumpled. Her pale brown eyes grew watery as she stood there, frozen, unable to respond.

Talia plunked down the haddock she'd been holding and moved quickly around the side of the counter into the dining area. She snagged Whitnee's books off the floor and said to Turnbull, "Get out."

Red-faced, Turnbull turned and stormed out onto the plaza, slamming the door behind him.

"Are you okay, Whitnee?" Talia slid a comforting arm around the young woman's shoulders.

Squashing away a tear with the heel of her hand, Whitnee gave a jerky nod. "Yeah, it's just . . . why did he have to be so mean? It wasn't like I was trying to knock him over!"

"I know. Of course you weren't." Talia tucked the two textbooks back into Whitnee's tote. "He's not a nice man, so don't let him get to you, okay? He's not even a customer. I don't think he's ever bought so much as a cup of coffee here." Talia knew that every person should be treated as a potential customer, but in Turnbull's case she made an exception.

Whitnee snuffled, and another tear fell onto her cheek. "Yeah, you're right. Jerks like that don't deserve the time of day, do they?" She forced her thin lips into a tepid smile. "I guess I better get into the kitchen, or Bea'll tan my hide. I'm already ten minutes late!"

Talia knew that Whitnee had recently turned twenty, but she found her to be a bit immature at times. Still, she couldn't help chuckling at the "tan my hide" comment. The tender-hearted Bea could barely bring herself to swat the occasional fly that found its way inside the eatery during the warmer months. She once spent the better part of an hour trying to persuade a persistent housefly to vacate the premises, a campaign that ended in a stalemate. Bea had just thrown up her arms in resignation when a customer strode in and out went the fly.

Talia stepped back around to the other side of the speckled aquamarine counter. With a groan, she stared at the poor haddock Bea had nearly lobbed at Turnbull. In retrospect, she almost wished she hadn't stopped her.

Talia swiped a napkin over the last traces of grease on her fingers, savoring the final mouthful of batter-coated, deep-fried haddock. Bea made her batter with a hint of lemon juice and a splash of malt vinegar, using a special recipe she'd brought with her from the UK. The result was—to use a tired cliché—to die for.

"You know, of course, luvvy," Bea said helpfully, "that the chief of police picks up his fish and chips on Fridays, not on Wednesdays." The kindly twinkle was back in her eyes, and her voice had regained that darling lilt she'd carried across the Atlantic from Edenbridge, in the county of Kent in England.

"Okay, it was a tiny fib." Talia grinned. "I couldn't think of any other way to get rid of that nuisance." She tossed the napkin, along with her empty plate, into the waste can.

It was after two, and the midday lull had taken hold. As much as Talia enjoyed the frenzy and bustle of the lunch rush, she relished this time of the day, when she and Bea and Whitnee could take a much-needed break. More than anything, Talia loved reconnecting with Bea, who'd been like a second mother to her since she was a teenager.

Talia still had to give herself an occasional pinch to remember where she was. A mere two months ago, she was occupying a plush cube in the offices of Scobey & Haight, one of Boston's up-and-coming commercial real estate firms. She'd endured the job for the better part of a year when she finally gave her notice to the manager. Adam Scobey, a thin-lipped man with a greasy comb-over, had found the swell of Talia's chest more gratifying than the commissions she'd been contributing to the company coffers. Shortly after Labor Day, she e-mailed him a polite resignation. She suffered through the two-week notice period, and on the last day skipped out of her cube and never looked back.

Chet Matthews, her almost-fiancé at the time, was furious when she left the job she'd worked so hard to snag. It was at Chet's urging that Talia had studied for the exam to become licensed as a commercial real estate broker. Prior to that, she'd been perfectly content working as a property manager for one of Boston's premier commercial landlords. But after acing the exam and jumping through all the necessary hoops, she'd landed the job Chet had pushed her to apply for. She knew within two months that she hated it, but she stuck it out for almost a year. Chet's refusal to support her decision to resign led her to a second, life-altering one: she ended their relationship.

"You're someplace else," Bea said, breaking into her thoughts. She waved a hand in front of Talia's face.

Talia laughed. "You're right. I *was* someplace else. Someplace I don't want to be ever again."

Bea nodded. "Then don't think about it anymore, luv." She reached over and squeezed Talia's hand. "Listen, Tal, I know this job is just a stopover for you until you find your niche again. But these last five weeks . . . well, I don't know what I'd have done without you. It's been such a joy, such a relief, having you here again. Howie's been out of commission for so long now . . ." Bea shook her head and reached for a napkin to dab at her leaky eyes.

Talia felt herself welling up, too. Bea was so special, such a treasure. Howie Lambert, Bea's husband of thirty-seven years, was recovering from a knee operation that hadn't gone well. He was still in the hospital, fighting an infection, and Bea's stomach was in a constant knot from worry.

"I'm just glad I could help, Bea."

Talia didn't want to tell her that she'd been posting her résumé online, hoping desperately to land a position as a property manager. Prior to working as a commercial real estate broker, she'd loved managing the rentals for one of the gorgeously restored office buildings on Summer Street in Boston. Negotiating with tenants and fulfilling their rental needs was so much more rewarding than the sales grind. For Bea, the timing of Talia leaving her job in Boston had been a godsend.

Talia was sixteen—nearly half her lifetime ago—when she'd gotten her first job at the fish and chips shop. A senior in high school, she'd squeeze in hours after school and work nearly every weekend. At the time, her folks had been going through a rough patch. Lambert's became her haven, her second home of sorts. It didn't matter if she was frying fish, mashing peas, or scrubbing tables—she'd loved every moment she was there.

Shaking away the memories, she glanced over at Whitnee. The girl had been unusually quiet through lunch. Normally she polished off a boatload of vinegar-spritzed fries, and at least two helpings of Bea's scrumptious mushy peas. Today she ate only a couple of fries and barely a spoonful of the peas.

"Whitnee, are you okay?" Talia said. "You seem a little down today."

Whitnee tugged on a lock of her straight, carrot-colored hair. "Yeah, I guess so. It's just . . . . I got a lot going on at school, and there's this one class I'm really sucking at—precalculus. Next week is the midterm, and I'm afraid I'm gonna flunk it." She shrugged her thin shoulders. "If I don't get a degree, it'll kill my mom. I'm really scared of disappointing her. I'm like, the only kid in our family who ever got into college!"

Whitnee was taking evening classes in business administration at Berkshire Community College. It was her first semester, and Talia had the feeling that the workload was overwhelming her.

Talia reached over and touched Whitnee's hand. "Is there anything I can do to help?"

"Not really." Whitnee's eyes were glassy with unshed tears. "I . . . just have to figure out how to study more efficiently. That's what my advisor at the school said."

Talia and Bea exchanged glances, and then Bea leaned forward toward Whitnee. "Listen, luv, I know your shift doesn't end till seven, but why don't you leave a little early today? You can use the extra time to study, or even take a walk and clear your head."

"That's real nice of you, Bea, but I . . . I actually need the money."

Bea sighed, chewing her lip. "Then how about you make up the time, in dribs and drabs? An hour here, an hour there. Maybe when midterms are over?"

Whitnee sniffled, and then gave Bea a thin smile. "Sure, I guess I could do that. Thanks, Bea." She emptied her plate into the waste can, collected her school tote, and scuttled out the door.

Bea turned to Talia with a sheepish look. "Poor girl, she looked so miserable. What could I do?"

"You did the right thing, Bea," Talia said. She grabbed a clean sponge and a bottle of lime-scented spray cleaner and began to wipe down the stainless-steel work counter.

With the exception of Mr. Ruggles, the retired lawyer who dined at Lambert's faithfully every Wednesday, the eatery was empty. Today he'd asked for a single order of mushy peas instead of his usual double, a sign that he was feeling especially low. His wife, Martha, had passed away three years ago, and according to Bea, he was lost without her.

Holding up a steaming pot of French-roast coffee, Talia

headed out to the dining area. "I'll bet you'd like a refill," she said to him with a bright smile.

"Oh, I surely would, young lady." He stabbed his fork through the last chunk of fried fish in his cone-shaped serving dish. "I'll take Bea's coffee any day over that sludge they serve at those chain stores!" He smiled at Talia, but the sadness in his faded brown eyes belied his good cheer. Having lost her grandmother six months earlier, Talia could understand the pain he must be feeling.

"I agree," Talia said, refilling his mug. "Can I get you anything else?"

"No, I'm fine, dear. But thank you."

From the kitchen, Talia could hear sputtering sounds coming from Bea. Before she had a chance to excuse herself to see what was troubling her boss, Bea burst into the dining area, gripping her smartphone as if it were a deadly weapon.

"Can you believe this?" Bea fumed, shaking the phone at her. "Now the bloody boob is badgering me by e-mail! How did he even get my e-mail address?"

Talia winced. She assumed Bea was talking about Turnbull, but with Mr. Ruggles sitting four feet away, a bit of discretion was in order. "Probably from the website," Talia said quietly. "Maybe we should—"

"Well, he's not going to get away with this," Bea said darkly. "Fire up the deep fry, Talia. I'm going to boil Phil Turnbull in oil!"

2

Talia had managed to get Bea calmed down, and the rest of the afternoon passed without any further distractions. The eatery had gotten busy again around four thirty, and by seven—closing time—they were both weary. Bea planned to head directly to the hospital to sit with Howie for an hour or so. Talia had paid him a visit the evening before, so tonight she was looking forward to relaxing with a light snack and a glass of wine.

She swung her Fiat into the stubby driveway of her nana's darling little bungalow. On the front lawn, a FOR SALE sign sat somewhat crookedly, the name and number of the realty company emblazoned across the bottom.

After Talia had left both her job and Chet, her mom had suggested that she move into the bungalow, at least until she figured out where her life—and her career—were headed. Her mom's twin sisters, Aunt Josie and Aunt Jennie, were completely on board with the idea, so Talia had moved her things in right away. At best it was a temporary solution, but she didn't want to think about a permanent place to live until she landed a new job . . . somewhere.

Or until someone made an offer on Nana's house.

The sight of the Realtor's lock box hanging over the doorknob sent a fresh wave of the blues washing over Talia. Nana's death this past spring had been shattering. Not a day passed that Talia didn't miss her. Now that the house was on the market, it wouldn't be long before it attracted a buyer. For its age, it was in decent shape, and it fit the category of homes brokers liked to dub "starters."

Inside, Talia dumped her purse onto the dilapidated tweed chair that her grandpop had been so attached to. After he died eleven years ago, Nana couldn't bring herself to get rid of the eyesore, in spite of the fact that she loathed it while he was living. "I know he's still sitting there," she would tell Talia with a catch in her throat. "How can I send it to the dump?"

By the time Talia had showered and thrown on a pair of jeans, along with her favorite UMass sweatshirt, it was after seven thirty. She hadn't given much thought to dinner, but since she'd had a filling lunch she opted for her default meal—a bowl of Rice Krispies with bananas. She was pouring a heap of cereal into one of Nana's pink-flowered soup bowls when her cell phone jangled.

"Hope you haven't eaten, because I'm on my way over with a pizza and a bottle of wine!"

"Rachel! I thought you had an open house at the school." Rachel Ostroski was Talia's BFF going back to their early school days. They'd kept in touch throughout their college years and still remained close. An elementary school teacher, Rachel was currently single and looking for love on one of the online dating sites.

"Yeah, but I was able to bail early. Only five parents showed up for my class," she said with a snort, "and even fewer for some of the others. So, are you in the mood for a slab or two of deep-dish pepperoni and mushroom? You can't say no because I'm already in your driveway, parked behind that strange little car of yours."

Talia laughed. "Then I won't say no. Give me a sec to flick on the porch light so you won't break your neck on the steps."

Talia dumped the dry cereal back into the box, and then scooted into the living room and flipped on the outside light. Seconds later, Rachel strode through the front door, pizza box in one hand and a brown bag in the other. Talia relieved her of the pizza and wine while Rachel stripped off her Burberry raincoat with its matching scarf. As usual, her friend looked as if she'd just stepped out of a page in *Vogue*.

"Honestly, is that cashmere?" Talia asked in mock disgust, gazing at Rachel's ensemble.

Rachel plucked at the stunning rose-colored sweater she was wearing over a black pencil skirt. With her thick mane of dark wavy hair, ocean blue eyes, and cheekbones that could slice a melon, she looked more like a runway model than a fourth-grade teacher. "Yeah, but only because I had to dress up for parents' night." She rubbed her hands together as she followed Talia into the kitchen. "Let's open up that pizza box. After the evening I've had, I'm starving. By the way, did you get a cat?"

"A cat? No, why?"

Rachel shrugged. "I thought I saw a little feline face peeking out from the side of the house. When I shut my car door, it took off."

"Must belong to a neighbor," Talia said.

Rachel sat down at Nana's scratched wooden table while Talia set two places with her grandmother's pink-flowered dinnerware. As Rachel opened the bottle of pinot noir and poured each of them a glass, Talia began filling her in on the events of her day, including Bea's meltdown over the e-mail.

"Ah, that's good wine," Talia said after sampling hers. "A nice change from chardonnay." She opened the pizza box, releasing the intoxicating aroma of spicy meat, basil, and mozzarella. They each grabbed a slice of the gooey pie, and for a few moments they munched and drank in silence.

"So, this Turnbull you were telling me about," Rachel said finally, a flush coloring her cheeks. "You said he's the guy who owns Classic Radiance?"

"Yes, he's the— Oh no, do you know him?"

Rachel took a bracing sip of her wine. "I dated him— once," she confessed, "a little over a year ago. Believe me, once was enough. What a consummate fool he was—a real piece of work." She gave Talia a wry smile. "I suppose I deserved it for letting myself be taken in by a pretty face. You'd think I'd be old enough to know better."

Talia gave her a flat smile. "We've all been there, fallen for *that*. I imagine he came off as quite the charmer at first, but that it wore off very quickly."

"You got that right." Rachel shoved the end of a second slice into her mouth. After she swallowed, she said, "He drives this big Caddy and brags about it, like it's the only car on the planet anyone with a brain would ever think of owning. And, get this—he keeps this big white towel draped over the back of the passenger seat so that—I kid you not— whoever sits there won't sully his precious leather seats with the oils from their hair."

Talia almost choked on a mouthful of pizza. She coughed and then washed it down with a hefty slug of wine. "Oh geez, he really is intense. Do you know if he was ever married?"

"Oh, he sure was." Rachel grimaced. "I had to listen to him rail on about the K-witch, as he called her, for half the evening. Apparently the two did *not* have an amicable divorce."

"Gee, what a surprise," Talia said. "I've come to a decision, though. I thought about it while I was driving home tonight. I'm going to confront Turnbull in the morning, this time without Bea. I'm not going to put up with him upsetting her every day. She's a wreck from all his pestering."

Rachel looked dubiously at her. "Better practice what you're going to say to him. He's got this way of twisting your words, especially when it comes to . . . well, anyway, just be careful. Not to change the subject, but have you heard anything from Chet?"

Talia shook her head. "I told you, Rach, he's not going to call. He has too big of an ego. Besides, I don't want to hear from him. I don't have anything left to say to him."

"So, it's really over then? No chance of you getting back together?"

Talia smiled at her friend over the burgeoning lump in her throat. "No, but I'm fine with it, honestly I am. We'd been going in different directions for longer than I wanted to admit. When he didn't support me after I left that horrid job, I realized that our lives, our goals, had drifted too far apart." She picked at a stray wedge of pepperoni that had stuck to the bottom of the pizza box. "Besides, he was going horseback riding nearly every weekend. I felt like I hardly ever saw him anymore. We were never going to find our way back to where we were in the beginning. I miss him, a *lot*, but I did the right thing."

And it *was* the right thing, Talia reflected, as they polished off the remaining two slices of pizza. Chet's anger over her leaving a job she detested had forced her to reassess the relationship. In doing so, she saw how vastly different they were. An investment counselor, Chet loved parties and socializing with clients, while Talia savored cozy evenings at home with comfort food, a good book, and her sweetheart at her side.

About a year ago, Chet had accepted a client's offer to go horseback riding at his sprawling home in northeastern Massachusetts. Chet had taken to the pastime like a frog to a lily pad, and before long it was all he wanted to do. Talia tried, she really did, to latch onto the sport, but she could barely lift herself onto the horse, let alone control it with two skinny strips of leather. The saddle felt like it was made of granite, and every time she dismounted the animal, all she could think of was getting home and taking a long soak in the tub. After three separate tries, she gave up. Life was too short to spend on something she truly hated.

"What about you," she prodded Rachel, anxious to change the subject. "Didn't you have a date last weekend?"

Rachel scowled. "I was hoping you wouldn't remember. It was an absolute disaster!" In typical Rachel style, she regaled Talia with a comical account of how she'd arranged to meet her date—a man she'd found on the online dating site—at a Thai restaurant in downtown Pittsfield. Every three minutes or so, and all through dinner, he'd whipped his comb out of his shirt pocket and scraped it over his balding head. The evening had gone south from there, ending with him trying to pull Rachel into a lip lock as they were heading into the parking lot toward their cars. By the time Rachel had finished telling the story, Talia was wiping the tears from her face.

Feeling thoroughly stuffed, Talia removed the dishes from the table and stacked them in the sink. "Well, I regret to say that I have nothing to offer you for dessert. If I'd known you were coming, I'd have stopped at the bakery for some brownies."

Rachel gulped back the last of her wine. "Yeah, well, don't let it happen again. Hey, did your mom tell you? My class is putting on a play for the residents at the Pines this Sunday. Can you believe I agreed to direct a bunch of fourth-graders in 'The Legend of Sleepy Hollow'? I must've had a mental lapse the day I told the principal I'd do it."

The Pines, actually the Wrensdale Pines, was the assisted living facility where Natalie Marby—Talia's mom—worked as the assistant director.

Talia grinned. "That sounds like fun! I wonder why Mom forgot to tell me about it."

Rachel wiggled a hand in the air. "Well, first it was on, then it was off. As of this morning it's on again, this time for good. I had a few parents who were afraid the play would be too scary for their kids, but when they finally sat down and read the script, they ended up changing their minds. We've already had three rehearsals, so the kids pretty much have their parts down pat."

"I read it so long ago I don't remember it," Talia said, "but it sounds like a blast to me."

"Oh yeah, it'll be a real trip." Rachel rolled her blue eyes at the ceiling. "Can you imagine getting twenty-three fourth graders into their respective costumes? I just pray to God one of them doesn't get stage fright and panic when they have to say their lines. Hey, you want to come? It starts at one, but we'll start setting up around eleven. I could really use your help."

Talia cocked a finger at her. "I'll be there. Maybe I should be the costume director or something."

"No, I've got a better idea." Rachel waggled her perfectly shaped eyebrows at Talia.

"Uh-oh. You're scaring me with that evil look."

Rachel laughed. "You, my friend, are now in charge of bringing the desserts. It'll be one more thing I can cross off my list. Cookies, coffee cake, whatever floats your dinghy."

Talia gawked at her friend. "Hey, now wait a minute. I didn't—"

"No, you didn't, so I did it for you." Rachel winked at her, and Talia knew she had been had.

Rachel stayed another hour or so. As she was leaving, she hugged Talia and quietly said, "I miss her, too."

Talia's throat tightened. "I know you do."

"I think I loved her as much as my own grandmother."

Her lashes damp, Rachel hugged Talia again and left. Talia locked the door behind her friend, feeling her spirits lift. Rachel had always had a way of dragging her out of a funk. She was compassionate and funny and supremely grounded—especially for someone whose family was Dysfunction Central. And, thanks to her friend, Talia was feeling considerably better about facing Turnbull in the morning.

Still, she had to think about what she was going to say to him. She couldn't just barge in there unprepared.

After washing the dishes, she fished around in the "junk" drawer in the kitchen until she found a small notepad, and then sat cross-legged on Nana's old green sofa. One by one, she listed the high points of the speech she intended to deliver. Her plan was to approach him early, even before his store opened, assuming she could get his attention by knocking on the store's front entry door. She would be polite, but firm. When she was through, he would be left with no other choice than to stay away from Bea and Howie.

At least that was the plan.

By the time she was through scribbling out her notes, her mind was frazzled. She stuck the pad into her purse so she wouldn't forget it in the morning, and then changed into a flannel nightshirt. After that, she watched a few of her favorite sitcoms. Finally, she snuggled under the covers in Nana's bed and picked up the romantic suspense novel she'd started reading the night before. It had gotten off to a roaring start, so she was anxious to get further into it.

At eleven, Talia closed the book and watched the highlights of the late news. When her eyelids began to droop, she turned on the nightlight and flicked off her bedside lamp. As she lay in her grandmother's bed, she spied a shaft of moonlight beaming around the edge of the shade. "Oh, Nana, I wish you were here," she murmured, feeling her eyes grow moist. "Or at least . . . I wish I knew you were okay, that you were at peace."

With a sigh, she floated her gaze over the darkened bedroom, smiling automatically at all the familiar shapes. She saw her grandmother's mirrored dresser with the lacy bureau scarf draped over it. Nana's favorite felt hat—the mauve one that she always wore to church on Sundays—hanging on the post of the dresser. The reading lamp resting beside Nana's puffy pink chair, where she always took care of her sewing repairs.

After a while Talia yawned, and her eyes closed. She was teetering on the edge of sleep when an odd scent tickled her nose. It smelled like . . . lilies of the valley. Nana's favorite dusting powder.

She opened her eyes. Something was different. Slowly, she sat up. She looked around, shifting her eyes from one object to the other until she realized what it was.

Nana's mauve hat was no longer hanging on the post.

It had fallen to the floor.

3

Talia felt refreshed the next morning, ready to take on whatever the day had to offer—even a confrontation with one Phil Turnbull. The sense that Nana had been with her the night before still clung to her. Had she only imagined the scent of Nana's dusting powder? At the time, it had seemed so real. Either way, the memory helped strengthen her resolve. And while she didn't relish the idea of paying Turnbull a visit, it had to be done. His days of badgering Bea and Howie were about to die a very quick death.

She'd already decided she wouldn't let Bea in on her plan until it was over. She wanted to accomplish her goal quickly, quietly, and without fanfare. Bea would only fret, and that was the last thing either of them needed. Talia had already rehearsed what she would say to Turnbull. She only hoped her preplanned speech wouldn't devolve into a nervous babble.

Avoiding the main drag, Talia maneuvered her Fiat along

the tree-lined residential streets of Wrensdale—a circuitous route that would bring her to the rear of the arcade. So familiar she could navigate it with blinders on, the route brought her past the town's older, well-tended homes, many with pumpkins, cornstalks, and other Halloween accoutrements staking claim to the front yards. One homeowner had created a graveyard of sorts, with "headstones" poking out from the lawn at odd angles, their skeletal occupants clinging to the slabs as if trying to escape their fate. Although she'd driven past this display nearly every day for the past month, it never failed to give her a giggle.

When she reached Birch Street, which ran parallel to Main behind the arcade, she spied a diagonal parking space that few vehicles other than her own would've been able to squeeze into—mainly because of the big car hogging the adjacent space. It was a Cadillac CTS, she noted, its wheels plunked carelessly over the painted line. Yet another reason Talia was grateful she drove a Fiat—it made parking *easy breezy*.

Talia slid her car into the vacant slot and shut off her engine. She scowled at the Caddy parked beside her, wondering briefly if it belonged to Turnbull. She grabbed her purse off the front seat and hopped out of her car. She leaned closer to the big car and peeked through the tinted window on the passenger side. Sure enough, a white towel was draped over the front seat—this had to be Turnbull's Caddy.

From where she parked, Talia could see the rear entrance to Turnbull's shop. To the right of the shop was the cobblestone walkway that led to the front of the store and to the plaza that formed the heart of the arcade. Now that she was so close, the prospect of facing Turnbull was beginning to unnerve her.

Drawing in a fortifying breath, she hoisted her purse onto

her shoulder and strode toward the cobblestone walkway. As she made her way toward the arcade, a cool October breeze rustled the trees, sending a flurry of dried leaves skittering across the plaza. When she reached the corner of the lighting shop, she stopped short and gazed across the expanse of cobblestone. All at once five centuries fell away, leaving her in sixteenth-century England.

The storefronts were Tudor in style, with herringbone brickwork painted white and the upper sections graced with cross timberwork. Above the door of each of the shops, a sign proclaiming the name of the establishment dangled from a scrolled iron bar. She grinned when she saw the sign jutting out from the entrance to Lambert's Fish & Chips. The eatery's name had been engraved in a whimsical script, below which was the image of a toothy blue fish popping a crispy fry into its mouth.

She smiled and continued over the cobblestone. Today she'd worn her lilac sweater under her maroon, 1950s-style flared jacket, along with a polka-dot scarf. Thick and woolly, the sweater protected her from the morning chill. By lunchtime, when slabs of battered haddock and chunky, hand-cut fries would be sizzling in the deep fryers, she'd probably be rolling up the sleeves. For now she was glad to have something warm to shield her from the stiff wind.

A sudden gust blew across the plaza, sending the tails of her scarf flying into her face. She pushed them back with her fingers, her heartbeat kicking up a notch. She wasn't sure why, but the feeling that her practiced sermon was going to backfire ripped through her like the stomach flu she'd endured this past winter. She hated to admit it, but Turnbull frightened her.

Which was ridiculous, when she thought about it. Turnbull

was a bully, and bullies were cowards in disguise. Besides, even if her ultimatum bombed, what could he do? Scream? Wave his arms? Toss her out?

Oh, for pity's sake, get it over with. You'll feel so much better after it's done.

Talia hitched her purse straps securely onto her shoulder and, with her head high, marched up to the front entrance of Classic Radiance. Her legs felt shaky, as if her kneecaps had been suddenly removed and replaced with dollops of Bea's mushy peas. Cupping her hand over her eyes, she peered through the diamond-patterned glass ensconced within the top half of the wooden door. The store was dark, but she could see the myriad outlines of the lamps and chandeliers that populated the showroom. A faint glow emanated from somewhere in the rear of the store. If a light was on in one of the back rooms, then Turnbull must be there.

Talia swallowed back the knob of dread that was forming in her throat. She was about to bang on the door when she decided to try the handle. To her surprise, the curved iron bar that served as the doorknob turned easily. She pushed open the door and stepped inside to a musical, tinkling sound. "Mr. Turnbull?" she called out. "Are you here?"

No answer.

Talia closed the door behind her. She skimmed her gaze over the showroom. The room wasn't pitch dark, but the low level of ambient lighting made everything look murky. For a few moments she stood there, motionless, fearful that if she moved in the wrong direction, she might knock over an expensive lamp. She hated to think of Turnbull's reaction if she were to break something.

"Mr. Turnbull?" she called again, a bit louder this time. "It's Talia. Talia Marby."

Still no answer.

Frustrated, she blew out a breath. After mulling her choices, she decided she had two. She could slink out of the store and pretend she'd never been there. Or she could head on down to the back of the store, find Turnbull, and have a little confab with him. It suddenly occurred to her that he might be in the bathroom. Which meant that even if he'd heard her yelling his name, he might not be in a position to—

The musical sound of the door made Talia jump.

"Talia?" The loud whisper came from behind her.

Talia knew that voice. She whirled around. "Bea! What are you doing here? You scared the liver out of me!"

"A better question is, what are *you* doing here?" Bea stuck her hands on her hips and gawked at Talia. "I'd just poked my head out to see what the weather was doing when I saw you open the door and come in here! How did you know the door would be open?"

"I didn't. It was sheer luck." By now Talia's eyes were beginning to adjust to the darkened showroom. With a sigh, she quickly laid out her plan for Bea. "I didn't want to tell you because I knew you'd want to come with me, and you have enough on your plate as it is."

Bea shook her black-tinted curls and grinned. "You crazy girl." The last word came out *gehhllll*. "Well, now that I'm here, there's no need for you to go in there alone. Let's go find Turn*bully* and give him a piece of our collective mind. Or is it minds?"

"If he's heard us," Talia said wryly, "he's probably already called nine-one-one."

Bea peered toward the rear of the store. "Is that a light on in the back?"

"I'm not sure. It's awfully faint. I called out Turnbull's name a few times, but he obviously didn't hear me."

Talia now saw that they were standing in a central aisle, about four feet wide, covered with a plush oriental runner. The runner led from the front of the showroom all the way to the rear of the store. With any luck, if they kept their feet on it without straying over the edges, they could avoid knocking over a lamp or tripping over a table leg. "Wait a minute, I just remembered something," Talia said. She slid open the zipper on her purse and dug out her keys. Her key ring had a mini-flashlight built into its ladybug design. She pressed the button that triggered the device, and a thin pin-point of light flickered on.

"Hey, that's cute," Bea said.

Talia aimed the beam at the floor, hoping to illuminate their way to the back of the shop. "It doesn't give out much light, but it's better than nothing." Talia sighed. "All right, it's now or never. But stay behind me, okay? And for heaven's sake, be careful!"

Talia called out Turnbull's name again, feeling suddenly ridiculous. Regardless of their innocent intentions, she and Bea were intruding. Why didn't they just wait until ten o'clock, when the store opened? Why skulk around like a pair of burglars? If Turnbull heard them, he'd have every right to call the police.

Or, maybe he'd cut out the middleman. Maybe he'd come blazing out of his office with guns blasting. Did Turnbull even own a gun? He seemed like the type who would enjoy packing heat, if for no other reason than to give the appearance that he was a tough guy. Talia rubbed away the shiver that was crawling up her arms. "Bea, I'm having second thoughts.

Maybe we should leave and come back later, when the store's open. I just got this eyeball-searing vision of the two of us in orange jumpsuits, strolling around the yard at the women's prison in Framingham."

Bea snickered. "Orange is definitely not my color. Still, we're here now. Why don't we just see if he's back there? He's probably not even in the store. I bet he went to Queenie's for a latte and a jelly doughnut. Every time I go in there for the paper, he's standing at the coffee station, chatting up that cute college girl who works behind the counter."

"Eww," Talia said.

"Eww, indeed. The poor girl always looks like she's trying to make a mad escape while the fool just stands there with a stupid grin, blathering on about himself." Bea pressed her fingers lightly to the small of Talia's back. "Come on, let's trot our bums back there and get this over with. If he's not there, we'll come back later."

"All right," Talia said glumly, "since it was my dopey idea in the first place."

Of course she hadn't counted on having a sidekick. With a sense that she was sticking her neck straight under the blade of a guillotine, Talia held out her ladybug light and began picking her way carefully along the fancy runner. The slender beam barely illuminated a few inches of space at a time. Bea at her heels, she made her way closer to the back of the showroom, eventually spying the open doorway from which the pale light was dribbling. It had to be Turnbull's office. Talia was ten or twelve feet from the doorway when her foot skidded on something.

"What happened?" Bea asked her.

"My foot slipped on something. Hold on a sec." Aiming

her beam downward, Talia spotted a slip of paper sticking out from under her sneaker. She bent low and retrieved it, and saw that it wasn't a slip of paper at all—it was a photograph. "It's a photo," she told Bea. "It probably fell out of someone's purse while they were lamp shopping." She held up her mini-light and shined it on the photo. She smiled as her light caught the face of the child in the snapshot—a little girl of about four or five with tight red curls and wearing orange plaid boots.

"What a darling creature," Bea said, peering at the picture over the crook of Talia's arm.

"I'll leave this with Turnbull, if we ever find him," Talia said. She moved toward the open doorway, which was now only ten or twelve feet away. All at once, she had a vision of Turnbull rushing out of the bathroom—wherever it was— and aiming a gun at their faces. Her insides felt liquid as she called out his name again. This time it came out like a squeak.

"The rotter isn't even here," Bea said with disgust, after no response from Turnbull came. "All this anxiety for nothing. We may as well leave."

Talia wrinkled her nose. "Bea, something's off." A bad feeling was beginning to nibble its way up her spine. Her first instinct was to grab Bea and flee, but a stronger one told her someone might need help. She moved to the open doorway of what now revealed itself as Turnbull's office. The light source, she realized, came from the large luminescent clock that hung on the wall opposite Turnbull's massive desk.

"See if there's a light switch," Bea suggested.

With her free hand, Talia reached around the doorframe and explored the wall. Her fingers landed on a switch, and she flicked it on. Fluorescent lighting flooded the room. She was so grateful to be able to see that she was tempted to do a dance of joy.

Or maybe not.

Talia stumbled backward onto Bea's toes, eliciting an "ouch" and a few other creative curses from her friend. She felt her knees wobble. The photo fluttered from her fingers. With a shudder, she turned and grasped Bea's arm. "I . . . think I know why Turnbull didn't hear us."

Massaging the crunched toes of her left foot, Bea peeked around Talia. She sucked in a noisy breath. "God save the Queen and McCartney."

Turnbull was lying on the floor, his head and one arm jutting out from behind his monster-sized desk. The one ice-blue eye that Talia could see was wide open. His gelled hair rested in a puddle of darkened blood. Protruding from the side of his damaged neck, just above the pressed collar of his cotton shirt, was the lime-green handle of a silver knife.

4

By the time Talia unlocked the rear door of Lambert's it was after one. A feeling of utter relief swept over her. The simple act of standing in the eatery's familiar kitchen went a long way toward erasing the horrors of the morning.

She peeled off her flared jacket, which now felt like a ship anchor, and slung it over a hook behind the door. Then she made a quick trip to the bathroom, where she washed her hands for a solid five minutes. The officer who'd taken her fingerprints had given her a solvent to remove the oily black ink. Still, nothing could take the place of a good scrubbing with soap and water and a hefty dose of elbow grease.

Unfortunately, even soap couldn't scour away the image that stuck in her mind. She couldn't stop seeing Turnbull's blue eye, staring and sightless, and that knife poking out of his neck.

Talia swallowed back the lump that had been blossoming

in her throat all morning. Drawing in a long, calming breath, she ran her fingers through her short blond hair. She shuddered, remembering the "interview" at the police station. They'd stuck her in a drab, claustrophobic room occupied only by a table and three wooden chairs. One entire wall was mirrored. Talia knew from watching TV crime shows that behind the mirror, someone would be watching her every move. Scrutinizing every blink of the eye or twitch of the lips. The idea of being spied on that way sent ripples of terror through her. And she had nothing to hide!

Not that she was blameless in this whole mess. It was Talia's crazy idea to sneak into the lighting shop. What was she thinking? Why didn't she just wait until opening time?

Because she didn't want Bea to find out, that's why. Now, thanks to her lovable friend being a nosy posy, she'd gotten them both into a hot pickle.

Police Chief Derek Westlake, who'd been three years ahead of Talia in high school, had escorted her into the interview room. Then a homicide investigator from the state police had arrived, tall and stately in his uniform, his expression appropriately grim. "Tell me again, Ms. Marby," he'd demanded, his mouth curved up on one side in a near smirk, "why you entered Mr. Turnbull's store when you knew it hadn't yet opened for business?" He'd posed the question at least five different times, his phrasing twisted with each separate attempt. Had he been hoping to elicit a Perry Mason–style confession? And each time she'd told him the truth, insane as it now sounded.

That painful boulder bobbed in her throat again. She couldn't stop thinking about Bea. The poor woman had looked terrified when a pimple-faced, twentysomething officer had loaded her into the back of his patrol car and slammed the door. Even though he'd assured her that she wasn't under arrest, she'd railed at him with all the fervor of a prisoner being wheeled to the Bastille.

"It'll be okay, Bea," Talia had screamed to her. But the sight of her friend's frightened face peering through the window of the cruiser had nearly wrenched Talia's heart out of her chest.

After her "interview," Bea had headed home to change. She and her husband, Howie, lived in a quaint, older subdivision on the outskirts of Wrensdale, about a ten-minute ride from the arcade. Knowing Bea, she was probably standing under the shower at this very moment, scouring her body with a steel wool pad and a bar of industrial-strength soap.

Talia slid her gaze over the stainless-steel work counter, still shiny and clean. An enormous colander of boiled peas sat beside a stainless-steel bowl, waiting to be whipped and creamed into Bea's delectable mushy peas. Over the years, Bea had improved on her original recipe by cutting out the extras and keeping it simple. The result was a luscious and healthy side dish even the pickiest of eaters couldn't resist.

Okay, get to work. The fish isn't going to batter and fry itself, is it?

She wasn't even sure if Bea planned to open for business today. After Bea's interview was over, she'd texted Talia that she was heading home to change and instructed her to meet her back at Lambert's. Maybe—

Oh God, poor Bea. Any other boss would probably hold Talia responsible for this entire mess and fire her. Talia knew Bea would never do that, but still, she felt wracked with guilt.

With a groan, she pulled a clean blue apron off the wooden shelf in the corner where Bea kept them neatly stacked. She slid it over her neck, then tied it in a bow at the back. The least she could do was look perky and ready to serve.

She'd just started to open the commercial refrigerator when the back door crashed open. Bea charged into the kitchen, spewing a chain of inspired expletives she could only have learned from her stint as a cook in the navy in the UK. But what truly startled Talia was the color of Bea's lips. Fluorescent green, they were smudged at the edges and gave off a weird, shimmery glint. Biting off a giggle, Talia decided not to mention it until Bea settled down a bit.

Talia closed the back door and peered at her friend—possibly her ex-employer—with concern. "Bea, are you all right?"

"No." Eyes blazing, Bea snatched an apron off the shelf, sending the rest of the pile toppling to the floor. She'd changed into black trousers and a long-sleeved gray T-shirt—an ensemble that matched her current mood, to be sure. She slung the apron around her neck, twisting it into a hopeless tangle even as she struggled to tie it in the back.

"Let me help," Talia said. She grabbed the bottom edges of the apron and twirled them until they were right side up. She pulled the ties around Bea's diminutive waist and secured the apron with a snug bow.

"Flipping coppers," Bea sputtered. "Who do they think they are?" She yanked open the door to the fridge, shoved a hand inside, and extracted a plastic bag filled with shredded cabbage. She turned to slap the bag down on her work area, and all at once, her shoulders sagged. Tears brimmed in her eyes, and she threw herself at Talia. "Oh, Talia baby, I didn't even ask how you were! What a dreadful, horrid woman I am. All I've been thinking about is how insufferable it was for me. I didn't even ask about you. Did the cops hurt you? Did they interrogate you? Did they make you sit in a hot stuffy room that smelled like last year's unwashed gym clothes?"

A smile tugged at the corners of Talia's mouth. She patted Bea lightly on the back. "Bea, I'm fine. And the worst I can say about the interview room was that it screamed for a coat of paint and a squirt or three of Febreze."

"Oh, Talia, you are such a gem," Bea said with a crooked green smile. "Whatever would I do without you?" Her neon smile faded. "What *will* I do without you?"

"Bea, you'll be just fine. But can I ask you a question? Why are your lips glowing green?"

"They are? Oh for the love of God and England! I must have slapped on that silly stuff I was saving for Halloween. That's what I get for putting on makeup without a mirror."

"It'll be perfect for Halloween, but since that's a few weeks away, why don't you switch to something more subtle for today?"

Bea scooted off to the bathroom. Since she hadn't said otherwise, Talia assumed she intended to open for business. She hauled a bag of potatoes out of the storage closet, set them next to the work area, and began the peeling process. It was a mindless task, one that gave her too much time to think. She couldn't stop obsessing about Bea. What if Howie didn't recover fully from his knee operation? What if Bea couldn't keep the fish and chips shop running on her own? She and Howie had always worked as a team, both in life and in business. What if—

An abrupt tap at the back door made Talia jump. She blotted her hands on her apron, dashed over, and opened it. Whitnee stood there looking utterly perplexed, her book bag dangling from one bony shoulder.

"What's going on?" Whitnee said, stepping inside. "I've been trying to get in for two hours, and the front door's still locked. Plus there's Staties all over Main Street taking up the best parking spots. And the lighting store has yellow tape around it!" She slid her bag off her shoulder, removed her windbreaker, and hung both on a hook next to Talia's jacket. Normally she wore a spotless T-shirt or sweatshirt over crisp jeans that hugged her slim legs. Today's wrinkled ensemble looked dredged from the bottom of the laundry basket.

Talia instantly felt guilty. Amidst the hullabaloo over Turnbull, she'd completely forgotten about the girl. "Hi, Whitnee. I'm so sorry, we should have called you. Someone killed Phil Turnbull in his store."

"Wh . . . killed? Did you say *killed*?"

"Bea and I"—Talia swallowed—"found him this morning, but the police think it happened last night."

That's what Talia had gleaned, anyway, from the questions the police had chucked at her with rapid-fire speed. Her whereabouts between the hours of seven and midnight Wednesday evening had been of supreme interest to them.

Whitnee teetered to the right, and for a moment Talia thought she might faint. Her face had gone milky pale. Tears spilled onto the girl's cheeks. Then she shook her head, covered her eyes, and began to cry in earnest.

"Oh, Whitnee, I'm so sorry," Talia said. "I shouldn't have blurted it like that."

Whitnee sobbed quietly into her hands for a minute, then sniffled loudly and wiped her eyes with the back of her fingers. "I'm sorry," she said and cleared her throat. "You must think I'm a baby or something. It's just . . . I never knew anyone who got murdered before. It took me by surprise."

"Of course. It's very understandable."

"I mean, I didn't even like Ph . . . Mr. Turnbull," Whitnee went on. "He was nasty to everyone, and he—oh God, I didn't mean it that way. Please don't tell anyone I said that!"

Talia smiled and squeezed Whitnee's shoulder. "Believe me, the police will have to search far and wide if they're looking for someone who *did* like Phil Turnbull." She hated speaking ill of the dead, but she couldn't ignore the truth. Nonetheless, he didn't deserve to die, and for that Talia felt terrible.

Bea stomped out of the washroom, her lips now free of their fluorescent shine. The moment she spied Whitnee's puffy face, she hurried over and hugged her. "There, there, luvvy, it'll all be okay. We'll get through this and go on like before." Bea sighed.

Whitnee hugged her back, then looked down with an embarrassed flush at her stained sweatshirt and crinkled jeans. "Sorry to look, like, so messy today," she told Bea. "My mom usually gets up early and does laundry, but she left work sick last night and she wasn't feeling so good this morning. By the time I realized I didn't have anything clean to wear, it was too late to run a load through."

"Aw, luvvy, that's okay," Bea said. "Under a nice clean apron, no one will see it anyway."

Talia tilted her head toward the front of the eatery. "Whitnee said the front door is locked, Bea. Did you lock up before the . . . police took you to the station?"

"I asked the copper to lock it for me," she grumbled. "I have to admit, the chap was quite obliging. Not bad-looking, either, if you go for the baby-faced sort. So, shall we open up for business? If all three of us get hopping, we should be able to open by two, wouldn't you say?" She looked far less sure than she sounded.

"Let me take a peek outside," Talia said. She slipped around the side of the counter and went to the front entrance. She opened the door and glanced out over the cobblestone plaza. The sun was bright, tempered by a chill wind. People had gathered in clusters, chattering to one another as they gawked and pointed in the direction of the lighting store.

Only one thing marred the appeal of the faux sixteenth-century village. Stretched across the front of Turnbull's lighting store was, as Whitnee had noticed, a length of yellow crime scene tape, punctuated by a series of orange cones. The tape fluttered in the stiff breeze.

Talia turned to Bea. "I agree, Bea. Let's open. People have to eat, right?"

"Bunch of looky-loos, all of them." Bea slammed the entrance door. "Don't these people ever eat? Has everyone gone crazy?"

Talia had just bitten into a fat, crispy fry sprinkled with a dose of malt vinegar when she heard Bea erupt over the depressing lack of customers. In spite of the horrible day she'd had, she was ravenous. A bowl of Rice Krispies with a sliced banana were the only food she'd eaten all day. Nevertheless, she felt guilty for stuffing her face when business had been abysmal all afternoon. She swallowed and said, "It's an aberration, Bea. It won't last. By tomorrow everything will be back to normal."

She hoped.

Wearing a dazed expression, Whitnee busied herself wiping down the work areas in the kitchen and putting away the condiments. She'd barely said a word all afternoon. In the tradition of Talia's nana—the quintessential Italian grandmother—Talia had tried urging her to eat. But Whitnee had waved away any offer of food, refusing even the mushy peas she normally gobbled with gusto.

Only three customers had come in for a meal all afternoon. Each one had taken their goodies outside so they could munch on deep-fried haddock and salty chips while they watched the crime scene technicians go about the tasks of photographing and collecting evidence. Judging from the number of people capturing it on video with their phones, it was quite the spectacle. It didn't look to Talia as if the techs were doing anything exciting, but the looky-loos apparently thought otherwise.

"I hope you're right, luvvy," Bea said wearily. "But since it's almost six and we haven't sold an ounce of food in over an hour, we might as well close early. How about we—"

The door to the eatery abruptly flew open, dispensing a heavyset, fiftyish woman lugging an overstuffed canvas tote. Talia recognized her—it was Whitnee's mom, Connie Parker. She'd been coming in every week or so to see her daughter, each time thundering through the eatery as if she owned the place. She always devised some dire excuse why she needed to talk to Whitnee, who kept her cell turned off during working hours.

Today the woman's gray-streaked hair stuck out from her head like the tines of an old rake. Beneath an open peacoat that had seen better decades, she wore a uniform-style polyester top that matched her pink polyester pants. Connie moved across the dining area, her thighs making a swish sound with each stride. "Where's my Whitnee?" she bleated. "Is she okay? I heard somebody got murdered right here in this plaza!"

Not in time, Talia moved toward the dining area with the

intention of cutting her off at the pass. Connie edged around the aquamarine counter and bumped past her as if she were a gnat, her gargantuan tote leading the way.

Whitnee's face reddened. "Ma, what are you doing here? I told you, you can't keep coming in here. You're gonna get me fired!"

"Then why didn't you call me? Didn't you get the messages I left on your phone?" Connie dropped her tote and threw both arms around her daughter. "There's a murderer loose. You coulda been killed!"

"I'm fine, and I told you, Ma, I can't talk on the phone when I'm working." Whitnee wriggled out of her mom's grasp. "You gotta go now, okay? You're embarrassing me."

"Okay, okay, so long as you're all right." Connie sent an exasperated glance in Talia's direction. "I guess it's a crime to worry about my daughter now," she huffed.

"You have every right to worry," Talia said kindly but with a firm undertone. "But I assure you that Bea, Whitnee, and I all look out for one another. We'll be sure Whitnee gets to her car safely. You have my word." She moved closer to Connie to encourage a swift departure.

"Yeah, yeah, all right. I can take a hint." Connie squeezed around the edge of the counter and trekked back into the dining area. Talia followed close behind to be sure she didn't try an end run back into the kitchen.

"Kids," Connie muttered. "I popped out three, and only one of 'em turned out decent. That would be Whitnee, in case you're wondering which one, and today even she's givin' me grief. She's a good girl, though, *most* of the time." She swiveled and shot a hard look at her daughter. "My other two—the both of 'em ought to join Deadbeats Anonymous. Can you believe my youngest never worked a day in his life?

He sits in his room playin' with his a-Pad all day. God knows where him and his brother go at night, but at least they go."

Talia went to the door to open it for her, but Connie hadn't quite finished her monologue.

"Well, at least Whitnee's going to school," Connie burbled on. "If she can keep comin' up with the tuition, that is. 'Course I heard some bosses repay their employees for the money they spend on college." Her small brown eyes homed in on Bea, who'd stood speechless during the entire Connie invasion. "I don't suppose you have any sort of deal like that?" she said sourly.

Bea shook herself out of her stunned silence. "I'm afraid not, Mrs. Parker. We're just a small—"

"Hey, never mind that Mrs. Parker stuff. It's Connie, okay? Anyhoo, I gotta go. Time to go clean the zoo. Night shift is a bee-yotch, if you catch my drift. No rest for the weary, huh? You just make sure my girl gets to her car like you promised."

Talia saw Bea let out a quiet breath of relief after Connie left. Whitnee looked as if she wanted the floor to swallow her in one giant gulp. Talia felt for the girl.

"I'm really sorry," Whitnee said in a tiny voice. "She's, like, a major worrywart, but she means well."

"Aw, that's okay, luvvy," Bea said. Fatigue had etched dark lines around her eyes. "She's a mum. She has a right to worry. Look, we're going to close up shop now. It's been a terrible day, a simply horrid one. I think we're all entitled to an early night."

"Can't argue with that," Talia said. After closing, she planned to head straight next door to Sage & Seaweed—the specialty bath and body shop adjacent to Lambert's. The owner, Suzy Sato, imported most of her products from

England, and the selection of scented bath salts was mind-blowing. The prices made Talia a little light-headed, too, but she reminded herself that every woman deserved a bit of luxury on occasion. A long soak in a scented tub later would go a long way toward soothing her frazzled nerves. The day she'd had would surely warm the chambers of the devil's heart.

They all pitched in to finish putting away the perishables. After Talia wiped down all the surfaces with lime-scented cleaner, Bea locked the door and they left. In keeping with her promise to Connie, Talia walked both Bea and Whitnee to their cars, which were parked in the town lot adjacent to Peggy's Bakery. The cold breeze of late afternoon had turned into a biting wind, but the sky was clear and scattered with stars.

"You watch who's around you," Bea admonished, sliding into her mud-brown vintage Datsun. "Until the coppers catch the killer, we could all be in danger. Where's your car?"

"I parked behind the lighting shop this morning, remember?"

"Dear God, luvvy, you're not walking back there alone. Hop in."

Knowing it would be futile to protest, Talia accepted the ride. She hadn't told Bea she planned to visit the bath and body shop—it would only worry her needlessly to think Talia was tromping around the arcade alone.

It was freezing inside the Datsun. Talia rubbed the arms of her jacket. The clunker didn't heat up very quickly, but Bea loved the old car. She'd bought it when she first immigrated to Massachusetts from the UK, and she refused to give it up.

Bea drove around the block and stopped behind the Fiat,

the headlights of the Datsun illuminating the quiet, darkened street. "Flash your lights when you get in your car," she told Talia. "And please be careful, luv, okay? There's a killer out there."

Talia leaned over and gave her friend a quick hug. She started the Fiat and flashed her headlamps, and Bea tooted and pulled away. Warm air blew out of the vents almost instantly. She rubbed her hands together to squeeze some warmth into them. All at once, she realized that Turnbull's Caddy was still parked beside her. Had the police realized it belonged to him? How long would they leave it there?

She drove around the block, this time snaring a spot on Main Street, only a pebble's throw from the arcade. Sage & Seaweed was one of the two shops closest to Main. A fast walk would take her there in less than a minute.

Talia locked the Fiat and scooted across the cobblestone to the bath shop. A shiver raced up her arms. She told herself it was from the cold. She didn't believe for a moment that she was in any danger.

Someone had wanted Phil Turnbull dead. It was as simple as that.

Wasn't it?

5

The spicy aromas of pumpkin, cinnamon, and vanilla swirled around Talia, enveloping her in a cloud of sensory delight. She inhaled slowly, each breath drawing her closer to the mythical Shangri-la. She began to feel lighter, more at peace. She now understood the attraction of aromatherapy. Sage & Seaweed had to be the best-smelling shop on the planet.

Well, except for Lambert's when the deep fry was in high gear, and the fish and the chips were sizzling in the baskets.

"Talia!" Suzy Sato dashed out from behind the long glass counter that ran along a portion of the rear wall. Springy reddish curls bounced around Suzy's head like mini Slinkys. She grabbed Talia and pulled her into a hug, her sky-blue eyes burning with questions. "I heard about you and Bea finding Turnbull," Suzy gushed. "My word, you poor thing.

Are you okay? You must be wiped. Come over here and tell me all about it." She took Talia's hand and tugged her toward the back of the store. "Sit," she said, pointing at one of the padded stools in front of the counter.

Inwardly, Talia groaned. She'd come in here to get away from the murder, not to talk about it. She'd already had to tell the awful story to both her mom and dad. When she'd talked to them earlier that afternoon, it had taken the better part of twenty minutes to convince her agitated mother that she wasn't headed to the pokey.

Suzy sidled around the other side of the counter, plopped onto her own stool, and plunked both elbows atop the glass. She gaped at Talia. "I heard Phil's whole *head* was nearly severed, that when you found him it was hanging by a *tendon*!" She gave a dramatic shudder, her eyes rolling back in her head.

"Suzy, there was no severing." Where did she hear such a thing? "And besides, I only caught a momentary glimpse. Once I realized he was, you know, gone, I pushed Bea out of the room and called nine-one-one. I hardly saw anything."

Okay, that part was a bit of a fib. But she had no intention of blabbing about the crime scene to Suzy, who would no doubt broadcast it on Facebook. Plus, the police had cautioned her against telling anyone what she saw. She did not need to add any more troubles to her day.

"But was there blood, right? Lots of it, I'll bet." Suzy clasped both hands against her ample chest. "Oh, it must have been horrible, simply terrifying. I'd probably have *fainted* if I'd been the one who found him."

Luckily, Talia wasn't the fainting type. She smiled sweetly at Suzy. "Anyway, Suzy, enough about the murder. I came in for some nice relaxing bath oil, or bubbles, or whatever you recommend. Tonight I want to put this entire day out of my head and have a long, luxurious soak in the tub."

Seemingly mollified, Suzy instantly morphed into sales mode. "Oh, I have just the thing! I'm so glad you came by. I've been experimenting with oils and creams, and I've designed my own blend of pumpkin bath oil. Perfect for the season, right?"

"Is that the luscious scent I detected when I walked in?"

Suzy grinned. "Yup. One of them." She slid aside one of the cabinet doors on her side of the counter. She reached inside and carefully removed a tall bottle filled with a thick amber liquid. "Now smell this," she said, removing the silver cap and waving the bottle under Talia's nose.

Talia closed her eyes and breathed in the scent. "Mmmm, that's heavenly. Did you say you made it yourself?"

"I did. I've been taking classes online. Eventually I want to have my own line of bath products, so I'm trying out some of the methods I learned." Suzy's blue eyes beamed. "I want you to take this bottle home and tell me what you think after you've tried it. No charge."

"Oh no, I couldn't—"

"I insist. You'll be my first tester." Suzy smiled, her eyes lighting up. Talia saw how excited she was about the prospect of creating her own product line.

"Thanks, Suzy. I'll look forward to my bath tonight."

As Suzy fussed with placing the bottle in a salmon-colored bag lined with a nest of silver tissue, Talia perused the various lip glosses perched on a circular display. She didn't want to leave with only a freebie—the least she could do was support Bea's neighboring merchant. Although she hadn't known Suzy all that long, she'd always felt a kind of camaraderie with the thirtysomething woman. And Suzy had always treated Talia as if they were the best of buds.

After narrowing down her choices, Talia snagged two tubes of seasonal gloss—a Vampire Smooch and a Butternut Squash. She dug out her wallet and pulled out a twenty. "Can I ask you something, Suzy?"

"Sure!" Suzy tucked the lip glosses into the bag with the bath oil.

"Phil Turnbull came into Lambert's on Wednesday. He told us you were on board with signing the petition against the comic book store. According to him, only Bea and Jim Jepson were the holdouts, and he was sure Jepson was going to cave."

Suzy swallowed, and her face flushed red. "That's . . . not true. I never told him I would sign." Avoiding Talia's gaze, she went back to fussing with the silver tissue. "Besides, why would I object to a comic book store?"

Talia chewed her lip. Was Suzy telling the truth? She could have sworn she saw Suzy's pupils dilate when she asked her the question. She hadn't meant to trap her in a lie—she was genuinely trying to find out if Turnbull had been deceiving Bea.

"No, you wouldn't, of course. Thanks, Suzy. I was pretty sure Turnbull was lying, but I just wanted to get your take on it."

The door opened and two customers strolled in. From their ages, Talia surmised they were a mom and her teenaged daughter. Since it was close to seven, they wouldn't have long to shop. But it gave Talia a chance to escape without embarrassing Suzy any further.

Suzy's face relaxed when she saw her new visitors. She pushed the bag across the counter toward Talia. "Let me know how you like the bath oil, okay?"

Talia stepped outside onto the cobblestone plaza. A white half-moon framed by a smattering of twinkling lights hung low in the eastern sky. Feeling instantly chilly, she tucked her scarf more tightly around her neck. In the window of Jepson's Pottery, a clay jack-o'-lantern grinned wickedly. Jim Jepson—Talia's high school geometry teacher turned potter—was no doubt working late.

The arcade was otherwise cloaked in darkness. The police tape, about the only thing visible on the darkened arcade, still stretched across the front of Classic Radiance like a long yellow snake.

Anxious to get home, at least to Nana's home, Talia had started toward her car when she spied someone emerging onto the rear of the plaza where Time for Tea, a specialty tea shop, sat perpendicular to the lighting store. Something about the person's shape suggested "female," but from this distance she couldn't be sure. The person was slight, and appeared to be clothed entirely in black.

Oh Lordy, it looked like Bea. She must have circled the block and parked behind the arcade so she could return to the scene and snoop.

But why? Surely she wouldn't be able to get in.

Talia watched Bea fast-walk toward Turnbull's shop and duck under the crime scene tape. Whatever her friend had in mind, it was nothing short of insane.

Talia shifted her polka-dotted Keds into third gear and raced across the cobblestone. Following Bea's lead, she dipped under the yellow tape and rounded the corner of the lighting store. She was just in time to see her friend punch at the keypad adjacent to the rear entrance.

Which was crazy. Bea couldn't possibly know Turnbull's entry code.

Talia felt her jaw drop when the door swung inward. She saw Bea scurry inside. As the door crawled to a slow close on its hydraulic hinge, Talia rushed for it. She caught it a nanosecond before it would have slammed shut, and then darted inside. A whiff of honeysuckle waltzed on the air, and in that fraction of a second she knew.

It wasn't Bea.

The door closed behind her with a soft click. Heart crashing in her chest, Talia dropped into a low crouch. The beam from a slender flashlight bounced over one of the walls. She held her breath, praying one of the bounces wouldn't stray to where she was huddled. All at once, she realized where she was—Turnbull's office.

Crickets and crumpets, not again!

Except that it made perfect sense. His office was located at the rear of the store, and that's exactly where she was.

Now, however, she was trapped. Her best hope was to hide until the intruder left, and then get the heck out of there. To her right, she made out the vague outline of a file cabinet. Still scrunched into a low stoop, she inched over to it. Her legs cramped painfully, but she kept going until—

Ach. The toe of her sneaker smacked something solid, making a dull thunk sound. Still clutching the bag from the bath shop, Talia dove behind the file cabinet. Her left hand skidded over something sharp—a pin? She palmed it just as a harsh fluorescent light flooded the room.

The intruder had found the wall switch.

Heart pounding like a jackhammer, Talia turned slowly. She stared up at the raven-haired woman with the flawless skin, the stunning blue eyes, and the perfectly manicured fingers curled around a silver gun. The woman pocketed her penlight so she could concentrate on the firearm, which she now gripped with both hands.

Talia's insides turned into one big jelly roll. "Jill Follansbee," she rasped. "What are you doing here? You killed Phil Turnbull, didn't you?"

6

"Are you crazy?" Jill Follansbee, the owner of Time for Tea, tilted her gun toward Talia's chest. "I didn't kill anyone. The minute I saw you, I figured *you* killed him."

Talia felt her limbs go numb. She'd ended up sitting on one heel, and a dent was forming in her rear end. Beside her was a stack of cardboard boxes—no doubt the object her toe had smacked into. Her voice seemed to come from far away when she said, "Of course I didn't kill him. How could you even think that?" A sudden rush of anger swept over her. Why was she explaining herself to a woman who had no more right to crash a crime scene than she did?

Crash a crime scheme. What in glory's name was she thinking?

Jill lowered her gun. "I have to admit, you don't look much like a killer. More like . . . Peter Pan," she said, with a pout of her full lips. "What are you doing here, anyway?"

"Can I stretch out my legs?" Talia pleaded, miffed at the Peter Pan comment.

With a sigh, Jill waved the gun in a circle. "Sure, go ahead."

Wincing, Talia straightened both legs out in front of her. Her purse had remained slung over her right shoulder, but the bag Suzy had given her was on the floor, its contents scattered. "When I saw someone dressed totally in black sneaking in here, I thought it was Bea."

"Bea! Are you psycho? She's shorter and at least ten pounds heavier than me."

"I was working with limited lighting. Give me a break."

Of course, with the lights on a closer look confirmed the obvious—Jill had at least three inches on Bea, and wore chic designer duds that Bea would've said made her look like a toffee-nose. Talia jabbed a finger at Jill. "And for the record, my hair is a smidge longer and a lot more stylish than Peter Pan's. But you—you knew the code to get in here!"

Jill did an exaggerated eye roll. "Anyone with even a quarter of a brain could figure out Phil's code. Besides, I've"—she flushed a deep crimson—"I've used it before."

"Can I get up?" Talia drew in a breath. "I mean, *may* I get up?"

Jill set the gun on Phil's desk and dropped into his chair. "I don't care. Do whatever you want," she said, tears blossoming on her long, thick lashes.

Talia gathered up the goodies that had spilled from her Sage & Seaweed bag, jammed them back inside, and pushed herself upward. Sliding her left hand into her jacket pocket, she fixed Jill with a piercing look. "You obviously came in here looking for something."

With a loud sniffle, Jill nodded. "Three nights ago I left my diamond and sapphire bracelet here. My husband gave it to me last year, on my thirtieth birthday. I have to find it before he notices it's gone. I wear it nearly every day."

Talia connected the dots. The picture that emerged was not a pretty one. "You and Phil were having an affair, weren't you?"

"It's hard to explain," Jill said miserably. "But, sort of, yes." She lowered her face to her hands.

"Why did you take the bracelet off in the first place?"

Jill lowered her hands. "Without getting too graphic, let's just say it was making the position I was in a bit too uncomfortable."

Talia felt her own cheeks reddening, and then a thought crossed her mind. She remembered the photo she'd found on the floor that morning, in the showroom—the snapshot of the little girl. She'd been holding it when she and Bea had gone searching for Turnbull, but when she saw his body she dropped it.

Had the killer left the photo there?

"Will you help me find it?" Jill begged, penetrating Talia's thoughts.

"The bracelet?" Talia rose to her feet and looked around the room. On the floor, where Turnbull's body had lain, was a darkened bloodstain. Fingerprint powder coated nearly every flat surface. "All right, but we can't spend much time in here. If anyone sees us, we're toast."

"This room doesn't have any windows. From outside, no one should be able to figure out we're in here." Jill leaped out of Phil's chair. "We were on the"—she swallowed—"desk when I took my bracelet off."

Oh ick. Ick squared.

"Then why don't you search the desk?" Talia suggested. Looking around, she saw a faded blue love seat resting against the far wall. "What about that sofa over there? Did you ever, um—"

Jill nodded sheepishly. "A few times, but I don't think it's there. If Phil had found it, he'd have returned it to me. *Or* . . . he told me once he had a secret hiding place in here, but I never found out where it was."

Talia suppressed a shudder. "I'll look there anyway. But let's put a time limit on it, okay? Five minutes, tops. Then we're out of here, whether we find the bracelet or not."

"Agreed."

While Jill rummaged through the desk drawers and rifled under the blotter, Talia stripped the cushions from the love seat and squeezed her fingers into its every nook and crack. A set of plastic gloves from the eatery would have come in darned handy, she mused, as her hand rolled over something hardened and rough that—pray God—was an old food stain. She made a mental note to start carrying a pair of disposable gloves in her purse.

Repellent as the task was, her search turned up nothing. It wouldn't surprise her if Turnbull had found the bracelet himself and pawned it for cash.

Talia couldn't help wondering what a classic beauty like Jill ever saw in a man like Turnbull, but she'd obviously had feelings for him. She remembered what Rachel had said about falling for a pretty face. Talia had never met Jill's husband, but it sounded as if their marriage was troubled.

Another thought occurred to her, one that shook her to the core. If Jill actually *had* murdered Turnbull, then Talia was aiding and abetting a killer. Sheer instinct told her Jill hadn't done it, but still—

At least while they searched for the bracelet, Talia could also look for the photo. It was the main reason she'd agreed to help, in spite of the nagging voice in her head warning her to get out of there. But if finding that photo could potentially tie the real killer to the crime, wasn't she right to stay and help?

"Jill, I've got nothing," Talia said after exploring every square inch of the sofa and underneath it. "We have to go before we get caught. I hate to say this, but even if the bracelet was here, the police probably found it and took it into custody."

"I'm afraid of that, too." Jill grabbed Talia's sleeve. "You won't tell the police about . . . me and Phil, will you?"

Talia wanted to rub the ache from her eyes, but then remembered where her hands had been. "No, but I think you should."

"But—"

"Your husband doesn't have to know," Talia said. "Just be honest and up front about it. Think about it, okay? If you know that you didn't—"

"I didn't. I didn't kill Phil!"

Oddly, Talia believed her.

"Then come clean about the affair, and let the police do their job. I don't suppose you have an alibi for last night?"

"I was home alone with my daughter. My husband was working late—one of his endless business meetings." She smirked as if she didn't care, but Talia could see the pain in her expression. "I would never leave my Carly at home alone. My mom sits if I'm out, but Wednesday's her bridge night."

Talia smiled at the child's name. "How old is Carly?"

"She'll be eight next month." Jill's eyes grew misty. "She's the love of my life, Talia. I can't get in trouble over this. I *can't*. She needs me."

For the second time that day, visions of a wardrobe designed around a single color scheme—orange—flashed through Talia's head. "Jill, we have *got* to get out of here. Do you want to grab a coffee somewhere?"

"Let's go to my shop. I'll brew us a pot of tea. I just have to fetch my gun."

"Wow. This is the most fabulous tea I've ever tasted." Talia savored another mouthful, swallowing slowly to keep the flavors lingering on her tongue.

Jill beamed as she stirred her own tea. On the table before them sat an exquisite blue cast-iron teapot etched with a serpent. "This is one of my new blends. It has a smidge of lavender, along with the faintest hint of blueberry. Scrumptious, isn't it?"

"Out of sight, as Bea would say."

Jill offered a weak smile. "Poor Bea. Phil really had been giving her a hard time, hadn't he?"

"Terrible," Talia confirmed.

"I don't know how everything turned bad so quickly. Phil . . ." She pushed a lock of her lush black hair behind one ear. "Look, I know he wasn't the most pleasant man to deal with, but he'd been under a lot of pressure lately. And now he's—" Jill's eyes grew watery.

"What kind of pressure?" Talia asked gently. She helped herself to another cup from the spectacular teapot.

"Mostly from his ex. She's a half owner in the lighting shop. I guess she wanted him to make some sweeping changes, changes he would've hated."

"Like what?" Talia asked.

"Pretty much a complete overhaul of the place. Plush new

carpeting, updated window treatments, that sort of thing. She felt the place was too stodgy, that it was deterring the younger buyers—especially the ones who had plenty of dough to spend and could easily go elsewhere."

Talia hadn't realized Phil had a business partner. Maybe the police should be looking at *her* as a potential suspect. Didn't Rachel say Turnbull referred to his ex as the K-witch?

"Jill, forgive me for being so blunt, but . . . honestly, what did you see in Phil? You are so amazingly gorgeous, you have a daughter you adore, this wonderful shop—" Talia broke off, realizing how insensitive she must sound.

Jill's voice grew quiet. "Phil and I have a history, Talia. We go way back. Oh, don't worry, I know he did everything in a skirt, so to speak." Her smile was achingly sad. "In the end, he always came back to me."

Yeah, for a guaranteed roll in the hay.

Talia had so many questions. Not the least of which was: what about your husband?

Jill laughed. "Now I can read your mind. You're wondering where my dear, devoted spouse fits into the picture."

"I guess so." Talia shrugged. "*Is* he devoted?"

"Oh absolutely—to his job. If I really want to rev up the fire in his furnace, I just give him a spreadsheet filled with scads of lovely numbers. Gets his *blood* flowing every time, if you catch my drift." The irony in her tone was unmistakable.

"Were you thinking of leaving him for Phil?"

Jill laughed. "Good heavens, no. Are you nuts? Phil would've made a rotten husband. He didn't like kids much, either." She frowned, and a tiny crinkle formed between her eyes. "I can't believe I'm speaking about him in the past tense. It seems so . . . surreal."

Talia felt a surge of sympathy for Jill. Right or wrong,

the relationship she'd had with Turnbull had been a significant part of her life. "Murder never makes sense," Talia said, and then a thought struck her. "Jill, do you have any photos of Carly? I'd love to see them."

A grin spread across Jill's face. "Oh gosh, I just got her school picture. It came out really good—well, of course I'd think that, right?" She went over to the oak counter that housed a sleek cash register, and reached underneath it for her handbag. She dug out her wallet and sat down again, extracting a photo from one of the slots. "Here, this is her third-grade picture." She gazed lovingly at the photo and then handed it to Talia.

"Oh, Jill, she's adorable," Talia said. The little girl's curly hair, a pale shade of auburn, framed a sweet, heart-shaped face. The impish twinkle in her dark brown eyes spoke of a child who was loved deeply and felt secure in her nook of the world.

Talia peered closely at Carly's face. Was she the same little girl in the photo Talia had found in Turnbull's showroom? There was a least a four-year age difference in the two pictures, and kids changed a lot from toddlerhood on. And even if the two photos were of the same child, did it mean anything? Couldn't it simply have fallen out of Jill's handbag during one of her assignations with Phil?

Talia didn't realize she'd been studying the picture so intently until Jill slipped two fingers over it and tugged it away from her. Talia flashed an innocent smile. "You're very lucky."

Jill stared at it again, her eyes filling with tears. It was in that moment Talia wondered if Carly was Turnbull's biological child. Yet another secret Jill was keeping from her husband?

Jill blotted both eyes with the tip of a manicured finger. "I guess we should go, but I want to tell you that I really appreciate your help tonight. And I'm sorry I pointed a gun at you."

"Yeah, I meant to ask you about that. Why *did* you have a gun?" Talia swallowed the last mouthful of her tea.

"I carry it for protection," Jill said tightly. "Don't worry, it's registered, and Carly never has access to it. She doesn't even know I carry it."

Talia nodded as if it made perfect sense, but she'd always had somewhat of an aversion to firearms. Why was Jill so concerned about her safety? Did she think her husband was a potential threat?

Jill collected their empty teacups and walked them over to the counter. Talia picked up the teapot and followed her.

"Thanks." Jill took the pot from her and set it down on a shelf beneath the cash register. "I'll wash these in the morning. No biggie. But before you go, I want to give you something."

Jill scurried over to an oak display shelf that lined one of the walls. She snagged a tall rectangular box off the shelf and went back to the counter with it. "This is a tea starter kit. It has everything you'll need to brew the perfect cup of tea. I'm also going to give you a tin of my strawberry-orange blend. Somehow I think it suits your personality. After you've tried it, be sure to let me know how you like it."

Talia studied the box, which contained a glass tea maker and all sorts of tea accessories. "Jill, I can't accept this. It looks so expensive. What if you gave me just a few tea bags to try out?"

At the words "tea bags," Jill feigned a spell. "Talia, no tea connoisseur would ever use anything except loose tea leaves, and they have to be brewed properly in order to be enjoyed. Trust me."

Talia smiled, but she couldn't help wondering if Jill's gift was a bribe of sorts. Still, it would be fun to experiment with brewing loose tea. It was something she could do with her mom and Rachel some lazy Sunday afternoon. "This is really sweet of you, Jill. Thank you."

"I'm thrilled to do it," Jill said with a sly wink. "And I guarantee, once you sample some of my luscious blends, you'll be begging for more. You'll probably end up being my best customer."

Before they left the tea shop, Jill gave Talia a quick hug. Talia waved to her as she strode across the cobblestone arcade toward Main Street, where her Fiat was parked. The temperature had dropped into the high forties, and a shiver boogied up her arms.

As she tossed her purse and her goody bags onto the passenger seat of her car, Talia thought over everything she'd learned. The tidbits she'd gleaned about Phil Turnbull had been nothing short of startling.

Not the least of which was the astonishing revelation that he'd loved Jill Follansbee.

7

At six twenty-five Friday morning, Talia's internal clock poked her awake. She hobbled out of bed, scrubbed her face, and headed for the kitchen. The long, relaxing soak in a pumpkin-and-spice scented bath the night before had gone a long way toward soothing her tattered nerves. She had to hand it to Suzy—the bath oil blend she'd created was delectable.

After a fast breakfast of wheat toast and orange juice, Talia threw on a pair of navy slacks, topping them with a mushroom-colored sweater. Around her neck she tied a square of sheer purple rayon. She fluffed the ends out to one side a la Audrey Hepburn, then threw on her flared jacket.

The morning air felt icy, despite the bright lemon ball in the sky that promised a stunning day. A coating of frost blanketed Nana's tiny lawn, reminding Talia that Halloween was nipping at her ankles. She should probably plop a few pumpkins on the front step, the way Nana had always done.

Talia groaned when she swung her Fiat into the town parking lot. Two enormous news vans had taken up residence along Main Street, squandering a slew of prime parking slots. She uttered a silent prayer that the arcade wouldn't soon be plagued by the media.

Using the key Bea had given her, Talia let herself into the eatery through the back door. Bea wasn't in yet—a bad sign. Normally she was bustling around the kitchen by eight o'clock, performing her daily "changing of the oil" in the fryers.

First things first: Talia fired up the coffeemaker. While the coffee brewed, she hauled a sack of potatoes out of the storage closet. She was filling a large pot with ice water when the kitchen door swung open.

"Morning, Bea!" Talia said brightly as her boss stomped in.

"Morning, luv." Bea looked around distractedly. Charcoal bags hung beneath her lower lids, and her eyes looked cloudy, without their usual sparkle. Spying the row of hooks on the door, she peeled off her fleece coat and slung it over the middle peg, next to Talia's flared jacket.

"Did you manage to get some sleep last night?" Talia poured each of them a mug of French-roast coffee, adding a dollop of milk to her own.

"Very little." Bea ripped open a packet of raw sugar and dumped it into her steaming brew. "I couldn't stop thinking about that bloo—blasted Turnbull." She slugged back several mouthfuls of the scalding java.

"I know what you mean. Yesterday was not a good day." Talia had already decided not to tell Bea about her encounter with Jill in the lighting shop. Neither of them should have been there. In the light of day, the entire incident horrified Talia. What had she been thinking, rummaging like a thief through a crime scene? Her only consolation was the certainty she felt that Jill had nothing to do with Turnbull's death.

"I got a call from the police chief early this morning," Bea said dismally. "The state police are going to ask every shop owner in the arcade to be voluntarily fingerprinted."

"That's not surprising," Talia said. "It's probably standard operating procedure in their little manual of murder."

Bea gasped over a mouthful of coffee. "The coppers have a manual of murder?"

"No, Bea. I didn't mean it literally. I only meant that it's probably part of a normal homicide investigation."

"Homicide," Bea grumbled. "I hate that word."

Talia reached for the coffeepot and topped off Bea's mug. "I wonder when the last murder was in this town. I mean, was there ever a murder in Wrensdale?"

Bea lifted her shoulders in a weary shrug. "Couldn't tell you that, Tal. I wasn't born here."

Talia still couldn't grasp the concept of Derek Westlake as chief of police. She'd been a freshman in high school when she was recruited by her class advisor to tutor Derek in English. He hated his English class—and reading—with a purple passion. As a guard on Wrensdale High's basketball team, he needed to earn at least a C or be kicked off the team. Talia had struggled to make reading enjoyable for him, but it had been an uphill battle for sure.

"You've got that glazed look," Bea said.

"I was just thinking about Derek when he was in high school. The real mystery is how he ended up being chief of police." Talia gulped down her coffee, then pulled the potato peeler out of the utensil drawer and grabbed a humongous spud from the bag.

Bea snickered. "Did you have a crush on him?"

"Hardly. But I tutored him in English for a while."

Okay, she might have had a *tiny* crush twenty years ago. Not even worth mentioning.

Bea drained her mug and plunked it in the commercial dishwasher. Her voice grew hoarse. "Westlake said the state police are handling the case now. The same detective from yesterday, Liam O'Donnell, is in charge. But get this. The coppers got some flippin' preliminary report in from the lab this morning." She looked at Talia, her green eyes filling with tears. "Oh, Talia, they think I did it. They think I killed Phil Turnbull!"

The next few hours dragged by in a haze, with Bea alternating between sobs and rants. Whitnee arrived a few minutes before eleven, her thin face drawn. She set to work making the mushy peas—her favorite thing to prepare. Talia tried to engage her in a few pleasantries, but received only a nod or head shake in return.

At eleven thirty, Bea asked Talia to flip the CLOSED sign to OPEN. Almost instantly, the door swung ajar.

"Hey, everyone." Suzy Sato poked her head inside, her reddish gold curls bouncing around her face. "How are y'all doing?" She stepped inside and gave Talia a quick hug.

Bea gave Suzy a faint wave with her wooden spoon and went back to stirring batter. Whitnee glanced over at Suzy but didn't acknowledge her.

"We're doing," Talia said. "By the way, that bath oil was

scrumptious. I dumped a pile of it in the tub last night and soaked for a good half hour."

"Oooh, I'm so glad you liked it. Um, I've got to get back to the shop, but do you and Bea have a minute?"

Bea wiped her hands on her apron and slipped around the side of the counter into the dining area. "Hi, Suzy. Didn't mean to be standoffish. I'm not having a very good day."

"Oh, Bea, I'm sorry to hear that." Suzy threw her arms around Bea and gave a hearty squeeze.

Bea shook her head and dabbed at her eyes with a napkin. "Don't mind the tears. I'm like a leaky faucet today."

"Well, listen," Suzy said. "I got a call from Jill Follansbee this morning, and she came up with a pretty good idea. You all know her, right?"

Talia bit her lip to keep from laughing out loud. "She owns Time for Tea."

"Exactly, and she got thinking about how slow things were yesterday. I mean, we *all* lost business, right?" Suzy rolled her eyes and ran her fingers through her curls. "I mean, it was so obvious that customers were staying away from the arcade in *droves*, wasn't it?"

"I guess so." Bea frowned. "It was frightfully dead in here, that's for sure." She slapped a hand over her mouth. "Oops."

Talia squeezed her shoulder. "It's okay to use the word *dead*, Bea."

"I know, I'm just so . . ." Bea swallowed and then looked at Suzy with misery in her eyes. "The coppers think I had something to do with Turnbull's murder," she choked out.

Suzy's mouth opened in shock. "Why, that's preposterous. What could possibly make them think that?"

Bea shrugged. "I guess I was the last holdout on the comic book store petition. Turnbull said Jepson had agreed to sign the petition. He claimed I was the only one bollocksing things up." She rearranged the folds in her soggy napkin.

Suzy's face turned bubble-gum pink. She looked at her watch.

"Plus, Phil and I had a big blowup that same day. If it hadn't been for Talia, I'd have nailed him in his smug face with a fish."

"I have a question," Talia said, gauging Suzy's expression. "Even if every proprietor in the arcade signed the petition, who's to say the landlord was going to take it seriously?"

"There's something in the by-laws," Suzy explained. "If the objection is unanimous, then it flies." She bit into her glossed lower lip. "Look, Bea, I know Phil told you everyone else was against the comic book store, but I, for one, was not. So don't believe everything you hear, okay?" She gave Talia a pleading look.

Talia opened her mouth to speak, but said nothing. What was Suzy trying to convey? Had she signed the petition or hadn't she?

"I've got to run," Suzy said, "so I'll get to the point. Jill has invited all the arcade owners to meet at her shop at seven this evening, after we all close. She'll serve snacks and tea, and we can all brainstorm. We need to find a way to entice shoppers"—she waved a hand at the kitchen—"and diners, back to the Wrensdale Arcade. Among all of us, we should be able to come up with some ideas, right?"

Bea looked as if she hadn't heard Suzy. Her eyes again grew misty.

Talia felt her own eyes filling. She glanced out at the dining area and then the kitchen. She loved this place—she had since she was a teenager. And Bea and Howie were family to her. She hated that so much bad luck had befallen them.

"It's Bea's call," Talia said. "I only work here, but I'll be glad to do whatever I can."

Bea nodded slowly. "Sounds fine," she said dully. "I don't want to stay too long, though. I visit my Howie at the hospital every night, and he'll worry if I don't show up."

"Of course." Suzy plopped a light kiss on Bea's cheek. "Our families come first. I think we all agree on that." She shot another look at Talia.

"See you after closing, then," Talia agreed. "Can we bring anything?"

"Only if you want to. Knowing Jill, she'll have enough goodies for all. Oh, and keep your eyes peeled for reporters today," she said in a stage whisper. "I saw one of them hanging around Queenie's Variety this morning. Dressed to the nines and trying to nab people for an interview as they were leaving the store."

With a wink and a wave Suzy left the eatery, leaving Talia to wonder. Was Suzy being honest about not objecting to the comic book store? Had Turnbull flatly lied about Suzy signing the petition?

So many questions, not enough answers. And now that Talia thought about it, where *was* that petition? She'd love to take a peek at it.

She was mulling that problem when the door slowly opened. Three elderly women shuffled in, their flat shoes stepping carefully over the blue-and-white tile floor. Vinyl purses hanging off their wrists, they huddled in a knot and looked around. "Are you open?" one of them asked, her bright blue eyes studying Talia's face.

"Yes, we are!" Talia graced each of them with a cheerful smile. "Welcome to Lambert's Fish and Chips. Is this your first visit?"

They all nodded. Talia guided them to a table near the far wall, where the cold air from the doorway wouldn't affect them. She offered to hang their coats but they refused, opting instead to drape them over the backs of their chairs.

"Oh my," one of them warbled, perusing the crisp, single-sheet menu. "Lil, you and I haven't had a proper fish and chips lunch since we visited Rodney in Maryland last year. This is going to be such a treat!"

Notepad in hand, Talia took their orders and brought each of them a mug of coffee. Bea had disappeared for the fifth or sixth time, no doubt to pay another visit to the "loo." In between bouts of tearful outbursts, Bea had been drinking coffee nonstop all morning.

Whitnee, too, had taken a quick break. She'd been shivering since she arrived and had to dash out to her car for a sweatshirt.

Back in the kitchen, Talia opened the fridge and extracted a container stacked with fresh haddock fillets. She set it down on the work counter next to the lemon, the large dill pickle, and container of mayo Bea had plunked there. Every morning Bea whipped up a fresh batch of tartar sauce—a concoction a local restaurant reviewer had dubbed "a tangy delight." Normally Bea would've had the tartar prepared by now, but her morning had been anything but normal.

Talia pulled on a pair of plastic gloves and set to work. First she lowered three fistfuls of chunky sliced potatoes into the smaller of the two deep fryers. Then she dredged three haddock fillets through a shallow tray of flour. Next, she coated each fillet thoroughly with Bea's special batter. She lowered them one at a time into the deep fryer reserved for fish only. Hot oil bubbled and sizzled, sending a tantalizing scent wafting through the kitchen.

From beneath the counter, she snagged three cone-shaped serving dishes forged from swirls of black wrought iron. Into each cone she tucked a paper liner that resembled newsprint. Talia thought the liners were a clever—and far more sanitary—improvement over the old English tradition of wrapping fish and chips in real newspaper.

After the potatoes had fried to a golden hue, Talia drained them and then divided them among the lined cones. Atop the "chips" in each cone, she carefully placed a crisp haddock fillet. For the final touch she sprinkled each one with a dash of malt vinegar. She set the cones on a large tray, along with three ramekins of mushy peas. Her own stomach was rumbling with hunger pangs by the time she delivered the meals to the ladies. All three women immediately dug in, and Talia heard them clucking their approval as she went back into the kitchen.

Talia was just refilling each of their coffee mugs when the door opened again. In strode a fair-haired young man wearing a hooded denim jacket and faded jeans. Talia squelched a shudder at the row of metal studs that lined his lower lip. How did the man eat, for pity's sake? In addition to the facial hardware, he had fleshy cheeks and a flattish nose, and a smirk that gave him the air of a know-it-all.

"Whitnee around?" he said to Talia, more a demand than a question.

Holding the coffeepot aloft, Talia forced a smile. "Yes, she is, although she had to run out to her car for something. Did you wish to speak to her?" She hadn't meant to sound so formal, but the young man's unsmiling arrogance unnerved her.

He looked around and sniffed the air like a hound trailing a scent. "I never been in here before. Smells good. Yeah, I wanna talk to her." Avoiding eye contact with Talia, his gaze traveled instead past the aquamarine counter and into the kitchen. Wearing an oversized navy sweatshirt, Whitnee had just emerged from the storage closet clutching a package of printed napkins. Talia hadn't even noticed that she'd returned.

"Yo, Whitnee," the visitor called out when he spotted her.

Whitnee stopped short, nearly dropping the napkins. After setting them down on the front counter, she scuttled into the dining area and sidled up next to him. "Pug, what are you doing here?"

He slid one arm around her shoulder and pulled her toward him. "Hey, what's the prob, babe? I thought you'd be glad to see me. You can't spare a few minutes to talk to your man?" His voice carried an edge that made Talia's hackles rise.

"No, I mean, sure, but—" Whitnee's face flushed redder than a ripe strawberry. "The thing is, the lunch rush just started and we're gonna be, like, crazy busy for the next few hours." Whitnee swiveled her head toward the kitchen. "I just don't want to get in trouble with my boss."

Poor Whitnee, Talia thought. She looked trapped between a fire and a flood. Talia quickly stuck out her only free hand. "Hi, I'm Talia. Whitnee and I work together."

The man gawked at Talia's hand as if she'd offered him a poisonous lizard. He snatched her fingers in a pathetic imitation of a handshake, then ran his own fingers through his oily, dishwater blond hair. "Pug," was all he said.

"His real name's Brandon," Whitnee said with a nervous giggle.

Pug glared at Whitnee, but said nothing.

Talia felt her heart sink. She couldn't imagine what Whitnee saw in this ill-mannered oaf. Whatever the attraction was, she only hoped it would fade before Whitnee got serious about him. That is, if he was even capable of being serious. The man wasn't ringing any chimes on the sincerity meter.

Feeling bad for Whitnee's obvious discomfort, Talia leaned toward the pair. "Hey, look," she said, in a conspiratorial whisper. "Why don't you two chat and catch up for a few minutes. I'll square things with Bea, okay?" She winked at Whitnee, who looked visibly relieved.

With that Talia flew into the kitchen and returned the coffeepot to the burner. Bea had reappeared and was unscrewing the mayo jar.

"Who's the bloke?" Bea hissed, shooting a scowl at Pug. She removed a sharp-edged knife from the utensil drawer and set it down on the cutting board next to the dill pickle.

"Boyfriend, I think." Talia lowered her voice to a whisper. "They just need a few minutes, okay?"

The wall phone jingled. Bea nodded and turned to answer it. Talia smiled when she saw Bea grab a lined pad and start scribbling down what appeared to be a sizeable order. She crossed her fingers and uttered a quick prayer that business was getting back to normal.

Out of the corner of her eye, Talia saw Pug saunter toward the counter at the same time she felt Bea tapping her arm. She turned to Bea, who shoved an order slip at her. Phone to her ear, Bea worked her eyebrows feverishly, apparently trying to convey a message. She jabbed her finger at the slip.

Talia looked at it. Bea had scrawled *D.W.* at the bottom and underlined it several times. "Derek Westlake?" she mouthed at Bea.

Bea nodded furiously, then turned again to answer the other blinking line. The takeout orders were coming in fast today, and earlier than usual.

Talia frowned at Westlake's order. Although she knew he ordered takeout every Friday for himself and a handful of his officers, she couldn't believe he'd had the nerve to place an order today, of all days! Hadn't he just told Bea she was a suspect in Turnbull's murder? For sure, the guy had one heck of a nerve.

Still, five orders of fish and chips was nothing to sneer at. Business was business, even if Westlake had implied Bea was guilty. Talia only wished she could add a plateful of common sense to his order, along with a helping of humility. The man looked good and he knew it.

Talia was dropping the requisite potato slices into the fryer when Pug smacked his palm hard on the counter to get her attention. "Hey, um, Talia is it?" he drawled.

Irritated, Talia glanced at him briefly, then turned and dragged a haddock fillet through the flour. "Yes, what can I help you with?" She swirled the fillet through the batter and lowered it carefully into the fryer.

Pug leaned both arms over the counter and grinned. "Hey, like, Whitnee says it was you who found that dead body yesterday. That is, like, so freakin' cool. I mean, that is righteously sick, know what I'm sayin'?" He cocked a finger at her, as if pulling a trigger.

Talia felt a flare of red-hot anger burst inside her. She grabbed another fillet, slapping it through the flour more roughly than she intended. "Yes, *Pug* . . . whatever your name is. It was *sick*, but not in the way you mean." She continued dredging, coating, and frying—moving in a rhythm that seemed to be getting ahead of her brain. "It was horrible, finding a man brutally murdered. I wouldn't wish it on anyone, not even—" She broke off, her hands shaking.

Pug gave his mouth an ugly twist. "Okay, lady, you don't have to get your thong in a knot. It's not like I killed the dude. Chill out, will ya?" He ran his forefinger over the metal fence beneath his lip.

"Pug." Whitnee tightened her fingers around Pug's upper arm and whispered something in his ear.

He shook her off roughly, then shot a menacing look at Talia. "I'm outta here," he said and stormed out.

Bea finally hung up the phone. She looked at Whitnee, then at Talia. "What's going on? What's all the bloody fuss about?"

"I'm sorry, Bea. That was all was my fault," Talia sucked in a breath. "I shouldn't have lost it like that."

Whitnee was shaking her head, her face drained of color. "No, it wasn't your fault. Pug shouldn't have talked to you that way." She looked at Bea. "I am *so, so* sorry he came in here, Bea." With a hitch in her voice, she hugged her arms to her chest and stared at the floor. "You're prob'ly sorry you ever hired me."

For the first time all morning, Talia saw Bea smile. "Aw, luvvy, I'd never be sorry I hired you. Was that chap your boyfriend?"

Whitnee nodded.

"Well then, it's water over the falls, isn't it. Let's all get back to work, shall we?"

"Oh my, I believe those were the best fish and chips I've ever had!" one of the silver-hairs trilled to Talia. "We're definitely going to make this a regular stop in the future."

The other two nodded, their faces beaming as they mined the depths of their vinyl handbags.

Smiling, Talia leaned forward. "I apologize if you overheard any unpleasantness," she said.

"Oh, we didn't mind at all," one of the other women tittered. "In fact, we were cheering you on. That young man was most obnoxious. I've never seen such rudeness."

"In my day," the stoutest of the three said, "our granddad would've taken a boy like that behind the woodshed and given him what for." Her face stern, she snagged a twenty out of her wallet.

The others nodded in agreement, and after calculating the tip they paid the bill. They scraped back their chairs and rose to leave.

"One last thing," the first senior said to Talia. "What do you know about the murder?"

Taken aback, Talia opened her mouth to respond just as the eatery's door swung open and Derek Westlake stepped inside. Tall and imposing in his crisp blue uniform, he tipped his hat to the ladies and nodded at Talia. All three seniors looked up at him, muttered hellos, and then scurried past him and out onto the plaza.

Saved by the bell, Talia thought, though she was less than thrilled to see Bea's accuser.

"Must've been the badge," he said with a shrug. With his long fingers, he straightened the gold shield pinned to his crisp navy jacket.

"Or the attitude," Talia quipped.

Westlake narrowed his dark eyebrows at Talia. She met his steely blue gaze straight on and said, "Your order is ready."

"Excellent. I'm starving." A smile hovered on his lips, but he wisely suppressed it.

Resisting an eye roll, Talia turned on her heel and went to the kitchen to retrieve his takeout order. Westlake strolled up to the counter.

Bea, meanwhile, was searching around as if she'd lost something. "Talia, did you— Oh," she said when she saw the chief.

"Hello, Bea," he said courteously.

Bea's green eyes glared at him. She pursed her lips but said nothing.

"Yours is on top," Talia said, handing him a tall brown bag with handles. "As always, it's marked EMP for extra mushy peas."

The chief smiled. "Great." He reached into the bag and pulled out a rectangular, red-checkered box. "I think I'll have a bite right now."

This time Talia did roll her eyes. Every week it was the same thing. Too hungry to wait until he was back at the station, he scarfed down half his lunch standing at the counter. He'd shown the same kind of impatience in high school, where he rushed through Steinbeck, sprinted through Dickens, and galloped through Hemingway as though his hat was on fire.

Talia planted a hand on her hips and shook her head. "Why don't you just sit down and eat your lunch here every week instead of taking it out?"

"Can't." He reached into the box and removed a golden length of fried haddock. "Gotta bring the boys and Abby their lunches. They don't want to eat 'em ice cold." He bit off a large chunk and began to chew slowly, savoring the taste. All at once, Westlake's face crumpled. He snatched a handful of napkins from the dispenser, and into it he spewed his entire mouthful.

Talia looked at him in horror. "Derek, what are you doing?"

Grimacing, he wiped his lips. "What am *I* doing? What are *you* doing?" He focused his gaze directly on Bea. "Are you trying to kill me?"

8

Bea trotted over to the counter. "What's the matter? What are you talking about?"

Westlake tossed his napkin into the nearby trash receptacle. He slammed the remainder of his takeout lunch on the counter and shoved it at her. "What do you call this? Green fish?"

Her legs wobbly, Talia pulled the box over for a closer look. After all, she was the one who'd prepared the takeout meals for Westlake and his gang. If anything was wrong, it was her fault.

A sudden giggle erupted from Bea, followed by an attack of roaring laughter that had her bending over at the waist. When Talia realized what she was looking at, she covered her mouth with both hands. "Derek, I am so sorry," she said, her smile peeking through her fingers.

"I looked everywhere for that pickle!" Bea howled, tears rolling down her cheeks.

"It's my fault, Derek," Talia bit her lip to keep from getting her own case of the giggles. "I got so flustered by one of our . . . customers, that I must have grabbed it by mistake when I was coating the fish." She reached for his takeout box. "Just give me a few minutes and I'll make a whole new—"

"Stop!" Westlake clamped his fingers over her wrist. "Hold on a second." He licked his lips a few times, then reached for the deep-fried pickle and took another bite. "You know what? This is actually delicious." His words came out garbled over a mouthful of food.

Bea grinned and clapped her hands with glee. "Look at that, Talia. I think you've discovered a new side dish!" She pointed at Westlake's takeout box. "Take that one off the bill—it's on the house today."

Westlake tossed his half-eaten pickle back into the box and tucked in the flaps. "Thank you, Mrs. Lambert," he said, digging his wallet out of his pocket, "but I'm afraid I can't accept a free lunch." He opened his mouth as if he wanted to add something else, but then closed it.

Talia's brief moment of levity faded. Pressing her lips into a firm line, she rang up the order and gave him change.

Westlake tipped his hat. "Ladies," he said with a nod. He grabbed the brown carryout bag and left.

Talia hesitated only for a moment. "Bea, I'll be right back," she said, and then followed him out the door.

"Derek," she said to his back when they were outside on the plaza.

He stopped and turned to her. "Yes?" he said warily.

"Bea told me the police think she killed Turnbull," she said, rubbing her arms against the nippy October air. "She said they supposedly found evidence that connects her to the murder."

Westlake's jaw hardened. "I'm not at liberty to discuss that," he said, his severe frown making crease lines in his brow. "Now, if you'll excuse me—"

"No, I won't excuse you! What is this so-called evidence? Can't you tell me? Doesn't the public have a right to know?"

Still facing her, he took a step backward. "I'll say it again. I am not at liberty to discuss the investigation. The state police are in charge now, so I suggest you direct any questions you have to them. Sergeant O'Donnell at the Berkshire Detective Unit in Pittsfield is heading up the case."

Talia stopped just short of stamping her sneakered foot on the cobblestone. "But you're the top cop in this town, and you've known Bea forever. You know she's not a killer!"

"Let me give you some advice, Talia." Westlake worked his jaw for a brief moment, while his gaze roamed the cobblestone arcade. "If you care about your boss, tell her to get herself a lawyer. And I would suggest she do it sooner rather than later. That's all I can say. Have a good day."

He turned and strode away, leaving Talia to gawk at him.

A good day? Was he kidding?

She stomped back into the eatery, where the heated air and delectable scents immediately warmed her bones. Bea was flinging potatoes into the fryer, and Whitnee was on the phone with more takeout orders.

"Everything okay?" Bea said in a low voice.

"I tried to extract some information from Derek, but his lips were zipped."

Bea's shook her head in disgust. "That's a copper for you. They never want to tell you anything, but they expect you to spill your innards."

Talia pulled the next order slip from the clip above the work counter, and all three worked in tandem through the busy lunch rush. Business was brisk—far better than Talia had expected, given the hype about the murder. It almost seemed as if the horrible crime had drawn people to Lambert's instead of repelling them. Fish flew into the fryer, potatoes sizzled, and mounds of mushy peas filled takeout containers like mini green mountains. For diners less inclined to go totally authentic, Bea offered helpings of her piquant homemade slaw, using a recipe she'd tweaked over the years. It was a concession she'd made long ago to those "fussy Americans"—a phrase she used with the utmost affection—who viewed mushy peas as nothing more than green blobs of toddler grub.

Talia wondered if the other shop owners, Suzy and Jill in particular, were experiencing the same uptick in customers.

Around two thirty the eatery slid into its usual midday lull. Bea had gone to the hospital to pay a quick visit to Howie, and Whitnee had opted to grab lunch at Queenie's Variety. Grateful for the break, and for a few minutes alone, Talia whipped up a snack for herself and dropped into a chair at the table tucked in the tiny alcove behind the commercial fridge. The space was just small enough to be hidden from view to anyone walking into the eatery.

Poking a fork into the scoop of mushy peas on her plate, she thought about Westlake's dire warning—his "advice" to Bea, as he called it. Talia still hadn't told Bea what he'd said about getting a lawyer. Did she really want to send Bea into a worse tizzy than she was already in? Or should she let sleeping pups lie and hope she'd never have to shake them awake?

For now, she'd settle for thinking about it. By closing time, though, she'd have to make a decision.

To tell or not to tell—

Wait a minute.

When Westlake picked up his order earlier, he'd mentioned that one of the takeout lunches was for Abby. Talia knew he meant Abby Kingston, the administrative whirlwind who kept the police department records shipshape. Abby had a little boy, Jacob, who was in Rachel's class. Earlier in the school year, Abby and Rachel had bonded over an incident involving a bully—a boy who'd been tormenting Jacob on a near daily basis. Rachel's kind and creative problem-solving had halted the bullying in its tracks. Both boys had benefited from her intervention.

Maybe Abby knew something about the so-called "evidence" against Bea.

Talia grabbed her phone from her purse and sent a quick text to Rachel. With any luck, she'd have an answer before the end of the day.

Talia barely had a chance to swallow the last bite of her lunch when Whitnee returned from her break. "Did you have lunch?" Talia asked her, hoping to engage her in a spot of conversation.

Whitnee nodded. "Turkey sub from Queenie's. They come, like, prepackaged, but they're pretty good."

"Sounds delicious." Yep. She was coming up with some real snappy lines today.

"I'll start wiping down the tables and chairs," Whitnee said. "It was pretty busy today, and I saw some kid spill tartar sauce on his chair. His mother just left it there, too. She was, like, oblivious." With a roll of her eyes, she pulled a clean cloth and the bottle of spray cleaner from beneath the sink.

Talia looked at Whitnee with concern. The girl's mood

was so melancholy that she had an urge to go over and give her a hug. She held back, sensing that such a gesture would make Whitnee distinctly uncomfortable. But something had put her in a blue funk today. Was she stressing over her spat with Punk, or Pug, or whatever his name was?

If she would only talk about what was bothering her, it might make her feel better. Talia realized that she knew very little about Whitnee—a fact she hoped to remedy in the not-too-distant future.

Since it was painfully clear that her coworker preferred silent companionship today, Talia busied herself tidying up the kitchen. She was putting away the container of slaw when she spied the jar of whole dill pickles in the fridge.

Hmmm.

Although Bea hadn't come back from visiting Howie yet, Talia felt sure she wouldn't object to a bit of experimentation. She removed a pickle from the jar and set it down on the cutting board. Pondering how she would attack the project, she stared at it for a minute. Then she grabbed a sharp knife and sliced it into even rounds, each about a quarter-inch thick.

On a large paper plate she sprinkled a layer of unbleached flour. She coated each round on both sides and set them aside. She returned the pickle jar to the fridge and removed the bowl of batter Bea had prepared for the dinner rush. The rush wouldn't begin until around four thirty, so Talia had plenty of time to "play" with her new idea.

After swirling each floured round in the batter, she dropped them one by one into the hot oil. The aroma triggered a Pavlovian response, and her stomach rumbled with anticipation. Talia inhaled deeply, unable to keep a smile from creeping across her face.

Whitnee returned to the kitchen and put away the cleaning supplies. She peered into the deep fryer and frowned. "What are you making? Those things look . . . weird."

Talia held up a finger. "Give me a few minutes and then we'll taste test them."

About three minutes later, when the rounds were crisp and golden, Talia drained them and set them on a plate. "Okay, they're hot, so be careful," she cautioned, offering one to Whitnee.

Whitnee shrugged without interest and took a round off the plate. She bit into it and immediately waggled her fingers in front of her lips. "Hot," she mumbled over the deep-fried pickle.

Talia grinned. "I warned you. Don't burn your mouth." She plucked one off the plate for herself, waved it through the air, and then bit into it. The flavor burst on her tongue. She closed her eyes, savoring the blend of the tangy pickle round and the crispy fried batter. Did the batter need a sprinkle of dried dill to enhance the flavor? Or maybe the tiniest bit of cayenne pepper to give it a little zing? What about a dipping sauce?

"Oh my gosh," Whitnee said, her eyes popping wide open. "That was, like, amazing. Can I have another one?"

"Of course!"

Between the two of them, they polished off the fried pickle rounds within five minutes. After Whitnee had gulped down her last bite she pointed at the empty plate. "Oh no, we didn't save any for Bea!"

"Don't worry. I'll make some fresh ones for her when she gets back. In fact—" Talia tapped a finger to her lips. She aimed her gaze at the fryer and felt a slow grin splitting her face. "I think I have a better idea."

9

Save for a few stragglers, the arcade was quiet. Too quiet,
Talia thought eerily, making her way toward Time for Tea
with Bea at her side. In her hands she clutched an oval plate
piled with fried pickle rounds. She'd prepared them at the
last possible moment before closing time, and covered them
with foil to keep them warm.

"That was a splendid thought, Tal," Bea said. "In all my
years of running a restaurant, I never thought of dunking
pickle slices into the fryer."

"Well, we can thank Whitnee's repulsive boyfriend for
the idea. If he hadn't ticked me off so supremely, I wouldn't
have grabbed that silly pickle from the cutting board in the
first place!"

Bea laughed. "Ah, well, sometimes things work out the
way they're supposed to."

"You seem a bit more cheery than you were this morning," Talia said.

Bea nodded, her hands shoved deep into the pockets of her black jacket. "I had a lovely chat with my Howie this afternoon. His color was a tad better, and the doctor said he might be able to go home in few days, if they can keep the infection under control. Whether or not he'll come back to work anytime soon . . . well, I'm not so sure about that." She lifted her shoulders in a shrug. "I guess time will tell, won't it."

Talia bit her lip with concern. "Does Howie know about . . . ?"

"The murder? Yes, it's not like I could keep it from him. He has a telly in his room, and the bloomin' thing is always on. Anyway, I made light of the whole incident. I don't need him worrying his poor self over me when his health is at stake."

"Like you could stop him," Talia said, knowing how close the two were. A wave of guilt swept over her. She'd visited Howie only once during his hospital stay. She made a mental promise to herself to pop in and see him either on Saturday or Sunday.

The two front windows of Time for Tea cast a soft, golden glow over the cobblestone at the entrance to the charming shop. Bea held open the door for her and they both stepped inside.

A host of aromas assailed Talia's senses. Citrus and cloves and pumpkin and apple, each scent vying for dominance in the cozy tea shop.

Suzy Sato had arrived early. Her springy red curls bounding around her face, she hugged Bea first, and then Talia. Her blue eyes looked brighter than ever—glowing, in fact. Talia wondered if it was Turnbull's untimely departure that made her beam with such apparent joy.

"Can I peek?" Suzy said, looking at the tray Talia was carrying.

"Absolutely." Talia pulled back a corner of the foil.

Suzy clapped her hands. "Ooh, they look scrumptious. What are they?"

"Deep-fried pickle rounds," Bea chimed in. "Talia's idea, and a brilliant one at that." She peeled off her jacket and tucked it under her arm.

"Why don't you set them over there," Suzy said. She indicated a long display counter, over which a runner the color of burnished gold had been draped. Atop the runner were several flowered teacups, each one in a different pattern. Two fragrant pots of tea rested on brass hot plates. Tiny paper containers of individual cream portions sat in a circle around a china bowl filled with raw sugar. At one end of the counter was an ornate silver tray stacked with an array of finger sandwiches. Talia squeezed in her own tray next to the sandwich platter.

"Hey, there, glad to see you!" Jill emerged from a back room carrying a plate of lemon slices sprinkled with a fine layer of powdered sugar. Her raven-colored hair had been pulled into an elegant French twist, and her eyes were exquisitely made-up. Her cobalt-blue dress—knitted mohair, Talia thought—caressed her soft curves. She looked at Talia for a long moment, as if to convey a silent message. Then she rested the plate near the sugar bowl and turned to Bea. "Bea, I think you'll enjoy some of the snacks I put out, especially the blends of teas I've chosen." With a teasing smile, she winked at her. "You Brits all love your tea, right?"

Bea returned the smile with a saccharine one of her own. "Yes, I suppose we do."

Talia moved past Bea to survey the goodies so her face wouldn't betray her amusement. If Jill only knew how fiercely Bea despised tea. She was a coffee person, straight to the bone. Even in her native England, Bea often claimed, she had never enjoyed tea. There wasn't a tea on Earth that ever pleased her, and for sure there never would be.

"Suzy, will you help me bring out some chairs?" Jill said. "We'll set up near the checkout counter."

Suzy trailed Jill into the storeroom, and they returned lugging a half dozen folding chairs. They were placing them in a half circle near the rear counter when the door swung open. A lanky, fiftyish man clad in a thin sweater and wrinkled navy chinos strode in, his shoulders hunched over his sunken chest. His face had a yellow, unhealthy cast, and he gawked at Talia through pewter-colored eyes as if he'd spotted an alien life form.

Bea nodded at him. "Good to see you, Cliff. I don't think you've ever met my colleague, Talia Marby. Talia, this is Cliff Colby. He owns the Clock Shop across the way."

"Oh, of course. Nice to meet you, Cliff." Talia held out her hand. "I've been meaning to pop into your shop and have a look around, but I haven't had the chance." Lord, could she have sounded any lamer?

With a glassy stare, Cliff shook Talia's hand. "Yeah, whatever." He dipped his thick eyebrows toward his nose. "So you're working for Bea and Howie?" His ragged fingernails raked her palm as he pulled his long fingers from her grasp.

"Yes. For now, at least." She avoided looking at Bea.

At least a foot taller than Talia, Cliff glanced over her head. His strange gray eyes shone when he spotted the food trays. Talia couldn't help comparing him to a bird of prey on one of those nature programs, gearing up to spring on some poor, unsuspecting mouse. "Those up for grabs?" he said. "What's under the foil?"

Bea excused herself and strolled toward the back of the shop. Talia reluctantly lifted the foil on the fried pickle tray so Cliff Colby could have a peek. "They're deep-fried pickles," she said, intercepting the question she knew was forming on his lips.

"Huh," he said. Without being asked, he stuck a hand toward the tray and grabbed three pickle rounds at once. He popped one in his mouth and chomped. "Geezum!" he said with a noisy swallow. He helped himself to two more.

While his hands were otherwise occupied, Talia quickly tucked the foil over the platter. "I don't want them to get cold before everyone arrives," she said.

Cliff assessed her with another hawkish look. When he turned his attention to the finger sandwiches, Talia saw her opportunity to escape. She hurried over to where the chairs were set up in a half circle and seated herself next to Bea. Following Bea's lead, she removed her jacket and draped it over the back of her chair.

Jill and Suzy had retreated to the storeroom again, which gave Talia the chance to talk to Bea. "Jim Jepson isn't here. Think he's ditching the meeting?"

"No. Jim's a good fellow. If he was invited, he'll be here." Bea turned at the sound of the door opening. "Ah, there's Jim now. We should be all ready to start. Now where did those other two disappear to?" she groused. "I really don't want to be stuck here too long."

As if by the wave of a magic wand, Jill and Suzy material-ized from the storeroom. Jill carried a small tray bearing plas-tic stirrers and cocktail-sized napkins, along with flowered china plates for the snacks. Spying Jim and Cliff, she beckoned everyone over to where the tea and treats had been set out. She smiled at the group. "Why don't you all help yourselves, and then we'll get started with a little brainstorming."

"I'll be right back." Talia scooted up alongside Jim Jep-son, the potter, whose gray hair hung in a neat ponytail over the back of his red flannel shirt. "Hey, Mr. J. How's it going?"

Jepson turned toward Talia, and his brown eyes danced with delight. "Hey yourself, Talia. It's good to see you. And please, it's time you called me Jim." He poured himself a steaming cup of apple-infused tea. "So, you're still over at Lambert's helping out Bea, are you?"

"Yes. It's déjà vu all over again. I don't know if you remember, but I worked there when I was in high school. I always loved working for Bea and Howie." She reached for a china plate rimmed with painted violets.

"As much as you loved my geometry class?" Jepson grinned at her. He slid two of the fried pickle rounds onto a rose-colored plate.

"Ah, good old geometry. I think the only thing I remem-ber about the isosceles triangle is how to spell it." English, she'd loved. Math, not so much. Talia helped herself to a sandwich of smoked salmon, along with another one of the irresistible pickle rounds. "I still don't understand how you went from teacher to potter. The kids all loved you."

Jepson shrugged and held a pickle round to his lips. "Kids are fickle. Times change. 'Nuff said, okay?" He popped the pickle into his mouth.

"Um, sure." Feeling a bit nonplussed, Talia poured herself a cup of the same tea Jim had chosen.

"Oh man, did you taste these things? They're fantastic." Jim reached for two more fried pickles.

"Bea and I made them," Talia said. She couldn't resist preening a bit. "Mr. J., I mean, Jim, do you mind if I ask you a question?"

"Fire away." He added an egg salad finger sandwich to his plate.

"Turnbull told Bea that you'd caved," she said quietly. "He said you agreed to sign the petition against the comic book store, and that Bea was the only holdout."

Jepson looked away. He nabbed a sugared lemon wedge and squeezed it into his tea. "He's a liar. I never volunteered to sign that ugly document." His nostrils flared. "It was elitism, in its purest form. I loathe that kind of snobbery."

Talia let out the breath she'd been holding. She wanted to believe him. But why had he looked away when she questioned him? Why was he still dodging her gaze?

"Thanks, um, Jim. I was sure he was lying, but I wanted to get it from the horse's mouth, if you catch my meaning."

Jepson's face relaxed. "I hear you." The opening lines of "Light My Fire" crooned from his shirt pocket. Juggling his cup and plate in one hand, he dug out the cell with two fingers. When he saw the caller ID, his face reddened.

Bea sidled up next to Jepson, her plate topped with three egg salad finger sandwiches. "Jim, how are you doing? Have you tried one of these creamed egg sandwiches? They're marvelous." She slapped her hand over her mouth and whispered, "Oops, sorry, I didn't realize you were on the phone."

Jepson immediately cut off the call and returned the phone to his pocket. He kissed Bea lightly on the cheek.

"It's great to see you, Bea. And no, I haven't tried the egg salad yet, but Talia tells me you and she are the creator of these . . . these . . . what are they again?"

"Deep-fried pickle slices," Bea said proudly. "And they were entirely Talia's idea. Isn't she a gem?"

"Oh *pshaw*," Talia joked.

"Attention, everyone," Jill called to the group. "If you'll fill your plates and cups and have a seat, we can get started. I know you all have other things to do, so the sooner we finish the faster we can go home."

They all took seats. Talia was pleased to see that everyone had taken a helping of deep-fried pickles, although Cliff Colby's helping was triple the size of everyone else's. The man was a hog!

"I first want to express my deepest sorrow over Phil's demise," Jill said soberly. "I know some of you had less than warm feelings for him, but he was a human being and a fellow shop owner, and"—her voice cracked—"and he didn't deserve to be murdered."

Bea nodded but remained silent. She'd barely poured a tablespoon of tea into her cup. She pretended to take a tiny sip.

"I agree," Suzy piped in, with a toss of her titian curls. "Phil could be infuriating at times, but there was a part of him that was really gentle and sweet."

Talia nearly choked on her tea. If there was a part of Phil Turnbull that was gentle and sweet, he'd certainly disguised it well. She looked over at Jill, whose eyes had grown moist, and immediately felt bad for her uncharitable assessment of the dead man.

"Suzy's right," Jepson said. "We had no right to judge him until we'd walked a mile in his shoes."

With that pronouncement, everyone turned their attention to the clock merchant. His plate balanced on his bony knees, Cliff shoved a sandwich of smoked salmon into his mouth. He looked up as if to say something, but halted when the door to Time for Tea flew open.

All eyes pivoted toward the stunningly pretty woman in the Red Riding Hood cape who promenaded toward them as if she owned the tea shop. Blond hair piled on top of her head in chic curls, she halted in her black-booted tracks and raked her gaze over the group. When her eyes landed on Jill, they locked. "Nice of you to invite me, Jill," she said in a glacial voice. "Or did you forget that I am now the proprietor of the largest shop in the arcade?"

Everyone froze, as if some invisible giant with a remote control had hit the Pause button.

Jill rose, and her face blanched. "Kendra, what are you doing here?"

The woman grinned wickedly, her sculpted lips the same shade of crimson as her magnificent cape. She seemed to revel in everyone's discomfort. "I thought you all might like to meet the new proprietor of the comic book store that's coming soon to an arcade near you—the Wrensdale Arcade, that is." With a sly wink she threw her head back and laughed—a low, throaty sound that set Talia's teeth on edge.

Jill clenched her fists at her side. "*You're* the one who wants to open the comic book store?" Her normally cultured voice came out in a mouselike squeak. She shook her head in disbelief. "No wonder he—" She broke off and sank onto her chair, her lips pressed together in a furious line.

The woman rolled her artificially long-lashed eyes at the ceiling. "Hardly, dear. That wouldn't be quite my style. By the way, for those of you who haven't met me, I'm Kendra LaPlante. Kendra *Turnbull* LaPlante."

Kendra. Turnbull's ex. The K-witch!

Jill looked too stunned to say anything further. Talia felt Bea nudging her with her elbow.

"Oh, um . . . hello, I'm Talia Marby, and I work at Lambert's Fish and Chips," she said to Kendra. She turned and smiled at Bea. "And this is Bea Lambert, my boss."

Bea bobbed her head at Kendra. "Pleased to meet you."

The others followed suit and offered a brief introduction—with the exception of Cliff Colby, who was so involved with the food on his plate that he didn't so much as throw Kendra a glance.

Kendra whipped a smartphone out of her designer handbag and punched it a few times. Flashing a devious smile, she held it to her ear. "You can come in, now, and meet your fellow shopkeepers." She stuck the phone back in her bag.

The door opened again, and this time a young man decked out in eighties-style punk shuffled in. His heavily gelled, sandy-brown hair stood out in pointy, blue-tipped spokes around his thin head, and his eyes were rimmed in black. Silver chains hung from torn denim jeans, the bottoms of which brushed the tops of his unlaced sneakers. Something about the entire getup looked contrived to Talia, but she couldn't quite pinpoint what it was.

"Ladies and gents, meet your new fellow shopkeeper—my stepson, Aaron LaPlante."

"Hey, everyone," the young man said without much enthusiasm.

Jill inhaled sharply. "What are you talking about? Are you saying that . . . *he's* the person who's going to run the comic book store?"

"You catch on quick. I'm putting up half the capital, and the rest is coming from his . . . trust fund," Kendra said, with a curl of her lip. "He'll either sink or swim, depending on how motivated he is to make a go of it."

The young man—Aaron—blushed to the tips of his pierced ears.

Talia found herself feeling bad for the guy. Kendra was treating him as if he were a trained seal she'd dragged in solely for their entertainment.

Aaron looked over the spread Jill had set out. "Is this stuff, like, okay to eat?" he asked of no one in particular.

Kendra waved a hand at him, a marquis diamond the size of a football winking off her left ring finger. "Go ahead and indulge. That type of food is just about your speed, anyway."

Jill paled. If looks could barbecue, Kendra would have been roasted over a flame and served up on a sesame bun.

"By the way, don't let his sluglike speech patterns fool you," Kendra said. "Aaron graduated with honors from the Art Institute of Boston, and in fact is far more intelligent than his looks would suggest."

Aaron glowered at Kendra, then reached for one of the flowered plates. In spite of his bizarre attire, Talia noticed, his hands appeared smooth and his nails manicured.

"Listen, we're getting off topic here," Suzy said. She reached over and gave Jill's wrist a supportive squeeze. "Mrs. LaPlante . . . Kendra," she went on, her smile like steel edged in lace. "We all came here tonight to discuss damage control. Our individual businesses have suffered since Phil's . . . demise, and we want to get things back to the way they were. If you have anything to contribute, please do. Otherwise, it would truly be best if y'all left."

Wow. *Way to go, Suzy,* Talia inwardly cheered. Beneath all those flouncy red curls was a woman with a backbone.

Kendra's eyes flickered with irritation. She lifted her chin. "Well, well, you're quite the little guardian of the flock, aren't you," she said to Suzy. "It actually seems you're rather astute. I have nothing to offer this ragtag group of whiners, and you surely have nothing to offer me. Personally, I have far bigger, far more *lucrative* fish"—she winked at Bea—"to fry. I only came here to introduce you all to Aaron. In the future, he'll be part of this little . . . troop, shall we say, so you may as well get used to him."

Talia felt herself swelling with anger at the demeaning way the woman talked about her own stepson, and right in front of him! She couldn't help wondering why Aaron didn't tell her to get stuffed.

She immediately answered her own question—money. Aaron obviously needed Kendra's infusion of capital to get his new comic book store up and running.

Jim Jepson, who so far had remained oddly quiet, shot out of his chair. "I, for one, will welcome Aaron to the arcade," he said, looking directly at him. "Aaron, my man, if you need any help settling in, getting the hang of things, feel free to stop in and see me at the pottery shop." Jepson sat down again and crossed one leg over the other.

Looking perplexed, Aaron frowned at him. "Yeah, thanks," he muttered, setting his still-empty plate next to the sandwich tray. To Kendra he said, "Maybe we should go."

"For once, a useful suggestion." Kendra waved her hand dismissively. "Ta-ta, all."

With a whirl of her cape, Kendra turned and glided toward the door. Aaron followed, just as Jill popped out of her chair and ran up behind Kendra. She grabbed Kendra's arm, and the two began a heated discussion that was just out of Talia's earshot.

"Blimey," Bea murmured in Talia's ear. "Talk about a *bee-yotch*, as Whitnee's mum would say." She scrunched her nose. "This apple tea tastes like worm juice."

Talia bit her lip to keep from smiling. "You don't have to finish it," she whispered back, perking her ears at the raised voices.

"—sitting pretty now, aren't you?" Jill hissed at Kendra.

"—none of your business, is it?" Kendra retorted.

In hushed tones, the two argued for a few more minutes. Then Kendra did a pirouette and stalked out the door, following by a glowering Aaron. Talia couldn't help letting out a sigh of relief.

"I apologize for that nasty intrusion," Jill said softly, reclaiming her seat. Her face looked splotchy. "I don't even know how she heard about our meeting."

Suzy looked down at her shoes, her cheeks pink. "It might have been my fault. She came into my store today, pretending she wanted to buy something. She must've picked up at least a dozen bottles of facial creams, read the labels, and then put them all back. She was making me so nervous that I started to babble—you know, just making small talk. I guess I must've mentioned the meeting to her." She looked at Jill remorsefully. "I'm sorry."

Jill patted Suzy on the knee. "No problem. Why don't we get on with things, then we can all go."

For the next fifteen minutes, everyone with the exception of Cliff Colby tossed out ideas. Talia wondered why Cliff had even shown up at the meeting if he had no intention of contributing. One look at his plate, heaped with a second helping of food, pretty much answered the question.

Jim Jepson agreed to display a few of his unique pottery pieces outside on the cobblestone plaza, where passersby could ogle them—something he'd been reluctant to do in the past for fear of breakage or theft. Jill and Suzy both decided to run specials through the weekend, and Suzy was going to put together some freebies in tiny gift bags to hand out to her customers. Although Jill didn't have restaurant facilities, her game plan for Sunday was to offer free samples of some of her English teas, along with freshly baked cranberry mini-scones from Peggy's Bakery.

Bea fidgeted in her chair. "I can do a 'two for the price of one' tomorrow," she offered, "to attract shoppers to the arcade. But I've got to say, business was quite perky today, wasn't it, Talia?"

"We did have a pretty good day. I guess when it comes down to it, people have to eat."

"Well, then, that sounds like a plan, Bea," Jill said.

"What about you, Cliff?" Talia was just irked enough and weary enough to prod the uncooperative shop owner.

Hearing his name, Cliff finally raised his head. "Oh, uh . . . I sell clocks, mostly vintage stuff. I can't do much more to push those." He shrugged. "You either need a clock or you don't."

About as helpful as a furnace in a heat wave, Talia thought wryly.

Jill pursed her lips at him and said, "Then I guess we're done. Although . . . wait a minute. How are we going to let people know about our specials? Does anyone here have a Facebook page?"

Suzy raised a hand. "My shop does. I'll post all of this tonight. It's somewhat short notice, but I think it will help."

Talia knew Bea didn't have a Facebook page for Lambert's, so she remained silent.

"Excellent, Suzy," Jill said. "Listen, I want to thank all of you for coming. I think we've proposed some solid ideas for getting the arcade back on track. Maybe the police will find the killer in the next day or two, and we can put all of this behind us." She sent a wintry glance in Cliff's direction. "I'll grab some plastic bags from the back and you can all help yourselves to the rest of the goodies. It's easier than my lugging them home."

Cliff launched himself off his chair and made a beeline for the food. Jim Jepson's cell chose that moment to ring again—the evocative plea to "Light My Fire" streaming from his flannel shirt pocket. Jim rose and stepped away from the group, answering the call as he did so. He moved until he stood a few yards behind Talia. Although she had no intention of eavesdropping, the shrill voice on Jepson's phone came through so clearly that she couldn't stop herself from listening in.

"I just found out he left another voice mail on my machine Wednesday morning. I thought you said everything would be okay. That you were going to . . . take care of it!"

"Everything *is* okay," Jim said tightly. "It's all going to work out, so just chill. I'm in a meeting right now. I'll call you when I get home." He ended the call abruptly and shoved the phone back in his pocket.

Whoa. What was that about? Talia wondered, slipping her arms into the sleeves of her jacket. Not that she had any right to know—the call was personal and had nothing to do with her. Still, the tone of what she'd overheard had been ominous, almost frightening. Not something she ever expected from the peace-loving Jim Jepson.

But . . . what if Jim had been referring to Turnbull's murder? What did he mean when he said, 'it's all going to work out'? The voice at the other end had sounded like a man's—a desperate man's—yet she couldn't be entirely sure. Cell phones had a way of distorting sound. The caller could easily have been a woman with a deep voice.

She had to stop thinking about it. If she didn't, it would drive her crazy.

"—ready, luv? You look like you've seen a monster." Bea's voice cut through Talia's roving thoughts.

"Oh, sorry, Bea. My mind was wandering. Ready to go?"

By the time they'd all divvied up the remaining sandwiches—the fried pickle supply was depleted—it was after eight o'clock.

"Your pickles were a hit," Jill said to Bea. "Are you going to start offering those at Lambert's?"

"Ah, well, who knows? That'll all be up to Talia." Bea sighed, and all at once Talia felt her mood sink. Bea was depending on her more and more. The realization made her insides twist. What was going to happen when the right job landed in her lap and she had to give Bea her notice? What if Howie never got well enough to return to working full time?

Talia scooped the empty pickle tray off the gold runner. "I'll pretend I'm Scarlett O'Hara and think about that tomorrow," she said to Jill. "Right now, all I want is a hot bath followed by oodles of sleep."

Suzy came up next to Jill holding a bag of four or five smoked salmon sandwiches. Her bubbly expression of only an hour earlier had vanished, and her blue eyes looked dull with fatigue. "I heard you mention a hot bath, Talia. I'm trying some new bath salts tonight—pearly almond with a hint of lilac. They came into the shop this morning from one of my new distributors."

"Sounds like just the ticket." Talia gave her a weak smile. "Save a bottle for me?"

"Sure thing." Suzy looked around in all directions, then leaned in close. Speaking quietly, she said, "You know, after meeting that weirdo tonight, I'm glad I did what I—" She stopped herself abruptly, and a bright pink flush crept up her neck, flooding her cheeks. "I mean, I— Sorry, guess I lost my train of thought. I can't even remember what I was going to say." She let out a nervous giggle that sounded forced and hollow.

"Oh, I do that all that time," Bea said with a wave of her hand. "Sometimes I wonder if I've left home in the morning without my head."

Everyone chuckled, but to Talia it was clear that Suzy had been about to blurt something. Something she hadn't intended them all to hear. Maybe something meant for Jill's ears only? The two seemed close. Talia sensed they shared confidences.

All the more reason Talia wanted to pry into Suzy's psyche a bit more. She felt sure Suzy had lied to her about refusing to sign Turnbull's petition.

Had Jim lied, too? Was that why he hadn't been able to look her in the eye when she'd asked him about it?

Despite her warm jacket, a shiver danced up Talia's arms. She had a sudden image of Phil Turnbull as puppeteer, controlling the strings of the arcade proprietors even from the grave.

As if he'd had some hold over them.

Some strange, manipulative hold that even death couldn't break.

Jill locked the door and they all stepped outside onto the cobblestone plaza. The night air, nippier than before, sneaked its icy fingers under the sleeves of Talia's jacket. She shivered and tucked her scarf more tightly around her neck.

Talia jumped when she saw that they weren't alone on the plaza. Several yards away, a man in a trench coat stood watching them, his hands resting protectively on the shoulders of the young girl standing in front of him.

"Mommy!" Clad in a short camel jacket over corduroy pants, the little girl broke away and raced over to Jill.

Talia realized she was looking at Carly—Jill's daughter.

Squinting, Talia studied the child. Was she the little girl in the mystery photograph? Did she bear any resemblance to Turnbull?

"Hey there, Carlycat!" Jill grinned and wrapped her arms around the child, pulling her close. "Aren't you cold, standing out here? Why didn't you and Daddy wait for me in the car?" Jill's gaze skittered to the man walking slowly toward her, but she didn't acknowledge him.

"She wanted to wait for you here," he said with a polite nod to everyone. "I promised I'd treat you both to a sundae at Scooped." His voice was Ivy League suave, his features pleasing but unremarkable. Even in the dark, his navy trench coat looked straight out of Brooks Brothers.

Jill introduced Carly all around. In a clipped tone she added, "And this is my husband, Gerry."

"What about the sundae, Mommy? Can we get one?" Carly begged.

"Of course, if that's what you want, sweetie." Jill kissed

the top of her head. "But I thought we were going to save that for tomorrow?"

"We can't. Daddy has to leave for a business trip in the morning."

Jill shot her husband a dark look. "On Saturday."

"It came up suddenly," Gerry said, avoiding her eyes. "I have a meeting in Tokyo on Monday."

Talia shifted her weight from one polka-dotted sneaker to the other. If there was a magic button she could press that would instantly transport her to her car, she'd be on it in a heartbeat.

"Luvvy." Bea tugged on the elbow of Talia's jacket. "We really ought to be going. Tomorrow's going to be a busy day, and we both need our beauty sleep."

"That's true. We really should fly. Thanks for hosting the meeting, Jill."

Talia and Bea issued hasty good-byes and fled toward their cars, Suzy in hot pursuit.

"Whew," Suzy said. "Thank God for you guys. That was *sooo* embarrassing, wasn't it?"

"It was uncomfortable, to say the least," Talia agreed. "By the way, I loved the way you handled Kendra at the meeting. I had the feeling she'd never been spoken to that way before."

"Thanks, but it had to be done. The way she bombed in there like a locomotive? I figured someone had to switch off her key."

They made their way across the plaza toward Main Street. Most of the downtown shops had gone dark, although tiny lights shone in several of the front windows. They passed

Talia's favorite gift shop—the Chortling Giraffe—where a string of orange lights flickered around the edge of the darkened display window. Beyond the glass, a trio of papier-mâché witches gathered in a spooky faux forest. Among the bare branches, several sets of fake staring eyeballs had been cleverly tucked. The witches hunkered around a black plastic caldron, maniacal grins plastered on their wart-encrusted faces. Talia smiled, imagining a mini-version of the scene on the mantel above Nana's never-used fireplace.

Not that she had time to decorate this season, or the inclination. She remembered the Realtor cautioning her not to load the house with tchotchkes. "The barer, the better," the broker had told her. "Buyers want to imagine their own personal touches there, not yours."

When they reached the town parking lot, Talia dug out her ladybug key chain. After ensuring that Bea and Suzy were safely ensconced in their vehicles, she beeped open her car lock. A moment later, Bea's ancient Datsun crawled up and idled in front of her. It wasn't until Talia flashed her headlights that Bea's car eased out onto the main drag.

A thought struck her like a hammer to the chest. She'd never told Bea about Westlake's advice to get a lawyer. She'd been stalling, dreading Bea's reaction.

But if she delayed telling her long enough, maybe she'd never have to. Wasn't it possible the police would have the real killer in custody by morning?

Didn't the police work around the clock to catch a killer?

She sure hoped so. Because the thought of them marching into the eatery the next day and arresting Bea for murder was just too horrible to imagine.

10

Talia zipped her little car into Nana's driveway and killed the engine. The bungalow was pitch dark. With an involuntary shiver, she vowed to buy a timer for one of the lights. Never again did she want to be forced to enter an unlit house.

Using the mini-light on her ladybug keychain for guidance, she climbed the front steps and unlocked the door. A sudden, plaintive cry gave her a start.

Mewww.

Talia let out a breath. The sound was animal, not human.

Heart thumping, she walked to the side of the porch, toward the sound. She flicked the beam from her keychain over the edge of the railing. An adorable feline face came into view—a furry, tricolored angel. The cat gazed up at Talia with a pair of moon-sized eyes.

Talia ducked inside the bungalow and plunked her handbag and the empty pickle tray onto her grandfather's ratty old chair. She flipped on the porch light and then, moving quietly, descended the steps. She hoped she hadn't already spooked the cat with the bright light.

It was still there—a darling calico, thin and shivering. Its face was mottled black and tan, and it had delicate white paws. Talia recalled reading somewhere that calico cats were almost always female, though she couldn't remember the reason why.

Moving slowly, Talia stooped and held out her hand. "Oh, sweetie, are you hungry?" she said in a soft, singsong voice. "Would you like something to eat?"

The cat took a few skittish steps backward. She looked ready to bolt.

Talia rose and retreated into the house, praying the cat would remain where she was. She returned with two plastic bowls—one filled with fresh water and the other with a can of flaked tuna. She wasn't sure if cats were supposed to eat "people tuna," but surely it was better than starving.

The calico kitty was still there. The moment Talia set the bowls down, the cat attacked the tuna.

Talia watched her scarf down food for a few moments, her heart melting for the little creature. If nothing else, the cat wouldn't go to bed hungry. Wherever her "bed" was.

She climbed the porch steps again and stepped into the cozy warmth of Nana's bungalow. The cat kept popping into her mind. Was she alone in the world, with no one to care for her? Had someone dumped her and fled, leaving her to fend for herself?

Nana had always wanted a cat, but her severe allergy to cat dander had put the kibosh on that notion. Chet, naturally, had an intense loathing of cats, so Talia never even brought up the subject with him.

For now, the least she could do was feed her little visitor. In the morning she'd check the animal shelter to see if anyone had reported her missing.

Talia washed the pickle tray and set it in the dish drainer, then nabbed a quick supper of Cheerios with low-fat milk. Curled up on Nana's sagging green sofa, she channel-surfed for at least half an hour. It struck her that the Friday night television lineup was alien territory. When she lived with Chet, their typical Friday evening consisted of drinks and dinner with a colleague or two from Chet's investment firm, followed by a late movie or the occasional sporting event. For Chet, the idea of spending an intimate Friday evening alone with Talia had all the allure of a trip to Mars. Not possible. Not happening.

With a sigh, she gave up trying to find anything that appealed. Random thoughts tumbled through her head, refusing to leave.

Her concern for Bea.

Her worry over needing a job *and* a permanent place to live. Plus, she hadn't seen her folks in several days and she knew they were getting antsy.

And the biggie—a murderer still at large.

At last, the bath oil Suzy had given her beckoned. Talia filled the tub and stepped into the steamy, aromatic water. The luscious scents of pumpkin and vanilla bubbled around her. She sank deep into the water. Closing her eyes, she tried to imagine she was lying on a tropical beach. A bright sun warmed her face, while the sound of the waves curling over the shore lulled her into peaceful drowsiness.

Without warning, a man emerged from the sea, intruding on her tranquil image. Red-rimmed eyes shone from a pale, angry face. A knife protruded from the ugly wound on his neck. Dripping wet, he trudged toward her, one arm outstretched. He drew closer, until she could see him clearly.

Phil Turnbull.

Talia's eyes jerked open. Good glory, she must have nodded off for a minute or two.

Or was Turnbull haunting her from the grave, trying to send her a message?

No, it was her—she was losing it. It was her overactive imagination, struggling to make sense of the murder.

One thing could not be denied—someone had hated Turnbull enough to want him dead.

Someone had seen to it that he would never again laugh or love, or peddle his lamps, or drive his treasured Caddy. Unfortunately, Turnbull had been a pro at making enemies. The killer could be anyone. Someone the police haven't even thought of.

It was all making her head throb. *Relax, relax.* She breathed in deeply and then exhaled, trying to slow her heartbeat. On her hit parade of murder, two suspects jockeyed for first place.

In the top spot—Kendra. The K-witch.

She'd crashed the meeting, but for what purpose? To rub their noses in the fact that her bizarrely clad stepson was going to set up shop in their midst?

According to Jill, Kendra also owned an interest in the lighting shop and had been strong-arming Phil to make changes he'd have hated. Talia suspected the word *compromise* did not occupy the pages of Kendra's personal dictionary. What if Kendra had taken matters into her own hands? Took the ultimate step and killed off the source of the objection?

Kendra had also made a cryptic comment about having

"bigger, more lucrative fish to fry." The woman had plans up her designer sleeves. Was it the lighting store she coveted? Somehow, vintage lamps and chandeliers didn't seem like her type of gig.

And what had Jill meant when she pulled Kendra aside and accused her of *sitting pretty*?

And then there was suspect number two—Suzy Sato. Talia hated adding her to the list. She genuinely liked Suzy. Still, a few things about the woman didn't add up.

Suzy swore she hadn't signed Turnbull's petition, but Talia was more convinced than ever that she was lying. The way she'd blushed and caught herself when she made the "weirdo" comment had been a sure tipoff.

Something else about Suzy nagged at Talia's memory— something she couldn't quite lasso into her consciousness. It would come to her eventually. Maybe if she slept on it, it would float into her brain, and by morning she'd have all the answers.

Yeah, right. In the words of Aerosmith . . . dream on.

Talia closed her eyes again and tried to unwind her jumbled thoughts. There was another suspect she needed to consider—Jim Jepson.

Before tonight, she would never have believed she'd be considering her former geometry teacher for the position of murder suspect. Mr. J.—Jim—was the quintessential pacifist. Then why had he avoided looking her in the eye when she'd asked him about the petition? The phone call was odd, too. Whispered. Urgent. Was it about Turnbull? Or had she read too much into it?

After pulling on her favorite sleep jersey—a knee-length purple affair embellished with ladybugs—Talia booted up her laptop. Of the seven property management companies she'd sent her résumé to, so far only two had responded. Both replies had been in the negative, although they promised to keep her "fine résumé" on file in the event of a future opening. The rejections had sounded eerily similar. Was there some database these people went to for stock responses?

She scrolled through her inbox, deleting the junk. She opened a message from her mom, sent a few hours ago: *Didn't want to bug you, honey, but are you okay? Dad and I are worried about you!*

Talia grinned. Her mom disliked texting, preferring to use e-mail. Talia e-mailed back that she was hunky doony, as her dad liked to say, and that she'd see her on Sunday at Rachel's play.

She scrolled down to the last e-mail. It was from Diamond Crown Properties, a property management company in Holyoke. Her pulse pounding, Talia opened it.

Ms. Marby, thank you for your résumé and for your interest in Diamond Crown Properties. Are you available for an interview next Friday at 9:00 sharp? Our company is expanding, and we have an opening for a property manager. Your excellent qualifications fit our needs, and we look forward to meeting you.

Yes! She scored an interview! She crafted a quick response thanking the sender—one Donna Franklin—and confirmed the appointment. But when she slid the cursor to Send, her mouse finger froze.

Was this what she wanted? Holyoke was only an hour or so from Wrensdale, in the central part of the state. She could buy a garden-style condo for herself, start building up some equity. Meet new friends.

So what was the problem? Why was she wavering? She couldn't stay in Nana's house forever. At best it was a stopover until she could find her own place.

In her mind, she pictured herself telling Bea she was bailing on her, and Bea's kindly face crumbling. Okay, sure, Bea knew Talia wasn't a forever employee. She was only helping out while Howie was laid up. Still, it would be a setback, especially with the present turmoil in her life. Bea was going to be crushed if she got this job.

Stop being ridiculous. You're thirty-four, for pity's sake. Time to get a life and a home.

Before she could overthink it, she clicked Send. Task accomplished, her mind drifted back to her suspect list. Maybe Google could perform a little magic.

The search engine brought up several links on Suzy. The first was a 2010 snippet from the *Wrensdale Weekly*. "Vermont Native Opens Fragrance Shop in Wrensdale Arcade." The article featured the opening of Sage & Seaweed. On the left was a photo of Suzy with her husband, Kenji Sato. Suzy's face was half hidden by an enormous pair of faux scissors as she pretended to cut a yellow ribbon in front of the charming new shop.

The remaining links mentioned Suzy in a cursory way, mostly relating to local charitable donations or fund-raisers. Talia searched for a Facebook page, but the only one she landed on was the one for Sage & Seaweed. She was surprised someone as gregarious as Suzy didn't have a personal page.

A search under Kendra's name brought up scads of links—everything from a fender bender with her Beemer to an Easter egg hunt sponsored by the Wrensdale Women's Council.

One particular link caught Talia's eye. The article, dated five months earlier, was from the *Berkshire Eagle*. "Wrensdale Resident Pitches Spa Designs to Planning Board." The short clip described Kendra LaPlante's intention to acquire a seventeen-acre spread near the town line and build a luxury day spa. The spa would offer everything from facials and massages to yoga classes and professional beauty consultations.

Bigger and more lucrative fish to fry.

So that's what Kendra was cooking up.

Later articles confirmed approval of the plan. Envisioning new tax dollars plumping up the town's coffers, the planning board members had unanimously approved the proposal.

So where was Kendra getting the funding for her grand project? Even the sale of the lighting shop wouldn't make a dent in the cost of the new spa.

It was all making Talia's head spin. She yawned, too tired to think anymore. She was about to power down when a chirp from her computer signaled a new e-mail. She opened her inbox. Her stomach flipped when she saw the name of the sender—Chet Matthews.

A tiny sprig of optimism bloomed in her chest. Did he have a change of heart? Did he want to apologize for his bad behavior? Scrap the past and give their relationship a fresh start?

Is that what *she* wanted?

She opened the e-mail.

Hey, Talia. Hope things are well. I hate to pressure you, but I wondered if you could come by soon and pick up the rest of your things. Your quilt is still here, and a slew of winter clothes. Do you want that table you bought in Rockport? It goes more with your décor than with mine. Anyway, if you pick a day, I'll arrange to be here. I can always work from home if necessary. How's the job search coming? Regards, Chet.

Stunned, Talia reread the e-mail.

Four years she'd lived with Chet. Loved Chet. Let him make all the decisions—which furniture to buy, where to vacation, how to spend every moment of her precious free time.

And since when had the décor become his and hers? Had she ever objected to the sleek, hard-edges pieces he'd chosen for the living room, and to which she contributed half the exorbitant cost? The single piece of furniture she'd chosen— the antique mahogany candle table—had been the only item in their condo she truly loved.

Swiping at the hot tears flooding her cheeks, she bashed out a terse response. *Monday is my day off. Will late morning work for you?* She didn't even type her name. Let him think she was too busy to be bothered.

With that, she shut down and slammed the cover of her laptop. Her cell rang from the depths of her purse, and she fished it out.

"Perfect timing," Talia said.

"Hey, you're still up." Rachel's perky voice held a trace of something Talia couldn't quite put her finger on.

"Is that rhetorical?" Talia sucked in a long sniffle.

"What's wrong?" Rachel said immediately. "Your voice is weird."

"Nothing's wrong, except that I'm a fool and a buffoon."

"*Not*," Rachel retorted. "What gives?"

Talia gave her a briefing on Chet's e-mail.

"The gall, the absolute nerve." Rachel's voice was tight. "Oh, Tal, I finally get it. You are *so* done with his sorry rump. I wish I could go with you on Monday to fetch your stuff."

"Don't be silly. I'll be fine," Talia said. "And I certainly don't intend to linger. I'm going to stuff my belongings into my car as fast as I can and then split like a torn seam."

"Will all your things fit into the Fiat?"

"I'll make them fit," Talia said, thinking about the candle table. It was about thirty inches tall. If she laid her clothes out flat over the backseat, she could rest the table across them. With a bit of luck, she'd still be able to see through the rear window.

"More importantly, Rach, did you find out anything from Abby?"

Rachel sighed into the phone. "I did. Abby sent me a text a few minutes ago. Here, I'll read it. 'Prelim report from lab showed victim died from knife wound to neck severing carotid artery. Weapon fillet knife with six-inch blade and molded rubber grip. At base of blade, miniscule traces of whitefish found. Estimated TOD between 7 and 9 PM.' "

Talia felt her limbs go numb. "Whitefish?" she whispered. "I don't understand. What would whitefish be doing on the knife?"

"I guess that's what the police want to know."

Talia took her mind back to the crime scene, to that horrible moment when she saw Turnbull sprawled on the floor. She'd seen the knife only briefly, but she remembered the handle had been green.

She tried to remember if she'd ever seen a knife like that among Bea's countless utensils. Bea did own loads of kitchen knives. Did she have one with a green handle? The report had said fillet knife. Bea didn't fillet her own fish—it arrived "kitchen ready" from the seafood supplier. Still, this was all going to look bad for Bea. Very bad.

"Sorry, Tal," Rachel said. "I wish I had more encouraging news. Unfortunately, there's one other thing."

What other bad news could there be? How could it get any worse?

"Someone, an elderly man, called the station late yesterday. He reported that on the day of the murder, he heard Bea threaten to kill Turnbull."

"But that's crazy! It's—"

And then, like a punch to the abdomen, the memory came to Talia.

Fire up the deep fry, Talia. I'm going to boil Phil Turnbull in oil!

Except for Talia, the only other person who heard Bea utter those words was their loyal customer, Mr. Ruggles.

On Saturday morning, Talia tugged open the creaky door of Queenie's Variety. She pulled it closed behind her—it always stuck if you didn't—and stepped into the warmth of the old place. The scent of brewing coffee and bakery delights drifted toward her from the snack station adjacent to the checkout.

Built in the late 1930s, Queenie's still had the same sagging linoleum and the same glaring lights blinking overhead. In the center of the store, in front of the supporting column, fake wood glowed in an electric version of the ancient potbellied stove that once occupied the same spot. On the post behind the stove was a yellowed photo of old Queenie, his hazel eyes sparkling beneath a pair of bushy eyebrows, his ever-present cigar clasped in his fingers.

Talia took a deep breath and inhaled the mélange of aromas. It reminded her of Saturday mornings when she was a kid. Her dad always brought her here for strawberry-frosted doughnuts delivered fresh from one of the bakeries in Pittsfield. Dad would put away three with ease, while she and her mom split the other three.

At the moment, even the cozy familiarity of Queenie's failed to cheer her. She was going to have to tell Bea what she'd learned from Rachel. She only hoped Bea wouldn't pull a nutty.

It was beginning to look as if Bea really did need a lawyer. There was only so much Talia could accomplish on her own, although she'd surely do whatever she could to help her friend.

Yeah, right. Like abandoning her for a new job?

She didn't want to think about that now. Besides, why was she already assuming that the job in Holyoke was hers for the taking? How egotistical was that? The company probably had a wealth of qualified candidates to choose from. What made her so special?

Feeling lower than a bear under a bridge, Talia scanned the aisles. She had no idea where the pet foods were located. She'd never had to buy for a cat. Her mom bought Sunny's food from her vet, since the aging cairn terrier had special dietary needs.

She trotted down to the back of the store. In the last aisle on the left, she found a surprisingly wide selection of cat supplies. She grabbed a box of dry kibble and a six-pack of wet food. If her feline visitor decided to show up again, Talia would at least be able to feed her a meal actually intended for cats.

Which reminded her—she'd meant to check the animal shelter's website to see if anyone had posted a "lost kitty" notice. Maybe after the lunch rush was over, she'd use Bea's computer to check it out.

Talia snatched a loaf of wheat bread off the shelf in the baked goods section. Arms now loaded, she headed to the checkout, four deep with customers, where Queenie's granddaughter, Rita, was busy ringing up sales.

While Talia waited, she turned and glanced around the store. She tried to remember if she'd forgotten anything. All at once, she realized who was standing in front of her.

It was Cliff Colby, wearing the same clothes he'd had on the night before. He acted nervous, shifting from one foot to the other, jerking his head all around. In his large hands he clasped several cellophane packs of cupcakes. Talia had no sooner opened her mouth to say hello to him when a bearded man shot out from behind the candy aisle. The man reeked of stale tobacco, and his dirt-brown eyes were glassy. He strode up to Cliff and slapped him hard on the shoulder. "Cliff, my man, fancy running into you here."

Cliff jumped. "Oh, um, hi. I didn't see you come in." His voice sounded jittery.

"I've been hoping to catch up to you, Cliffy." The man's voice was singsong, too syrupy to be genuine. "You're gonna have that *package* ready for me today, right?"

Talia inched backward a few steps. She could see Cliff's face only in profile, but it was definitely ash gray.

"Um, yeah, except it's not quite ready yet. I'll have it tomorrow, though, for sure. I mean, if that's okay with you."

The man's eyes drilled into Cliff. And then, as if he'd just spied her out of the corner of one glazed orb, he shifted his gaze to Talia. His jaw hardened, even as his scary eyes brightened. "Well, looky here, *cousin* Cliff. There's a pretty lady standing right behind you with an armload of nice treats for her *kitty cat*. Why don't you let her get in front of you?"

Cliff swiveled his head toward Talia, and she'd have

sworn his face went even grayer. "Oh, hi. I didn't see you there. Um, yeah, sure, go ahead."

"Hi, Cliff." Talia smiled at him. "But I'm fine, really. These things aren't heavy at all. You stay right where you are."

The bearded man grinned at her with crooked teeth. "Are you sure, little lady? Because my cousin Cliff here is nothing if not a gentleman. Aren't you, Cliffy boy?"

Talia stifled a shudder. This guy was downright creepy.

"Oh absolutely, I'm sure. But thanks for the offer."

With a nod, the man tipped his grimy Red Sox cap at her. "I'll be by later," he said to Cliff. "You can *bet* on it." He clapped Cliff's bony shoulder once more and then sauntered out.

Talia blew out a breath of relief. Who was that guy? Was he really Cliff's cousin? The way he'd said the words *kitty cat* made her feel as if bugs were crawling up her arms.

She peeked around Cliff and saw that his hands were shaking. "Cliff, are you okay?" she said quietly.

"Of course I'm okay. Why wouldn't I be?" he snapped.

The line moved, and Cliff was next. He plunked his cupcakes onto the counter and mumbled something Talia couldn't quite make out. Rita got it though. Her expression neutral, she nodded and went to the Plexiglas case that housed the lottery tickets. She pulled out a long accordion of glossy orange scratch tickets—five-dollar ones, Talia noticed—and then folded them and gave them to Cliff.

Cliff paid for the tickets and then began mining his pockets for enough change to cover the cupcakes. He was short by eleven cents. Rita took the shortage from the "Need a Penny?" cup next to the cash register. He tore out of the store before Rita had a chance to bag his purchases.

Talia felt something akin to a rock drop to the pit of her

stomach. Cliff had just spent at least a C-note on scratch tickets, yet he could barely scrape up enough to buy his cupcakes.

She'd seen it before. Up close and personal.

It was the addiction that almost shattered her mom and dad's marriage.

"Got yourself a cat now, Talia?" Rita's grin, framed by a wide face and graying eyebrows, was a near perfect replica of the one in her grandfather's photo.

Talia shook away her agitated thoughts. "No, not really. It's just . . . well, there's a stray kitty I've been feeding until I can figure out who her owner is."

"I see." Rita's lips gave a slight quirk. "That'll be ten twenty-nine."

Talia handed her a ten. "Let me see if I can scrounge up twenty-nine cents," she said, rifling through the change in her wallet. "Oh geez, wouldn't you know, I've got twenty-six." She plopped the coins on the counter and held up one finger. "Wait a minute." She stuck her hands in the pockets of her jacket. Sometimes she had a spare penny or— "Ouch!"

Something in her pocket had pinched her. No, not pinched—jabbed. She removed the object from her right-hand pocket and held it to the light. It was a thin shaft of black metal with a pointy tip, about three inches long.

"Looks like an arrow," Rita noted, taking three pennies from the cup.

Talia shrugged and stuck the thing back in her pocket. And then it came to her.

Whatever it was, she'd found it on the floor in Turnbull's office the night she tripped over the stack of boxes. She'd shoved it in her pocket and forgotten about it.

Rita bagged the order and handed it to Talia. "Or a hand from a clock," she said.

12

Talia scurried through the back door of Lambert's at precisely two minutes past nine. "Sorry to be late, Bea. I picked up a few things at Queenie's and I had to go put them in my car." She stripped off her jacket and hung it on the back of the door. "I'll get started with the—"

"Grab yourself a cuppa and sit down, luvvy," Bea said softly. She was seated at the corner table, her hands curled around a mug of coffee. Her dark hair looked neat but unwashed, and her face was devoid of makeup.

Talia prepared a cup of coffee for herself and sat down, her heart smacking her rib cage. "Is something wrong, Bea?"

Bea chuckled, and Talia was glad to see even a ghost of a smile from her. She'd abandoned her dreary ensemble of the day before in favor of a forest-green top and brown corduroy slacks. Not exactly a burst of color, but a definite improvement.

"After I left you last night I went straight to the hospital," Bea said.

"Is Howie okay?"

Bea nodded. "He's getting there, but they won't spring him until the infection's fully gone."

Talia breathed out a sigh. For a moment she thought Howie had taken a downturn. "Weren't visiting hours over when you got there?"

"They were, but the nurses there are such loves. They let me pop in and see him for a few. Anyway, we got to talking about things. Life. Work. Our health. We've decided we're both getting a bit long in the tooth to keep up with running a restaurant."

"You're only fifty-nine!" Talia cried.

"I know, Tal, but that's nearly retirement age, isn't it, and my Howie is sixty-three."

"Where is this coming from, Bea? Is it because of Turnbull's murder? You had nothing to do with that!"

Bea's face fell. She took a sip of her coffee. "Of course I didn't, but the coppers have me pegged for it, don't they?"

"But they're wrong, and when they find the real killer, I'm going to make them all eat crow. Deep-fried crow, at that—and Derek Westlake gets the biggest chunk!"

Bea's tinkling laughter filled the air. "Ah, Talia, you are such a gem. Is it any wonder I love you like my own daughter?"

"Bea, please don't make any sudden decisions. Wait until the murder is resolved and Howie is back on his feet. You'll look at it through different eyes, I promise."

Bea shook her head. "It's decided, luv. We've tossed around the idea in the past, but this time we're serious. Come next spring, Howie and I plan to be living in one of those lovely condos in Myrtle Beach. Howie has a chum there, you see, and he's been hounding us for years to move down there. Mild climate, no bloody snow to shovel, the ocean right at your feet."

"But . . . what about Lambert's?" Talia choked out, feeling her eyes brim with tears. "This wonderful place has been the mainstay of the arcade. I can't imagine the town without it."

"Well, you see, luv, we've got that all figured out, too." Bea paused and gave her an enigmatic smile. "Talia, Howie and I want you to buy out Lambert's. You'll take over the lease, buy out all the business assets. If you need a loan, we'll work out something that's more than fair. We've made a good bit of money living our dream, Tal, and you've always loved it here. We can't think of any better hands to leave it to."

Stunned, Talia sat back and gawked at Bea. "I . . . I don't even know what to say, Bea. Of course I love this place. I always have. It's been a second home to me. But I'm not a restaurateur. At home I live on Cheerios, for God's sake. When I come in here, I just follow your lead."

Bea looked at her curiously. "You mean like you did yesterday, when you battered and fried those pickles and brought them to the meeting?"

"But Bea, that only happened because I accidentally fried a pickle. I just wanted to see what it would taste like if I fried up smaller slices. End of story."

"Beginning of story," Bea said gently. "Just think, Tal. You could rename the place, do whatever clever things you'd like with it. Sometimes, when I look at your face, I know you're cooking up ideas in that lovely head of yours. Why, yesterday, I saw you gazing at that clock in the dining area for a good five minutes. You were thinking of how that wall would look with a different clock, weren't you?"

Talia opened her mouth in shock. Bea was right. How could she have known?

She'd been picturing a pottery clock shaped like an octopus, each of its eight tentacles curled around a French fry. She'd gone so far as to wonder if Jim Jepson would be able to create something like that in his shop.

Talia gave her lips a wry twist. "I guess you know me too well."

Bea laughed, and then her expression turned serious. "Tal, all we ask is that you think about it. You studied business at university, didn't you?"

"I did, but—"

"Then you have one leg up already! Howie and I didn't even go to college and we made this business work." She tapped her hand to her chest. "Success starts right here, Talia. And if there's one thing I know about you, it's that your heart has always been at Lambert's. I see it in your eyes every time you walk through that door. This isn't a job for you, is it? It's what you love to do. For the love of Mike, you came in here at two minutes after nine this morning and apologized for being late."

"I . . . don't see your point."

"Talia, luv, your workday starts at ten, remember? I told you that when you first came back, but you've been coming in every day at nine without giving it a second thought. What does that tell you?"

"It . . . I don't . . . I mean—"

Bea laughed out loud.

"I guess I'm just so used to showing up at my office at nine, I didn't even think about it." She couldn't deny anything Bea was saying, yet it all seemed so sudden. "But if you and Howie move away, I'll never see you again."

Bea laughed. "Ah, luv, we'll come back at least twice a year for a visit. We might even plunk our arses at your place—wherever that is—to save on a hotel." She winked at Talia. "Howie's frugal that way, you know."

"You'll always be welcome at my place, even if I'm living in a shoe box." Talia leaned over and hugged Bea, then sat down again. "Seriously, this is a lot to think about. You don't need an answer today, right?"

"Of course not," Bea assured her. "It's a bit of fodder for the brain mill, is all. But once this silly business with the police is behind us, we'll want to start making plans."

Talia nodded over the lump forming in her throat. How could she tell Bea she had an interview scheduled, and for a job that sounded perfect for her?

How could she tell Bea the police found traces of white-fish on the murder weapon?

"I promise to give it serious thought," Talia said, "and I'll give you an answer soon. I need to talk to you about something else, though."

Bea hopped off her seat and refilled her coffee mug. "Top off?" she asked to Talia.

Talia nodded, and Bea filled her mug. "Bea, I don't like the way this investigation is going. When I chased Westlake out the door yesterday, he told me you should get a lawyer." She heard her own voice cracking.

Bea patted her hand. "No worries, Tal. I've already called our regular fellow. You know the one I mean—he did our wills for us."

"But can he handle criminal cases?" As in homicide?

"He's had his share of them." Bea's face turned grim.

She set the coffeepot back in its slot and sat down. "He's never had a murder case, but he's defended some real rotters in his day."

Talia stirred a few drops of half-and-half into her mug. "But you're not one of them, Bea," she said, her voice breaking. "You're one of the kindest people I know, and you're innocent."

Bea's face fell, and her eyes sprouted tears. "You're right. I never thought of it that way. It's probably harder to defend the innocent than the guilty, isn't it? Oh, Tal, what will Howie ever do if I have to go to prison?"

Talia stared at the ceiling to halt the flow of her own tears. She swallowed and then pulled in a calming breath. "You're not going to prison. Tell me what your attorney said."

"So far, not very much. He's made an appointment with that state police chap. Liam something, I forget his last name. I might need to leave later for another interview."

A wave of relief washed through Talia. Not at the interview, but from knowing that Bea was finally getting help from someone who knew the system and could figure out how to protect her. She knew Bea's attorney only by reputation, but everything she'd heard about him was positive. Still, defending a client on a murder rap was a whole 'nother satchel of peas.

They finished up their coffee and began the daily food prep. Talia lugged potatoes out of the storage closet while Bea removed the outer leaves from a large head of cabbage. Allowing her thoughts to meander, Talia pictured herself as proprietor of the eatery. She'd be making all the decisions—whom to hire, how to deal with difficult customers, how to keep the place financially afloat. The idea was overwhelming, and yet . . .

The idea of actually stepping into Bea and Howie's collective shoes sent an odd little zing through her.

Talia was pulling the potato peeler from the utensil drawer when the knives caught her eye. Had Bea ever owned a knife like the one that was used to kill Turnbull? She moved her forefinger over the myriad knife handles. Paring knives, serrated knives, chopping knives . . .

. . . and two fillet knifes with sleek wooden handles. Not a colored handle in sight.

Which meant nothing, Talia admitted to herself. She released a breath and closed the drawer. If she didn't stop obsessing, she'd never get any work done.

Her encounter with Cliff Colby at Queenie's suddenly popped into her head. Watching him buy those lottery tickets had been like opening an old wound and watching it bleed.

She was fifteen when the gambling fever first grabbed hold of her dad. It started with little things. He'd begun coming home late from his job at a tax preparation franchise, using tax season as an excuse. Then his behavior changed. Before her eyes, she'd watched her easygoing dad transform into a short-tempered ogre. He'd snap at her for every tiny thing— even berating her one evening for keeping the television volume too low because she was trying to study for an exam.

Although her mom never said so, Talia knew she suspected an affair. She couldn't count the nights her mom had kept her dad's dinner warm, only to toss it down the disposal and grind it to shreds when he slunk through the back door at ten or eleven.

But if her dad was having an affair, why did he always look so unhappy, so beaten down? Talia knew it was something else.

Then the bill collectors started calling. Rude, insensitive, demanding. Her mom had tried hiding it from her, until one day the oil company refused to make a delivery. After they'd shivered for two nights in a frigid house, her mom finally broke down and told her.

Talia knew she needed an escape. She'd just turned sixteen when she applied for the part-time job at Lambert's. She began spending every free hour there, doing every menial task Bea and Howie assigned to her. Eventually she learned how to safely operate the fryer, and before long she was serving up fish and chips to the customers as if she'd done it all her life. At the end of every shift, she'd notice that the aroma of hot oil and condiments had clung to her clothes. She'd worn the scent home like a cloak of sanity in her otherwise topsy-turvy life.

It wasn't until her mom threatened to take Talia and leave that her dad faced his addiction squarely in the eye. Once he sought help, everything changed. The credit vultures stopped circling. Things slowly improved at home.

Talia thought about the "arrow" she'd stuck in the pocket of her jacket. Could it really be a broken hand from a clock, as Rita had speculated? If so, why was it on the floor of Turnbull's office? Maybe later, if things got quiet for a few minutes, Talia would pay Cliff a visit and put him on the spot. A nagging feeling was beginning to creep into her bones. She knew she had to check it out.

In the meantime, they needed to be prepared for a very busy Saturday.

"Bea, I just thought of something," Talia said. "How are we going to advertise our two-for-one deal today?"

"Ach." Bea stuck a hand on her hip. "We need one of those sandwich board thingies to stick out in front. Do you know where we can get one on short notice?"

"A real sandwich board might be pricey." Talia tapped a finger to her lips. "Know what? I'll bet we could make our own. We could buy two of those stiff, poster-sized sheets from the crafts store on Elm Street, tape them into a V shape"—she demonstrated by tenting her hands—"and write our own message on it."

Bea snapped her fingers. "Maybe Whitnee could stop by there and grab them on her way in this morning."

"Mom's friend Millie works there part time. I'm pretty sure she's there Saturday mornings. Let me make a few calls."

Within five minutes, Talia had it all arranged. Millie agreed to have two neon orange poster boards waiting for Whitnee when she arrived, along with a black marker. Whitnee, who answered her cell immediately, said she'd be happy to make the pickup. She didn't need to worry about paying, since Talia already charged the cost to her own credit card. She also agreed to come in early, since she had some time to make up anyway.

"Let me know how much that all came to," Bea said, "so I can reimburse you."

"No, Bea," Talia said firmly. "The cost was minimal, and besides, we're in this together."

Bea looked at Talia, and her eyes filled with tears. "Then you and I had best get our lovely buns in gear. I predict we're going to be frying up a mountain of fish today!"

"Whitnee, that looks fantastic." Talia beamed. "I love the way you drew those fish. They actually look thrilled that they're being dunked into a vat of hot oil!"

They were standing outside on the cobblestone plaza,

assessing the merits of the sandwich board they'd created from the bright orange posters. Whitnee's artwork delighted Talia. She hadn't realized how talented the girl was.

Her cheeks flushing, Whitnee shoved a strand of carrot-colored hair behind one ear. "Do you really think so? I couldn't decide how to make the fish smile, so I gave them faces that were sort of, you know, human."

"You did a super job, Whitnee. I am truly impressed."

The board was already attracting potential customers. A middle-aged couple with a young boy in tow approached the sign and read the message. "Do you like fish, honey?" the woman said. She tousled the boy's dark curls.

"Yup. I like potato chips, too."

Talia bent toward the child, whose brown eyes were the size of checkers. "I'll tell you a secret," she said. "In this restaurant, chips is the code word for French fries."

"I like those even better! Can we eat here, Grandma?"

The woman laughed. "Of course we can, in another hour or so. Let's shop a bit first. Maybe we can buy you that DVD you keep hinting at."

With a promise to return at lunchtime, they strode off toward the shops on Main Street. A pang of loss went straight to Talia's heart. Her own nana had been exactly like that—kind, loving, indulgent to a fault. She swallowed hard and dashed inside Lambert's, Whitnee trailing her like an obedient pup.

"Luvvy," Bea said to Whitnee, "you'd best make an extra batch of mushy peas today. I expect we're going to be handling a crowd."

Whitnee nodded. "Sure thing, Bea."

"So, did you do anything interesting last night?" Talia inquired, trying to sound casual. She couldn't help noticing that Whitnee was in far better spirits today. She wondered if anything in particular had triggered her sudden upswing in mood.

Whitnee smiled shyly, and her light brown eyes glowed. "Pug and I had this, like, really nice dinner? At this cool place on Pontoosuc Lake? It was kind of an anniversary dinner. We met at the lake two months ago, at a party at my friend's folks' cottage. So Pug got this awesomely romantic idea that we should celebrate our anniversary on the lake, too."

Talia removed a glass batter bowl from an upper shelf. She couldn't imagine the metal-studded Pug being anything close to romantic. He seemed to have all the grace and sensibility of a gourd. Still, she had no right to judge. As young and innocent as Whitnee looked, she was an adult and had the right to date whoever she pleased.

"Sounds like you had a great time," Talia said with as much sincerity as she could muster.

A mysterious grin split Whitnee's thin face, and she flushed a deep crimson.

Uh-oh. Did Whitnee have a secret? Had Pug proposed? Or was their two-month-anniversary date the first time they'd—?

Ugh. Talia didn't even want to think about it.

They worked in tandem to get everything prepped for the two-for-one special they were offering. Talia pictured a horde of hungry diners storming through the door at eleven thirty. The idea sent an odd little thrill through her, and she caught herself smiling.

Bea's relaxed mood of earlier that morning had faded. Although she'd managed to whip up a double batch of slaw, she'd spent much of her time either on her cell or in the bathroom. From the tidbits of conversation Talia had picked up, she gleaned that Bea's attorney had been in touch with the state police.

"That does it," Bea said furiously, shoving her phone into her pants pocket.

"Wh . . . what is it, Bea? What's wrong?" Bea's face was a frightening shade of purple, and her hands were clenched into tight fists.

"That was Mr. Patchett, the bloke who's representing me. That state copper wants to meet us at two this afternoon, at my house."

Talia exchanged glances with Whitnee, whose expression was suddenly pained. "Bea, if you're worried about leaving Whitnee and me alone here, you don't—"

"Aww, luv, I'm not the slightest bit worried about that." Bea waved away the notion. "It's what he said that has me so bleeping mad. Can you believe this one? The state police want me to surrender my passport. They're afraid I'll try to flee the country!"

13

By the time the noon hour rolled around, Lambert's was hopping. Talia and Whitnee worked assembly-line style, with Talia as fry cook and Whitnee adding the final side dishes to each of the orders. Bea answered the phone and rang up orders robotically, in between delivering meals to the customers seated in the dining area. In spite of Lambert's being busier than Talia had ever remembered, they'd been able to keep up with the orders.

So far.

The dining area was filled to capacity. The low hum of chattering customers melded with the delectable scent of fried fish and chips, producing a sound Talia loved—the sound of success.

"Looks like your sandwich board performed magic," Talia whispered to Whitnee. She simultaneously dredged two slabs of haddock through the tray of flour.

Whitnee giggled at the compliment. "I'm sure it wasn't just the poster, but it sure is busy, isn't it? I've never seen the place so . . . overflowing." She plopped a scoop of mushy peas into a round container, snapped a cover over it, and set it next to a mound of fried fish and chips in a takeout box. After closing the box she handed it to Bea, who rang up the order for the customer.

Talia was just going to the fridge for another box of haddock fillets when she spied a familiar-looking young man waiting his turn at the counter. His sandy hair curling around the collar of his charcoal suede jacket, he smiled shyly at her through startlingly long lashes. She'd definitely seen him before, but where? The young man let a hunched, elderly gent with a cane go in front of him, then peeked over the man's head and greeted Talia with a little wave. "Hey," he said, "remember me?"

And then she got it. "Oh my gosh, Aaron?"

Aaron LaPlante grinned. "I had a feeling you didn't recognize me."

"I didn't, at first," Talia admitted with a laugh. "Your hair, your clothes . . . well, just about everything is different."

One corner of his mouth quirked up in a smile. "I was under orders last night. Kendra told me to look as"—he made air quotes with his long, manicured fingers—"punky and grungy as possible. She wanted everyone to be grossed out when they saw me." He rolled his gray-blue eyes at the ceiling.

Interesting, Talia thought. So the punk gig had all been an act. Now she desperately wanted to talk to Aaron. He could probably tell her plenty about Kendra. He might even know where she was the night Turnbull was killed.

She was about to ask Aaron if she could speak to him privately when she saw him lean toward the old man in front of him and place a gentle hand on his shoulder. "Sir," Aaron said, "I'm alone today, and don't have anyone to share the two-for-one special with me. Would you mind if I treated you to your fish and chips?"

The old man's faded eyes brightened. He turned and offered Aaron his wrinkled hand, which Aaron clasped with a friendly shake. "That's awfully kind of you, young fella. I was going to ask for a senior discount, but I believe I'll take you up on that."

Talia saw tears pool in the old man's eyes, and she flashed Aaron a grateful smile.

Bea took their order and rang it up. She hadn't recognized Aaron, and it was obvious her mind had been elsewhere during the entire exchange. When it was time to box up their meals, Talia whispered to Whitnee that she'd take care of this one. She gave the elderly man his lunch bag and wished him a good day.

"Aaron, do you have a minute for me?" Talia said, handing him his takeout bag.

He handed her a twenty and she gave him the change. "Sure, but it's kind of noisy in here. Can we step outside?"

Bea shot Talia a strange look and then nodded her approval. "I'll cover for you, Tal. Go ahead and take a break."

So, she had been listening.

"Back in a flash," Talia promised, and then followed Aaron outside. She didn't want to leave Bea and Whitnee any longer than she had to, but she couldn't pass up the chance to extract information from Kendra's stepson.

Aaron strolled out onto the plaza and glanced around the arcade. "Too bad they don't have any benches out here. I mean, the cobblestone lends a charming ambiance, but sometimes people like to sit for a few and just take in the scenery, you know?"

Talia smiled. She'd often wondered the same thing. "That's okay, I only have a few minutes to spare. Aaron, why did Kendra want you to gross us all out? What did she have against the arcade owners? I don't think any of them even knew her."

"Yeah, but she was pi . . . ticked off big-time that they all signed Phil's petition."

"Bea didn't."

Aaron shrugged. "Maybe she didn't know that. Anyway, she was determined to have me open a comic book store here. It was all a plot to get under Phil's skin." His sandy eyebrows dipped over his eyes. "Kendra loves to play games, you know? She isn't happy unless everyone in her perfect little world is squashed firmly under her thumb."

"But a comic book store would be good for you, right?"

"No." Aaron scowled. "Don't get me wrong, I love comic books. But I don't want to sell them—I want to design them. It's been my dream since I was in grade school. I'm an artist, not a shopkeeper." He flushed. "No offense to anyone here, but it's just not my thing."

"Then why are you letting Kendra pressure you?"

His face darkened. "When Kendra doesn't get her way, she takes it out on my dad. He's like, you know, really passive. I guess that's how she got her claws into him in the first place. But I hate it when she browbeats him." He barked out a laugh. "Besides, Phil was an enormous boil on my butt, pardon the language. Cripes, I couldn't stand that man."

Talia glanced toward Lambert's, where a foursome of giggling teenagers had just paraded through the front entrance. She couldn't waste any more time. "Aaron, one last question. Did Kendra hate Phil enough to kill him?"

Aaron laughed out loud. "Everyone hated Phil enough to kill him." He shook his head. "But Kendra wasn't around that night. She had her usual Wednesday night spa appointment at Always You. She never misses it. I mean, like, *never*."

"Aaron, you've been very helpful." Talia pointed at his bag. "I owe you another fish and chips meal for letting yours get cold. Come back any time. It'll be on me."

"Nah, it'll be fine. But I'm going to bring my dad here soon. He loves fish and chips. His housekeeper made fried cod for him a few weeks ago, and it came out awful. She's strictly a meat-and-potatoes type—had no idea what to do with an actual fish."

Talia laughed. "Doesn't Kendra cook?"

"Oh please. The only thing Kendra ever cooks up is a scheme to make more money."

"Hey, I've got to run. Come in again, Aaron. I'd love to meet your dad. By the way, that was sweet, the way you paid for that elderly man's lunch."

"Well, it was a two-fer, right? No skin off my wallet." Aaron winked at her. "Catch you later, 'tater."

He sprinted off across the arcade, and Talia paused in front of the neon orange sign.

Yes, it was a two-fer, except for one thing. At Bea's instruction, Whitnee had inscribed, in crisp black letters, the words *half price for one*.

"I'm about run off my feet today," Bea grumbled. She looked at her watch and groaned. "It's quarter till two. I'll have to leave soon. Are you sure you two will be okay? It's been awfully busy . . ."

"We'll be fine," Talia assured her. "We're in a mini-lull right now, so Whitnee is going to take her break, and then I'll take a quick one."

Bea leaned over and hugged her. "Wish me luck, luv."

"Of course I will," Talia said, "but you don't need luck because you're innocent. Remember that, okay?" Talia wished she could believe her own words, but in truth she was terrified for Bea.

Whitnee surprised Talia by giving Bea a fast hug. "Good luck," she whispered in a crackling voice.

After Bea left, Whitnee reached for the book bag she'd left hanging on the door hook. "I'm just going to sit in my car for twenty minutes. I've got a calc test on Monday. It helps if I can squeeze in some extra study time here and there."

"Sure, take your time, Whitnee," Talia said. "Is it hard for you to concentrate at home?"

Whitnee's cheeks turned pink. "Um, it's kind of noisy there. My older brother is always blasting music. It's, like, hard to keep a train of thought."

Poor girl, Talia thought. Her home life sounded like a bad dream.

The dining area was quiet now, with only a few stragglers. Talia went into the kitchen and loaded the dirty mugs and glasses into the dishwasher. She washed all the serving cones with a clean, soapy sponge and hung them on a rack to dry.

After a twenty-minute break, Whitnee returned. "Hey," she said, hanging her book bag on its usual hook behind the kitchen door. One handle didn't catch, and the bag sagged sideways. A thick, dog-eared magazine caught Talia's eye, and she couldn't resist sneaking a peek. Although she couldn't see which mag it was, the one thing she could see made her insides sink. At the top left corner was an elaborate, hand-drawn heart with the initials *W + P* inscribed in the middle in purple ink.

Talia sighed. Whitnee really did have it bad for Pug, and she deserved so much better.

"Get any studying done?" Talia smiled at her.

"Not that much. I was dying for chocolate, so I went over to Queenie's to get a Hershey's bar."

A Hershey's bar. Talia loved them, too, but she preferred the almond ones. She wondered how a deep-fried chocolate bar would taste. And what if the batter was chocolate, too? Would she have to freeze the bar first to get the right consistency?

With a shake of her head, she chuckled at her silly idea. She definitely needed a break.

Talia snatched up her jacket and slid her arms into the sleeves. She remembered the strange metal arrow that was still in her pocket. "Be back in a few," she said to Whitnee. "My cell's on, so call me if you need me. I won't be far."

Using the front entrance, Talia stepped out onto the plaza. Dark clouds had gathered, hinting at a storm. Shoppers chatted and mingled as they trod over the cobblestone, some with salmon-colored bags from Sage & Seaweed looped over their arms. Talia crossed directly over to the Clock Shop, opened the door, and went inside.

At first, the jumble and tumble of the store's contents startled her. Clocks of all sizes were jammed willy-nilly onto the shelves. There seemed to be no pattern to their placement. Talia suspected some of the clocks might be valuable, but surrounded by so much clutter it was hard to tell the trash from the treasures.

At the far corner of the shop, Cliff Colby sat on a stool behind a glass counter that was packed with yet more clocks. He was bent over a sheet of paper on which he appeared to be scribbling. When he saw Talia, he jerked his head up. He quickly stashed the paper under the counter.

"Hi, Cliff." She waved at him.

"What do you want?" His mouth turned down in a scowl.

Talia walked up to the counter and folded her hands over the glass. "I hope you don't talk that way to all your customers."

He smirked. "You're a customer all of a sudden?"

Talia didn't have time to waste. She reached into her pocket and fingered the metal arrow. "You heard that Bea and I found Turnbull's body Thursday morning, right?"

"Yeah? So?"

Talia had to be careful. She didn't want Cliff to know she'd found the arrow *after* Turnbull's body had been removed. "I found this on the floor in Phil's office that day," she said. She pulled the arrow out of her pocket and held it up.

Cliff looked at it and shrugged. "And I care, why?"

"At first I wasn't sure what it was," Talia went on. "Then someone pointed out to me that it looked like the hand from a clock."

At the word *clock*, Cliff snapped his head toward the object. His eyes narrowed, and then his face drained of color. "I . . . guess it could be from a clock. What difference does it make?" His attempt at sounding nonchalant flopped like a landed tuna.

"Think about where I found it, Cliff," Talia pressed on.

Cliff swallowed. His Adam's apple bobbed as if he had

a lightbulb in his throat. "I don't . . . I mean . . . Oh cripes," he finally said, "it's probably from the clock Phil smashed against the wall. Leave it to a nosy dame like you to find it."

Pay dirt.

"Maybe you'd better tell me the whole story," Talia said.

Cliff looked away. One of his knees jiggled. "I owed Phil some money. I thought I'd be able to pay it back pretty quickly, but then I ran into some, you know, bad luck."

Talia nodded. She knew exactly the kind of bad luck he was talking about.

"So anyway, I had this gorgeous antique clock I thought he might like—a Seth Thomas mantel clock with a double dial, walnut case. Real beauty of a timepiece, and in perfect condition. It wasn't worth anywhere near what I owed him, but I thought it might appease him temporarily."

"But it didn't."

"No." Cliff's voice quaked. "I guess he was having a bad day because he smashed the clock against the wall in his office, face-first. It was so stupid of him—the clock was worth a grand. 'You owe me cash, not clocks,' he screamed at me. The clock broke, and the face got shattered."

Talia slipped the arrow back into her pocket. "How much did you owe Phil?"

Cliff's shoulders drooped. "Seven and a half grand."

Not a fortune. Certainly not enough to kill over, unless Cliff had been truly desperate. Talia had the feeling that what he owed Turnbull was only the tip of an extremely fast-moving iceberg.

"Um, does anyone else know you found that?" Cliff asked in a mousy voice.

"Not yet." Talia knew it sounded like a dangling threat, but Bea's freedom was at stake. "Cliff, I'm not trying to hurt you. I understand your problem better than you think I do. But the bottom line here is that the police are homing in on Bea as their primary suspect. I do not intend to let her go to prison for a crime she had nothing to do with."

Cliff chewed one side of his lip. "Are you freakin' kidding me? The cops think . . ." He looked away. "But that's just crazy."

Talia shook her head. "They're doing their job, Cliff. Bea's the one who refused to sign Turnbull's petition, and she'd had words with him earlier that day. That makes her suspect number one on their hit parade." That and a bunch of other things Talia had no intention of sharing. And in spite of all the people who had strong reasons to hate Phil, poor Bea was the one who'd threatened to boil him in oil on the very day someone else killed him. And in front of a witness. What kind of rotten luck was that?

All at once, Cliff got antsy. "What do you want from me? I didn't kill him either. You're wasting my time."

Talia let her gaze wander around the disorderly shop. She was stalling, hoping he'd blurt out some useful tidbit that she could take to the police. When she saw that he wasn't biting, Talia leaned over the glass counter and said, "Cliff, do you know who might have wanted Phil dead? Have you told the police everything you know?"

"Not that it's any of your business, but I already talked to the cops." He pointed a bony finger at her. "Now get out of here. I don't have to talk about my personal life to a *fry cook*."

Talia gave him a stiff nod. "You need help, Cliff," she said quietly. "If I were you, I'd find it before it's too late."

With that she spun on her heel. She was almost at the door when he called out, "Wait! What are you going to do with that minute hand?"

Minute hand. He'd known perfectly well what it was.

Talia turned and graced him with a flat smile. "I haven't decided yet, Cliff. I'll let you know."

She closed the door hard and was crossing the arcade when she realized a man was leaning against the façade of the vacant antiques store next to the Clock Shop. In his hands was an open newspaper. She hurried toward Lambert's, turning as she reached the entrance. The man had lowered the paper, just enough to reveal his face from the nose up. His stare burned through her, and a chill zipped straight down her spine.

It was the same scary guy who'd been bothering Cliff in Queenie's that morning. The same creepazoid who'd made her want to scrub her skin raw.

With a shudder, Talia plunged through the front door to Lambert's. The toe of one of her Keds caught on the tile, sending her tripping toward the nearest table. She grasped onto the back of a chair to right herself. When she looked down, she saw that her hands were shaking.

Luckily, no one was in the dining area to witness her klutzy move. She headed into the kitchen, where Whitnee was busy whipping up another batch of mushy peas.

"Figured we'd need more for the dinner rush," Whitnee said, smiling. "We nearly ran out at lunch time." She reached into the utensil drawer for the masher. "Are you, like, okay? Your face looks kinda red."

"Yeah, I'm fine." Talia looked at the bottom of her sneaker and laughed. "Sometimes rubber soles are a—"

The entrance door thumped open. Talia's heart leaped in her chest, until she saw who it was.

Connie Parker again—Whitnee's mom.

The gargantuan tote was gone, replaced by a supersized

plastic purse that stuck out from under one shoulder like a shiny white tent.

Her mouth agape, Whitnee took in her mother's polyester ensemble beneath the ever-present peacoat. "Ma, what are you doing here again? You going to work on Saturdays now?"

Connie slogged toward the kitchen. "I'm workin' extra hours to make up for bein' sick the other night. And I thought you were comin' home for lunch," she whined, waving a wrinkled brown bag at her daughter. "I even made those brownies you like with the colored candies in 'em." Head down, Connie made a beeline for the gap between the speckled blue counter and the wall.

This time Talia was ready for her. She quickly stepped into the opening, blocking Connie's access.

"Do you mind?" Connie said rudely, jiggling the bag in Talia's face.

In spite of being half the woman's size, Talia stood her ground. "I'm sorry, Mrs. Parker, but I can't allow you into the kitchen. The state has health laws, and we have to comply with them. The kitchen is for employees only. No exceptions." She knew she sounded ridiculously formal, but how else could she get through to this bulldozer of a woman?

Connie's jaw dropped. Her gaze shot to her daughter, then back to Talia.

"However"—Talia cleared her throat—"since it's quiet at the moment, you can visit with Whitnee for a few minutes at one of the tables in the dining area. If you'd like, I'll even prepare some fish and chips for you. It'll be my treat."

Connie stuttered backward a few steps. "Well, I guess that'd be okay. No fish, though—just French fries, and lots of 'em. And some of that coleslaw, too."

Whitnee slammed down the stainless-steel bowl of

partially mashed peas. "Ma, why don't you go home? Bea pays me to do a job—not to socialize, and not to have you barge in here any time you feel like it!"

Talia gave herself a mental slap. Why, oh why, had she offered the woman a free meal? Why had she interfered?

Connie blinked several times and her face reddened. "Well, little miss smart mouth, isn't that a nice way to talk to your mother. And after everythin' I've done for you." She pointed a fat finger at her daughter. "Maybe I ought to rent out your room to someone who appreciates it. Maybe you'd like to come home some night and find a smelly boarder stinkin' up your bed."

Talia sneaked a glance at Whitnee. The girl's eyes were closed, and her complexion had gone pasty.

"Do whatever you want," Whitnee said through clenched teeth. She jammed the masher into the mound of peas and began crushing the pulp out of them. "I love this job and I'm not gonna risk losing it. You can rent my room out to any bum you want. I'll move in with Pug and his roommate."

Connie's small eyes narrowed into slits. "I mighta known," she said with a sneer. "Once you give it away the first time, it's a free-for-all, isn't it?"

"All right, Mrs. Parker, that's enough," Talia said. "Now I will have to ask you to leave."

Connie looked at Talia as if she were a spider on her shoe. "Don't worry, I'm goin'. But that one"—she jabbed a finger at Whitnee—"better come home with her tail between her legs, or else."

Talia watched the woman stomp out the door and then went over to Whitnee. The girl was standing stock still, but her entire body trembled. "I'm sorry, Whitnee, I shouldn't have interfered. That was all my fault."

Whitnee shook her head. "No, it wasn't. You were just being nice. She just, like, can't accept that I'm a grown woman. She pokes her nose into everything I do, like I'm a child."

"I know. Some moms hate to see their kids grow up. When I first went off to UMass, my mom cried for a week."

"She did?" Whitnee stabbed the masher into a clump of peas.

"Yup. Even more embarrassing, my dad showed up at my dorm on my third day at school with a big Tupperware container of all my favorite snacks. He was afraid I'd starve on the dorm food, which was notoriously awful."

Whitnee sniffled. "You must have really nice folks."

"Well, of course I rolled my eyes and pretended to be mortified," Talia said, "but in truth, I was thrilled to see him. Plus, I scored a boatload of peanut butter cups that lasted me a month!"

Whitnee sighed. "I guess I overreacted about her showing up with those stupid brownies. She was only, like, trying to be thoughtful. 'Course now she's seriously mad at me, so I'll have to deal with that when I go home."

Talia's heart broke for the girl. She really did seem to have a chaotic home life, and her mother clearly had a nasty bent. Talia shuddered to think what it would be like to live with a woman like that. She went over to Whitnee and touched her forearm. "Hey, look, if it gets too hairy at home, you can always give me a call. There's a pullout sofa at my nana's. You'd be more than welcome to bunk there for the night."

"Thanks," Whitnee choked out. "I really appreciate that."

Whitnee went back to her pea mashing, which turned out to be cathartic. Her thin face began to relax. Soon her head was bobbing to a tune that only she could hear.

Talia peeked out at the dining area, which, fortunately, was empty. In that respect, Connie's timing had been good. No customers had been around to witness the "row," as Bea would have called it.

When she thought about it, Talia still couldn't believe she'd confronted Connie that way. Never before had she taken so bold a stand! She'd behaved almost as if—

—as if Lambert's Fish & Chips already belonged to her. As if this were *her* culinary home away from home, not Bea and Howie's.

Chuckling to herself, Talia wondered why she'd never taken a stand like that with Chet. Why she'd let him make all the decisions, without any input from her. Even on matters that affected them equally, it never occurred to him to ask for her opinion.

She'd never forget the Thursday evening he'd made a trip to the specialty bath shop in Belmont without even asking her if she wanted to tag along. He'd returned with a set of aqua horse-themed accessories for the bathroom—towels, shower curtain, throw rug, toothbrush holder—the works. After arriving home, he'd plopped a perfunctory kiss on her cheek, dropped his purchases onto the sofa, and then asked her to wash everything so they could start enjoying their new bathroom décor right away!

Kicking Chet from her thoughts, Talia scrubbed her hands, dried them, and pulled on a fresh set of disposable gloves. She began lining up the ingredients to prepare the next batch of batter for the dinner rush. She'd checked the haddock supply after the lunch crush had ended, and they were good for the rest of the day. Lambert's was closed on Sundays, and the seafood supplier from Boston would be there early Monday morning with fresh reserves.

Talia was grateful she didn't have to work on Sunday. Much as she loved the eatery, she desperately needed a break. Rachel's play was tomorrow. Talia was eager to see the kids perform "The Legend of Sleepy Hollow" at the assisted living facility.

Which reminded her of her folks. Both her mom and dad had been e-mailing and texting her frantically since the morning she'd discovered Turnbull's body. *Are you okay? Do you want to talk about it? Are the police harassing you? Do you want to sleep here?* She'd been feeling guilty for not calling them, but sometimes their histrionics drove her over the edge. She'd put them off with reassurances that she'd be seeing them on Sunday at the play.

A sudden stab of guilt poked at her. Witnessing that horrible scene between Connie Parker and Whitnee had made her realize how blessed she was to have such loving and supportive parents. She really needed to cut her folks a little slack.

Talia measured the dry ingredients and added them to the bowl she used for preparing the fish coating. Slowly, she poured in the club soda, along with several splashes of malt vinegar. She glanced at the clock. Twenty to four, and Bea still hadn't returned. Not that Talia had expected her back that soon, but she was worried about how things were progressing.

Her thoughts traveled to Kendra as she whisked together the ingredients. In Talia's mind, that woman should be at the top of the suspect list. Had the police even considered her?

Means, motive, opportunity. Didn't the police have to prove all three?

As for means, anyone could get their hands on a fillet

knife. The gourmet shop on Park Square in Pittsfield carried all kinds of funky utensils. If Kendra wanted to frame Bea for the crime, all she had to do was buy a piece of fish at the supermarket, stab a fillet knife through it, and then use the knife to kill Phil. Easy peasy.

Motive shouldn't be hard to prove. Before Phil's demise, Kendra owned a half interest in the lighting shop. Now she owned the whole thing. The math couldn't be simpler. Plus, any number of people knew they despised each other.

Opportunity was a bit more problematic. Aaron claimed Kendra had been at her weekly spa appointment at the time Phil was murdered. According to the text from Abby, the medical examiner had estimated the time of death at any- where between seven and nine PM. Was that time carved in stone?

Talia covered the batter bowl with plastic wrap and tucked it into the fridge. The spa Aaron referred to—Always You—was a well-known destination for locals and tourists alike. The only one of its kind in the area, the gray, stone monstrosity sat on a landscaped hill only a few miles outside the Wrensdale town limits. At best, it was a seven- or eight- minute ride from there to the lighting shop. Double that, and add the time it would take to confront and murder Phil . . . with careful planning and a pocketful of luck, Ken- dra could have pulled it off in under half an hour.

But did she? And wouldn't someone have noticed her leaving the spa?

Talia peeled off her disposable gloves and tossed them into the trash. "Whitnee, I need to make a quick call on my cell. Do you mind if step outside for a few minutes?"

Whitnee shrugged. "Sure, no problem."

Talia grabbed her jacket and slipped it on. For this call she needed privacy.

She dashed out to her car, which was parked in the town lot. Once settled in the driver's seat, Talia found the number for Always You and punched it in. A singsong female voice answered the line. "Always You, the place for an always beautiful you! How may I help you?" The last note ended on an upward lilt.

"Hi, there, my name is Ms. Sunday." Technically not a fib, since Talia's middle name was Domenica, which was Italian for Sunday. "I'm Kendra LaPlante's assistant?"

"Of course," the voice said smoothly, though Talia detected a cool undertone. "What can I do for you?"

"Um, Ms. LaPlante was at the spa Wednesday evening? She's almost positive she left her small cosmetics bag there, because she can't find it anywhere. I'm wondering if anyone might have found it and turned it in?"

"One moment please."

Talia fidgeted as the woman left her on hold for well over two minutes. Had she been made? Maybe she'd overdone the ditz routine.

"Thank you for waiting," the voice returned. "Since Ms. LaPlante always enjoys our deluxe spa treatment, I'll put you through to the technician in charge of that department."

A whole department for it? "Thanks," Talia said airily, but her heart was pounding. "That would be super."

After another minute or so, she was put through to a woman whose voice sounded like a twelve-year-old's. "Hello, this is Misty Manners," the youngster chirped. "May I help you?"

Misty Manners? If that was her real name, Talia would

eat one of her Fiat's wheel covers. Talia repeated her story, embellishing it with a few giggles and a description of the imaginary cosmetics bag. When Misty finally spoke, her voice was hesitant. "I see. Well, I'm afraid no one has turned in a stray cosmetics bag."

Talia heaved a loud groan. "Oh, bummer, that's too bad. She was *so* sure she left it there. Do you know the exact time her appointment was for?"

"The time?" Misty said warily. "Why do you ask?"

Uh-oh. Talia scrambled for an answer. It wasn't as if she could say: oh, I just wanted to establish her alibi for the time of her ex-husband's murder.

"Oh, you know, um, I'm just . . . trying to retrace her steps that day. Like, if she was there *after* her eye doctor appointment, I might be able to figure out where else she could have left it." Talia dropped her head on her steering wheel. That didn't even make sense! Misty was sure to see through the ruse.

"Oh, of course." Misty's girlish voice relaxed. "Let me check for you."

Talia breathed out a relieved sigh as the sound of fingers flitting over a keyboard filtered through the phone.

"Okay, here we are," Misty said, "and now I do recall, because I was working that evening. Ms. LaPlante arrived here promptly at six thirty. She had her age-busting facial and eye treatment—that takes about an hour and fifteen—after which I escorted her to the south wing for her full body massage." After a long hesitation Misty added, "She finished with her mani-pedi, and then . . ."

For a moment, Talia thought she'd lost the connection. Misty seemed to have dissolved into the ozone.

"Sorry, I had to put the phone down for a minute," Misty

said, her voice a few notches lower. "I thought my boss was waving me over."

"You were saying she had a mani-pedi?" Talia prompted.

"Yes, that was her last treatment, at eight forty-five. Although . . ."

Another lengthy silence. Blast the girl!

"Um, sorry," Misty said. "Yes, her mani-pedi was at eight forty-five. I believe she left right after that."

"Eight forty-five," Talia repeated. Seemed late for a mani-pedi. "How late are you open?"

"On Wednesdays and Thursdays we stay open till ten, although our last appointment is at nine," Misty said. "Obviously if a customer's appointment goes a little over the time limit, we remain open as long as we need to. We *never* make a customer feel rushed."

"Oh goodness, well, that's an excellent policy." Talia was babbling now, but as Bea always said, *in for a ha'penny, in for a quid*. "So a mani-pedi probably takes about forty-five minutes, right? Do you know what time Ms. LaPlante paid for her . . . services?"

"Ms. LaPlante has an account with us," Misty said, her tone now bubbling with suspicion. "We bill her on a monthly basis."

"Oh right," Talia said. "I should've remembered that."

"Shall I call you if the cosmetics bag does turn up?" Misty said stiffly.

"No need. Thanks for your time, though." Talia disconnected before Misty could ask any more questions.

Darn. Kendra's alibi seemed solid. Still, there was something in Misty's voice, plus all those long silences, that had definitely seemed off-kilter.

Talia hopped out of her car just as Bea was swinging her

old brown Datsun into the parking lot. A puff of relief escaped Talia. Bea was still a free woman. Talia caught up with her, and together they headed back to Lambert's.

"How did it go?" Talia asked, almost afraid to hear the answer.

Bea shot Talia a grim look, her small feet barreling along the sidewalk. "I had to surrender my passport. That state police chap was a tough bugger. Asked me the same blasted questions, over and over. I tell you, Tal, I thought my head was going to spin clean off my neck."

Talia slid her arm through Bea's. "I know giving up your passport seems drastic, Bea, but it won't be for long." She hoped.

They strode past Peggy's Bakery, where the dual aromas of yeast and cinnamon wafted out from the propped-open door. Peggy was smart—she knew how to entice customers! The tantalizing scent suddenly reminded Talia that she was in charge of bringing desserts to the play on Sunday.

"What were you doing in your car?" Bea asked.

"I . . . had a quick personal call I needed to make."

Bea gave her an odd look but said nothing. They ducked into the alley behind Lambert's and scurried inside through the kitchen door.

"Hey, you're back!" Whitnee said to Bea, looking pleased to see her. She lifted a basket of crispy fries out of the fryer. In the adjacent basket, two fat chunks of battered haddock were sizzling their way to golden perfection.

"Yes, I'm back, and it looks like you're doing one bleeding good job, luv." Bea squeezed Whitnee's arm affectionately.

Talia hung her jacket and then peeked into the dining area, where two elderly fellows were seated at one of the tables. She turned back to Whitnee. "Sorry I took so long, but you obviously have things under control."

Whitnee beamed, and a flush crept into her pale cheeks. "Thanks. I kinda like being on my own here once in a while. It's sort of fun, you know, being in charge. I mean, as long as it doesn't get too crazy." She inserted paper liners into a pair of serving cones. "Are you, like, okay, Bea?"

Bea slipped on a clean apron, her face unreadable. "I've got problems," she said in a low voice.

The three worked through the dinner rush in near silence. By quarter to seven, the dining area had emptied out, and the last phone order had been prepared. Judging by the number of customers they'd served, the "two-fer" had been a ringing success.

"Come over here, luvs," Bea said, motioning Talia and Whitnee over to the table in the alcove at the back of the kitchen. "Before we close up, I need to talk to you both."

Whitnee looked at Talia, a panicked expression on her face. They each took a seat, and Bea leaned toward them. "The cops think I murdered Phil, and I'm afraid my lawyer and I didn't do much to convince them otherwise."

"What happened, Bea?" Talia folded her hands over the table. "Can we help in any way?"

Bea shook her head, and her eyes brimmed with tears. "Turns out the knife that killed Turnbull had traces of white-fish at the base, near the handle."

Talia already knew that, and a wave of guilt swept over her for not having divulged it to Bea sooner. "What about fingerprints? The real killer's prints must've been on the knife." Unless he, or she, was cunning enough to have wiped them off.

"Ah, well, that's a problem, too. There were lots of prints on the knife handle, you see, although some were too smudged to be useful. It's as if the flipping thing was never washed." Bea's eyes flashed with indignation. "Unfortunately, they couldn't match any of the prints to anyone in the national system, or database, or whatever it is the coppers use."

"But . . . *your* prints weren't on the knife, right?"

"No," Bea muttered softly, "and that's exactly the problem. The investigator, that O'Donnell fellow, thinks I wore a pair of disposable gloves to murder Turnbull."

Talia blew out a long sigh. "Did they show you a picture of the knife?"

"Actually they showed me the real thing—in a plastic bag, naturally. I'd never seen it before. I've never owned a knife with a handle like that. It was a fancy piece of work, let me tell you. Not something a practical soul like me would ever buy."

"What about your attorney?" Talia said. "I thought he was supposed to help you."

"He did help, Tal. He objected to more questions that I can count." She sat back in her chair and scrubbed a hand over her face. "And the questions I did answer, I answered truthfully, but that O'Donnell bloke just kept badgering me."

"Bea," Talia said, "if the knife had been yours and you'd used a disposable glove to murder Phil, then the other prints should match mine or Whitnee's, right? Assuming the police think the knife came from Lambert's."

"That's exactly right, luv. They couldn't explain the other prints. All of the arcade owners voluntarily submitted to fingerprinting, but none of their prints are on the knife, either. It's the main reason the cops didn't detain me."

Whitnee looked at Bea with a worried face. "I . . . I don't know much about these things, Bea, but it sounds to me like, you know, the evidence against you is all circumstantial."

"That's exactly what my lawyer said." Bea smiled at her. "Maybe I should have you on my legal team. Or maybe what I really need is my own detective. Someone who's not trying to string a rope around my neck." She gave Talia a wide-eyed look. "Someone like you, Tal. Didn't you tell me a story once about how you tracked down a stolen rabbit?"

"I did?" Talia chewed one side of her lip. She thought back to her school days. "Oh yeah, Rachel's brother's rabbit. Gosh, I'd forgotten all about that. How did you even remember that story?"

"Well, all those years ago, when you first started working here, you had a lot of heavy things on your mind," Bea said gently. "To distract you, I used to ask about your childhood. You know, what kinds of things you liked to do when you were growing up."

"And I told you the rabbit story." Talia frowned.

"I want to hear it," Whitnee piped in. "I had a rabbit of my own once."

"It's not much of a story. Rachel's little brother, Noah, had gotten a rabbit for his birthday—his seventh birthday, I think." Talia recalled how desperately the little boy had wanted that rabbit, how he'd begged his parents to buy one for him.

"A white one?"

"No, it was black and white—a darling little bunny. His folks bought it at a pet store, along with a big cage. They were very particular about their home—didn't let the kids breathe in it—so they made Noah keep it in the garage."

"Ugh," Bea said. "With all those exhaust fumes?"

"During the day they left the garage door open, and Noah was forever taking Punky—that's what he named him—out of the cage and plunking him on the lawn to play. In spite of his name, the bunny always stuck close to him—he never tried to go very far."

"So what happened?" Whitnee said impatiently.

Surprised at the girl's tone, Talia continued. "He'd had the rabbit for several weeks, and then one morning discovered it was gone."

"Stolen?" Whitnee said.

Talia nodded. "Yup. There was a side door into the garage, and even though it had a twist lock on the doorknob, Noah never remembered to lock it. The poor kid was heartsick when he found that cage door hanging open and his beloved bunny missing."

Whitnee shivered. "What did he do?"

"Well, Rachel and I—we were nine or ten at the time—helped him make 'lost bunny' posters. We tacked them up all over the neighborhood and inside every store and restaurant that would let us hang one."

"Poor little boy," Whitnee whispered, almost to herself.

Talia shot her a glance and went on. "About a week after Punky went missing, I was in the checkout line at Queenie's with my mom. I noticed a little girl, all by herself, standing in front of us holding a basket filled with carrots and lettuce. Totally weird for a kid, I thought. At that age, all I ever wanted to buy were peanut butter cups and Snickers bars. Anyway, I recognized her—she was a fifth-grader in my school. Her name was Oriana Butterforth. The kids used to poke fun at her name, but I always thought it was exotic and enchanting."

"Did you follow her?" Whitnee asked.

Talia smiled. "Not quite, but my suspicions had definitely been aroused. As soon as I got home, I looked up her last name in the phone book. Turned out her family lived on Hampton Avenue, only three streets away from our house. I asked Mom if I could ride my bike for a while, and as soon as I'd turned off from our street, I was barreling toward Oriana's."

"I'll bet I can guess the ending." Whitnee grinned.

"Well, when I got there, I didn't see any sign of the rabbit. The Butterforths lived in a two-family house and didn't have a garage, so I knew the rabbit had to be somewhere in the house, maybe even in the basement."

"What did you do?" Whitnee said urgently.

Talia shrugged. "The only thing I could think of. I rang the bell, and when Oriana opened the door I told her I *really, really* needed to use the bathroom."

"Did she let you in?"

"Oddly enough she did, though she looked totally perplexed. She pointed at a staircase, and I raced upstairs. I remember it bothered me that she seemed to be home by herself. I found the bathroom, flushed the toilet, and then started snooping. Which wasn't too hard, since the apartment only had two tiny bedrooms. Sure enough, in the first room I looked, I spotted the makeshift cage she'd constructed for Punky. She'd duct-taped two big cardboard boxes together and made the bunny a cozy little home. It was pretty clever, actually."

Whitnee's eyes widened. "Did you call the police?"

"Let her finish the story, luv," Bea said softly.

Looking chastised, Whitnee shrank lower into her chair.

"Punky was in the box munching happily on a carrot," Talia continued. "I was so relieved that he was okay, I never heard Oriana creep up behind me. But when I turned to leave there she was, these huge tears streaming down her cheeks. I'll never forget her face—it was so sad. 'You have to give him back,' I told her. She nodded, reached into the box, and picked up Punky. She handed him to me, and I rode all the way home with him sitting in my bicycle basket."

"Yesss!" Whitnee pumped her fist.

"Noah was thrilled to have him back, but I felt horrible. I couldn't stop seeing Oriana's tiny, freckled face drenched in tears." Talia looked away and rubbed her hand over her forehead. "I remember asking my mom, if I saved enough from my allowance, could I buy Oriana a rabbit of her own? But Mom said no, because that would be rewarding her for stealing. When I think back, I wish I'd done it anyway."

And she wished Bea had never reminded her of the rabbit story. Oriana had looked so shattered that day when Talia cycled away with Punky. It was probably why she'd pushed the memory from her mind. She hadn't thought about Oriana Butterforth in a very long time. Oriana and her mom moved out of town a few years later, and Talia never saw her again.

Whitnee seemed entranced by the story. "Talia, you really are a detective. If you were that smart when you were nine, then you can, like, definitely figure out who killed Phil!"

"I appreciate your confidence," Talia said, "but that's a pretty big stretch."

"Not really." Bea pounded her small fist on the table. "That story tells me you have the imagination to hunt down the clues and put them together. Of course, I've always known you were a clever cookie." She gazed at Talia with affection, and then looked at her watch and sighed. "Ah, look at me, keeping you hardworking girls here so late. Let's close up, shall we? But you think about that, luv, okay? Along with that other matter we talked about this morning." She gave Talia a meaningful wink.

Talia couldn't help smiling. She didn't deserve Bea's blind faith in her. Should she divulge her suspicions about Kendra? Let her know she'd been checking into Kendra's whereabouts at the time of the murder?

No, that would only raise Bea's hopes, and she wasn't ready to do that—not yet. Talia's "case" against Kendra was about as strong as cotton candy—all spun sugar and fluff, with no real substance.

As for the "other matter"—the idea of taking over Lambert's—Talia had to confess that the idea was beginning to get under her skin. During the course of the day, she'd caught herself fantasizing about it several times. Thinking about the changes she'd make, but without destroying the essence of Bea and Howie's original dream. There was so much she could do, both with the menu and with the eatery itself.

For now, though, she'd have to force it from her mind. Nothing was going to happen until Turnbull's murderer was caught and Bea's name was cleared.

They all left together through the front entrance. "Are you seeing Pug tonight?" Talia said to Whitnee, pulling the collar of her flared jacket more tightly around her neck.

"Not tonight. Pug has to work until, like, midnight. He got a job at that new burger joint. The one that opened last month?"

"I've heard of it," Talia said. "It's in that funky strip mall on Pittsfield-Lenox Road. What does he do there?" Okay, so she couldn't suppress her perverse curiosity about Whitnee's repulsive beau.

"Oh, you know, he, like, waits tables, helps clean the kitchen after closing time, that sort of thing." She lifted her thin shoulders in a world-weary shrug. "I guess I'll just poke around the mall for a while and then go home. Not much else to do."

"My offer stands," Talia said quietly. "If you need a place to stay—"

"Got it," Whitnee said brusquely. She turned her back on Talia and stared out over the arcade.

Touchy, Talia thought to herself. She didn't know what to make of Whitnee's roller-coaster moods, but decided to cut her some slack. Clearly the girl lived under stressful conditions. Having Connie Parker for a mother would make anyone snappish.

The plaza was empty, and eerily quiet. Even Jim Jepson's jack-o'-lantern had gone dark. On the street behind the lighting shop, the brittle leaves from the fading maples whispered in the cold breeze. The yellow police tape around Turnbull's place was gone. Did that mean the police had collected all the evidence they needed?

In the corner shop, Time for Tea, lights shone through the front window. Was Jill still there?

Bea secured the front entrance to Lambert's. "All right now, luvs, we have to walk to our cars together. I never thought I'd see the day when I didn't feel safe here." She shook her dark head sadly. "If the coppers ever catch the real killer, I'm going to throw a big party. And you two"—she slipped an arm through each of theirs—"I can't do enough to thank you. You've been here for me every minute."

"Bea, we're only doing our jobs," Talia said. "And the police *are* going to find the killer. Maybe they just need a little push in the right direction." She looked over at the tea shop. "Listen, I think Jill is still in her shop. I need to bend her ear for a few minutes, so I'm going to pop over there and see if she has time for a chat."

"You be careful!" Bea cried. "Never mind, Whitnee and I will walk you over there, won't we luvvy?"

"I guess so," Whitnee said in a peeved tone. "I've got no place else to go."

Why was Whitnee acting so strange? Talia wondered as they headed toward the tea shop. Ever since Talia had told the rabbit story, she'd seemed jumpy, almost to the point of surly.

Give her a break, Talia reminded herself. They'd all been as jumpy as fleas since Turnbull was murdered. Why should Whitnee be any different?

A sudden gust of wind sent a cold blast down the back of Talia's neck. She shivered, and the memory of the weird guy who'd been watching her earlier slammed into her brain. Was he still hanging around? The idea that he might be close by sent another chill through her.

"Let me see if Jill's in, then you two can go to your cars," Talia said, unhooking her arm from Bea's.

Peeking through the glass, she spotted Jill tidying up the shelves in the tea shop. The sight of all the beautiful teapots gave Talia a momentary lift. She knocked on the door and called Jill's name, hoping she wouldn't startle her.

Jill turned abruptly. When she saw Talia waving at her through the glass, her face relaxed. She set down the flow-ered teapot she was holding and scurried over to unlock the door. "Well, hey, you're here late," she said, lifting her gaze to Bea and Whitnee. "Can I help you all with something?" Jill's words were gracious, but her tone was flat.

Talia scrunched her face in a *sorry-to-be-a-pest* kind of

way. "We were just going out to our cars when I remembered something I wanted to ask you. Can I come in for a sec?"

"All of you?" Jill leveled a hard look at the trio.

"Ah, no," Bea said lightly. "Whitnee and I are leaving, aren't we, luv? Have a good evening, Jill."

But Whitnee didn't move, nor did she speak. She stood staring at Jill, her face a pale mask in the faint light that drizzled from the tea shop. Only when she realized Bea was tugging at her elbow did she finally turn away. The two hurried off toward the town lot, leaving Talia alone with Jill.

"So, it's just us chickens," Jill said, an uneasy flutter in her laugh. The subtle scent of honeysuckle swaying around her, she ushered Talia inside the shop.

"So, how was your day?" Talia said. "Lots of sales?" Her stab at sounding casual made her voice come out like a squeaky hinge.

Jill flashed a brief smile. "I'm sure you didn't come over here after hours to inquire about my day," she said evenly. "What can I do for you, Talia?"

Hmmm. Why the sudden frost? "Sorry. I know you want to close up, so I'll get to the point. Last night when we all met in here and you were arguing with Kendra, I overheard you say she was sitting pretty. Do you mind if I ask what you meant?"

Jill lifted her chin, then shrugged. "I suppose it wouldn't hurt to tell you. Phil had a sizeable life insurance policy naming Kendra as beneficiary. Now that he's"—she swallowed—"gone, Kendra will be able to collect on it."

Life insurance. That hadn't even occurred to Talia. "A large policy?"

"Depends on your viewpoint, but two hundred fifty grand is large by most people's standards."

Whoa. A cool quarter mil.

"In my book it's a queen's ransom," Talia said. "So why did he leave it to his ex-wife if he hated her with such a passion?"

Jill folded her arms. "Quite simply, it was a deal made with a she-devil, that being Kendra, of course. Poor Phil. I'm sure he didn't expect her to be collecting on it so soon. Nor did I," she added in a thin voice.

"A deal in return for what?" Talia prodded. Okay, casual was out the window. Pushy was in like a gale-force wind.

"In return for leaving him alone, for letting him run the shop the way he wanted to, without all the glitz and the showy trash she wanted to infuse into the place."

"Maybe it's me, but that just doesn't ring true," Talia said. "Why did she care? Was she really all that wild about vintage lighting?"

"Of course not. It was just another way to stick it to Phil."

"But the life insurance policy wasn't enough, was it, because Phil was relatively young and healthy. So she found another way to torment him. She persuaded her stepson to take over the old antiques shop and open a comic book store he didn't even want. Jill, did it ever occur to you that Kendra could be the killer?"

Jill gave out what might have been a belly laugh if her abdomen hadn't been as flat as an iron. "Kendra, murder Phil? Are you kidding? She'd have to risk chipping a nail, for God's sake!"

Talia felt taken aback. "Honestly, Jill, I'm a little surprised at your reaction. I Googled her. I know all about her grand plan to build a spa on the land she's buying from the town."

Jill shook her head. "I hear what you're saying, and believe me, there's nothing I'd like more than to see Kendra doing hard time." She toyed with the diamond-studded heart that hung from her neck on a chain. "But Kendra would never take a risk like that. She's too smart. And how did you know about Aaron?"

Talia smiled. "He came into Lambert's today for fish and chips. We had a short but very interesting chat. I liked him—he seems genuinely devoted to his dad."

Jill sagged against the adjacent display counter. "I begged Phil to forget about the comic book store, but he couldn't let it go. To him, it meant another win for Kendra." She mimed licking her finger and swiping it down over a chalkboard. "He just couldn't watch that happen. It was making him crazy." Her blue eyes welled with tears. "Every so often, it hits me that he's gone," she whispered. "It hurts."

Talia still couldn't make sense of Jill's relationship with Turnbull. It was a puzzle with pieces so warped they simply didn't fit together.

"Jill, I know I'm prying, but what was really going on with you and Phil? What is it I'm not seeing? And please don't tell me it was his good looks. As women, we both know that gets old very fast."

The tiny lines next to Jill's eyes deepened. "Then you may as well sit down. This will take a few minutes."

"Am I keeping you from your daughter?" Talia said, feeling more than a twinge of guilt.

"Yes, but she's in good hands. She and my mother are going to watch a movie and order a pizza, so they'll be fine until I get home."

They sat at one of the small tables in the front of the shop. Jill folded her elegant fingers on the table in front of her. "Phil and I knew each other since high school. We lived in the same neighborhood, in a town just outside of Hartford. Went to a pretty rough school. Phil was a year ahead of me, and a fairly good student. He was a loner in a school where most of the boys hung out in gangs." She smiled, and her face took on a dreamy look. "Phil never tried to fit in. That was one of the things I admired about him. He wasn't very macho, but he was *sooo* good-looking. Gorgeous eyes, wavy blond hair with a hint of auburn, perfect skin."

"You had a crush on him." Talia smiled at Jill.

"Kind of." Jill flicked an imaginary crumb off the table. "Anyway, this one afternoon I was walking home from school. I was almost there when three of the seriously bad boys from school appeared out of nowhere. They'd been lurking, waiting for me. Two of them grabbed me, started squeezing me in a really nasty way." Her face flushed, and she rubbed at her cheeks. "The other lowlife just stood there, leering at me, laughing. I'd never been so terrified."

"I can only imagine," Talia said, a shiver running through her.

"They started pulling me toward this junky car that was parked on the street. I was sure I was going to be taken somewhere and raped . . . and God only knows what else. I tried screaming for help, but the ringleader—this creep named Wally—put his ugly hand over my nose and mouth so I couldn't breathe."

Talia tucked her hands under her arms. "Wasn't anyone around to witness this, or to help?"

Jill paused and shook her head. "No, no one. I was starting to see spots, when all of a sudden, they just . . . let go."

Her blue eyes were alight. "Like a bold knight from a fairy tale, there was Phil, wielding a baseball bat. Before I could blink, two of the scumbags were writhing on the ground. Phil had whacked them in their family jewels." She laughed, but without mirth. "The third coward took off so fast I could almost see his dust. Oh, Talia, if you could have seen Phil. He was like a Norse god. When he turned to ask if I was okay, my legs slid out from under me, and I collapsed against that crappy old car. His eyes so were full of worship—he held out his hand and pulled me to my feet. I realized, then, that he adored me."

"He was your hero," Talia said.

"Yes, and I know it sounds nuts but Phil's always been my hero, in spite of his faults. And believe me, they were numerous." Her laugh flitted through the tea shop.

Yeah, no kidding. "Did those jerks get arrested?"

Slowly, Jill shook her head. "No," she said. "One of them had a father with some half-baked connections, so it all got swept under the rug. I didn't care—I was too ashamed for anyone to know."

"But you didn't do anything wrong!"

"I know. It's the old dilemma, isn't it?" Jill stood abruptly. She went over to a shelf where a celery-colored teapot with a hummingbird-shaped spout sat with its lid slightly askew. With her slender fingers she straightened the lid, then moved the pot back a smidge.

"Sorry. That was driving me insane," she said, dropping back into her chair.

"Jill, is that why you carry a gun, because of that assault?"

"Exactly. And believe me, if anyone ever tries to hurt Carly or me, I will use it." She aimed a finger at Talia and pulled an imaginary trigger.

Talia shivered under her flared jacket. "So you knew Phil since high school."

Jill nodded. "We stayed close through the end of his senior year, then he got a scholarship to Springfield College. After that, we saw each other mostly on weekends. But after I graduated high school, my folks moved to Wrensdale. Even though it wasn't that much farther away, it changed everything."

As distance often does, Talia thought. She remembered vowing to stay close to many of her high school buds, only to find that time—and maturity—had sent them scattering like spent dandelions. Thank heaven for Rachel, her loyal and lasting friend. She couldn't imagine their friendship ever fading, even if they lived a thousand miles from each other.

"I couldn't afford college right away," Jill said, "but I landed a clerical job at Gerry's accounting firm." She laughed and shook her head. "One glance and he was hooked. As was I. Gerry was so charming, so classy, so . . ."

Rich? Talia almost blurted.

". . . well, so sophisticated," Jill finished. She fingered the jeweled heart again. "Even more amazing—he was divorced and available. Before I knew it, we were engaged."

"How did Phil take the news?"

"Like you'd imagine. First he flew into a rage, then he stopped speaking to me altogether. By that time, I didn't care. In my own way, I'd outgrown him."

Talia shifted her purse from her shoulder to her lap. "How much did Gerry know about Phil?"

Jill blinked. "Almost nothing. After I married Gerry, I lost track of Phil for a long stretch. Then I had Carly, and honestly, nothing else really mattered to me. It wasn't until she started first grade that Gerry encouraged me to start a business. He sensed I was getting bored, and he was right."

"When did Phil pop back into your life?"

Jill glanced at the wall clock—a rose-encrusted teapot with thorns for hands. "About three years ago. He'd been checking me out on the Internet, and one day he just showed up here."

"Were you happy to see him?"

Jill hesitated, then a smile crept across her face. "The second I realized who he was, I went all melty. He was my first love, you know? Anyway, he was working for an insurance company in one of the Boston 'burbs, but he hated it. When he found out the lighting store was up for sale, he saw the opportunity to get close to me again. Weirdly enough, he grew to love that business. He had a sense of aesthetics that surprised even me."

Talia propped her chin on her fist. "Did you want him to be that close?"

"I didn't know what I wanted. He wasn't the same Phil anymore. He'd grown jaded and hard. Full of himself." She looked away, her eyes filling. "But he still owned a piece of my heart, and with Gerry gone so much I was horribly lonely. It felt so good to be with Phil again. His womanizing didn't matter to me—I blamed myself for that. Anyway, we started having the occasional tryst at the—"

"Wait a minute." Talia held up a hand. "Why was Phil's womanizing your fault?"

Jill's eyes blazed like blue fire. "Don't you get it? Phil changed because of *me*. Because *I* broke his heart all those years ago."

Talia was beginning to feel like someone had stuck her brain in the deep fryer and left it on High. "No, Jill. Whatever Phil became had nothing to do with you. Whatever bad choices he made were his own."

Jill buried her face in her hands and shook her head.

"Jill," Talia said gently, "I'm sorry to ask you to relive this, but I'm trying to help Bea. The police think she killed Phil and I know she didn't. I think Kendra's involved somehow. When did—" Her cell phone chose that moment to ring. Talia excused herself to check the caller. When she didn't recognize the number, she shoved the phone back in her purse and continued. "When did Kendra enter the picture?"

Jill folded her hands. "He met her one weekend at a charity gig at the Red Lion in Stockbridge. Gerry was away on business that weekend, and Mom and I had taken Carly to Disney World. I found out about it when I got back."

Talia shook her head. "I can't see the attraction, other than the obvious."

"That's because you don't know Kendra," Jill pointed out. "She likes her possessions wrapped in pretty packages, even if the contents are a bit spoiled. And when she sets her sights on someone, she doesn't stop until she's wrapped her coils around him and embedded her fangs firmly into his neck."

"I get the picture," Talia said. Had Kendra done the same to Aaron's dad? "Did she know about you?"

Jill laughed. "She found out soon enough. The marriage barely lasted ten months. In that short time, unfortunately, she managed to get control of a half interest in the lighting shop. Phil was smart, but Kendra was smarter—and more cunning."

"What *does* Kendra do, by the way?" Talia asked.

Jill narrowed her eyes, and Talia thought she spied a hint of envy. "She started by opening a couple of chic boutiques for women—the kind that cater to the upper crust. She did so well that she started to invest in other types of shops. Each time she did, their sales soared. It kills me to admit it, but Kendra is one of the savviest businesswomen I've ever known."

And now she's building a new empire—a spa to die for. Did Turnbull die for it?

"So tell me," Talia said. "Did Kendra dump Phil? Or was it vice versa?"

"You were right the first time—Kendra dumped him. See, here's the thing. As much of a witch as she is, she's a loyal witch. When she realized Phil was a cheater, she shed him faster than she shed one of her many skins. Finding ways to hurt him became her new pastime. A woman scorned, and all that."

It was all starting to make a crazy kind of sense to Talia. Jill's attachment to Phil. His obsession with vetoing the comic book store. The odd piece that still didn't fit was Kendra. Not that she wasn't Talia's number one suspect. She definitely was. But why kill Phil? Was she so desperate for the life insurance money that she would take that big a risk?

There was so much more Talia wanted to ask, not the least of which was whether or not Jill had gone to the police with her story. Jill's prints were all over Turnbull's office. Surely the investigators had discovered that by now. And the bracelet—did the police find it? Wouldn't that have Jill's prints, too?

Talia settled for one last question. "Jill, did Carly ever own a pair of orange plaid boots?"

Jill stared at her. "That is probably the strangest question I've ever been asked. The answer is, *are you kidding me*?

Do I look like the kind of woman who'd dress her child in orange plaid boots?"

At that, Talia had to laugh. "I guess not." She pictured Carly wearing plush suede boots lined with fleece, the kind that would keep her feet toasty warm and look charmingly stylish as well.

But the little girl in that photo wouldn't leave Talia's head. Talia didn't know why, but she felt sure the child with the orange plaid boots was somehow connected to the killer.

14

After leaving the tea shop, Talia hurried over the cobble-stone plaza in the direction of the town lot. Bea would've popped out a batch of kittens if she knew Talia had made the trek to her car, short as it was, by herself.

The lot, illuminated by sodium lights in each of the four corners, was empty save for her turquoise Fiat and three sedans that were parked adjacent to one another. Talia's feet picked up speed as she drew closer to her car. She'd no sooner opened her door when her cell rang again. She jumped inside, locked the doors, and dug the phone out of her purse. "Hello," she said, slightly out of breath.

"Ms. Sunday?"

For a moment Talia was baffled. Then she remembered—it was the name she'd given to the woman at Always You. "Yes, this is Ms. Sunday."

"Oh, good." The young voice sounded relieved. "I got

your number from the caller ID on the phone at the spa. This is Marya . . . I mean, Misty. From Always You?"

Talia sat up straighter, her mental antennae on high alert. "Yes, Misty."

"Um, there's something I wanted to tell you before. You know, when you asked about Kendra LaPlante?"

"Oh yes, of course," Talia said, trying to keep her tone even. "Did you find her cosmetics bag?"

"Well, no. We didn't find anything like that. But there's something else. Something I couldn't talk about while I was at the spa."

Talia felt her heartbeat do a little tap dance. "What is it, Misty?"

"Um, remember I told you Ms. LaPlante had a full body massage? At seven forty-five?"

"Why, yes, I think you did say something like that."

"Well, um, I'm really good friends with the masseuse—the woman who always does her massage? She told me something the next day that was kind of strange." Misty paused. "So, okay, here's the thing. My friend had no sooner started Ms. LaPlante's massage when Ms. LaPlante jumped off the table. She claimed she had severe intestinal cramps and had to go to the bathroom."

"Oh dear. That must've been quite embarrassing—for both of them."

"I guess," Misty said. "But here's the weird thing. Ms. LaPlante never came back to finish her massage. She just . . . disappeared for almost an hour."

Talia struggled to keep her voice calm, but a tiny voice inside her was leaping to some lofty conclusions. "I see. Well, she must have been in some distress. Did anyone . . . go to the bathroom to see if she needed help?"

"That's just it," Misty said. "After about ten minutes my friend went to check on her. She couldn't find her anywhere in the south wing—not in the bathroom or in the dressing area."

Because she went to the lighting shop to murder Turnbull.

"Misty, you said she had a mani-pedi scheduled at eight forty-five. Did she show up for that?"

"Yeah, she did. Like nothing ever happened. She never said a word about bailing on her massage. Or about feeling sick."

"I guess she was embarrassed," Talia offered. *Or she didn't care to share with anyone that she'd just murdered her ex.*

"And get this," Misty went on. "When my friend opened her tip envelope on Thursday—all of our customers leave tips privately that way—she said Ms. LaPlante gave her *double* her regular tip. Double!"

Of course. To keep her from blabbing about Kendra's disappearing act.

"At first she thought Ms. LaPlante was just being nice because of the way she'd ditched her massage." Misty snorted. "Like that would ever happen. Ms. LaPlante is the *least* nice person I know."

"She can be difficult," Talia said mildly.

"Anyway, when the police found out that man who was murdered was Kendra's ex, they came here and started asking a lot of questions. They wanted to confirm Ms. LaPlante's alibi for Wednesday evening."

Talia jerked up so fast in her seat her knee hit the steering wheel. Squelching an expletive, she said, "The police were there? Did your friend tell them what happened?"

"No." Misty sighed. "She was afraid she'd get fired. Ms. LaPlante is our best customer. Every week she spends a fortune at the spa. The owner—our boss—kisses her behind, if you catch my meaning," Misty added with disgust.

"Misty, that's no reason to lie to the police. Murder is a serious crime!"

"She didn't lie," Misty protested. "She just . . . kept some stuff to herself."

This was big. This was huge. Talia was more convinced than ever that Kendra had murdered Turnbull.

Then Misty dropped a stink bomb on her.

"Ms. Sunday, I'm taking a majorly huge risk telling you all this. The way things are these days I can't afford to lose my job, and neither can my friend. If you repeat what I said, I'll deny it to the ends of the Earth."

Talia felt her jaw drop. "*What?* You've got to be— Is your friend there with you? Can I talk to her?"

"That's none of your business, and she's not talking to anyone." Misty was getting snippy now, and defensive. Talia wanted to reach through the phone and shake the girl.

In the next instant, Talia chided herself. Any second now, Misty could hang up and leave her with nothing. She remembered what her nana always said. *Put a smile in your voice— it shows.*

"Misty." Talia stretched her lips into a grin. "If you didn't want me to tell this to anyone, why did you call me?"

After a pause, Misty said, "I figured anyone sneaky enough to pretend she worked for Ms. LaPlante to wheedle information out of me ought to be able to figure out how to tip off the cops. *Without* getting me and my friend in trouble."

"I—" Talia began, but Misty was gone. The girl had hung up.

Oh Lord, now what? On top of everything else, she was freezing. She hadn't even started her car. She turned on the engine and flipped on the heat as high as it would go.

Ever since she'd found Turnbull's body Thursday morning, her mind had been on overload. Too many secrets, too many lies—all tumbling through her head like a load of mismatched socks in the dryer.

Maybe it was time to sort. To see which ones matched up to the truth and which ones needed to be chucked.

Something Jill said a few nights ago had stuck in her head like a bookmark. *Anyone with even a quarter of a brain could figure out Phil's code.* Talia punched in Rachel's speed-dial number on her phone.

"What up, pixie pie?"

Talia laughed. Sometimes Rachel was too funny. "If I treat you to pup-dogs from Deeno's, are you up for a little snooping?"

15

"I can't believe you recruited me for a B and E," Rachel said wryly. She swiped a tiny napkin over her ketchup-stained lips and squinted at the scrap of paper clutched in her fingers.

"It's not a B, just an E," Talia defended. "If we figure out the code we're only entering, right? If we don't figure it out, then we won't get in. Besides, it's not a crime scene anymore, so are we really doing anything illegal?"

Rachel waggled her hand back and forth. "That'll be for a judge to decide."

Talia groaned.

"Just kidding." Rachel laughed. "This reminds me of the time we snuck into Ms. Zimmerman's class to search for her grade book."

Talia nodded. "Tenth grade," she said. Their history teacher's grade book had gone missing one day, sending the woman into a minor tizzy. Over the next two days, Talia noticed that Todd Tetford, a fellow student and all-around class clown, kept grinning up at the ceiling with a satisfied smirk. Sure enough, when she and Rachel sneaked into the classroom after hours, they found the grade book hidden above one of the panels of the dropped ceiling. They turned it in immediately but couldn't convince the principal that they themselves hadn't filched the grade book. It wasn't until Todd fessed up to the crime that they were finally let off the hook.

"Now, what do you have on your list?" Rachel said. "So far I've got *lock*, *open*, *lamp*, and *lite*—that's L-I-T-E."

Talia popped the last bite of her third dog into her mouth, savoring the guacamole topping until the last swallow. Deeno's might be a dive, but their pup-dogs were miniature rolls of heavenly, spiced mystery meat on butter-grilled potato buns. She grabbed Rachel's heavy-duty flashlight and shone it on her own list. "All I've got is *light*—the regular spelling—*vintage*, *classic*, *radiance*, and *Caddy*, with a Y."

They were sitting in Rachel's Jeep Cherokee on Birch Street, each with a list of possible passwords to the keypad at the back of the lighting shop. Outfitted in sleek black leggings, black lace-up combat boots, and a black cowl-neck sweater, her wavy brunette hair tucked into a tight knot at the back, Rachel looked as if she'd stepped off the set of the latest Bond movie. Talia glanced down at her own pitiful version of "spy" clothing—a pair of navy sweats and the army green ski cap she'd had since the sixth grade.

"I still can't believe you snuck in there Thursday night with Jill." Rachel laughed. "I'd love to have been a mosquito on the wall when you were rummaging around in that sofa. And by the way, you violated the BFF Code by not telling me about it sooner."

"*Unh*-uh. Technically, I'm still in the seventy-two-hour grace period."

"Shootski." Rachel snapped her fingers. "Forgot about the grace period."

"I have a lot more to tell you, but I want to get this over with first. Besides, it wasn't one of my finer moments." She crumpled her greasy Deeno's bag and set it on the floor of the Cherokee. "Okay, I'm ready if you are. Why don't we start with your passwords and see how far we get."

"If by some miracle we manage to get in," Rachel said, "do we know what we're looking for?"

Talia told her about the photo of the little girl in the orange plaid boots. Jill mentioned Phil had a secret hiding place. What if the child in the snapshot is Phil's biological child? Could he have stashed more photos like it in his hiding place? Was he blackmailing someone? Was someone blackmailing him? But if that were the case, how did Kendra fit into the picture?

"Let's try to find the secret hiding place," Talia said, "and we'll go from there."

They climbed out of the Cherokee and made a fast dash to the back door of the lighting shop. Talia shot a nervous glance over her shoulder. Birch Street was dark, and blessedly quiet. The staid old houses that lined the street were hunkered down, their shades drawn against the cold October night.

"Let's try yours first," Talia said, holding her ladybug light over the keypad. "Somehow they seem more logical."

One by one, Rachel punched in the words on her list. Nothing.

"They're all a bust," she said, huddling close to the back door.

Talia tried the words on her list next, with the same results.

"Thwarted by technology," Talia muttered. "And Jill said anyone with a quarter of a brain could figure out Phil's code."

"Hmmm," Rachel said. She punched in another word. This time they heard a distinct click.

Elated and terrified at the same time, Talia pushed open the door. "Good job, Rach! What was the code word?"

"What else?" Rachel said drily. *"Phil."*

"You're a regular Double-O-Seven, aren't you?"

"Double-O-Crazy is more like it," Rachel said. "Come on, let's work fast and get out even faster."

They closed the door quickly. In the windowless room, a feeble light seeped from the luminescent clock on the wall. Rachel stared at the clock for several moments, then flicked on her oversized flashlight and bounced the beam around the room. "Ugh. Everything's covered with powder. Must be fingerprint powder, right?"

"I assume so," Talia said, "but this time I came prepared." She whipped two pairs of disposable gloves from her pocket and handed a set to Rachel.

"Ah, perfect." Rachel looked at the clock again. She tucked her flashlight under one arm while she slid on the gloves.

Talia went over to the gaping doorway that led to the showroom and closed the door. That way they could turn on the overheads in Turnbull's office without fear of any light seeping into the showroom and illuminating the front windows. She flipped the switch to the overhead lights—the same switch she'd flicked on that horrible morning when she'd made her gruesome discovery. Was it only two days ago? It seemed an eternity had passed since she'd found Turnbull's body.

"Ah, let there be light," Rachel said. She set down her flashlight atop the stack of boxes near the rear entrance. "On the way over here I got thinking about this catalog Noah has. You know how he collects gadgets?"

Rachel's adorably hunky brother was thirty-one, with an IQ that hovered in the stratosphere. Excruciatingly shy, Noah suffered from extreme anxiety, and rarely left the stately home on Milan Drive that he and Rachel shared with their mostly absent mother. Solely through online classes, he'd earned master's degrees in both German and Spanish, and now worked from home as a translator for an international law firm based in London.

"Of course I do." Talia smiled. "Noah has more gadgets than the ingenious Mr. Bond himself."

"You got that right. He has this one catalog that specializes in items with secret compartments. You know, desks, bookcases, coffee tables." She offered some more examples, and they split up the room and began their search.

For the next ten minutes, they scoured the office. Anything that might conceal a secret opening was poked, pulled, prodded, and pried. The result was a disappointing *zippo*.

Talia plunked herself on the floor in front of a narrow bookcase choc-a-bloc with lighting catalogs. She pulled out each one and shook the pages, hoping to dislodge a photo or letter or anything Turnbull might have tucked away from prying eyes. By the time she'd searched the last one, she heaved a disappointed sigh.

All at once, she noticed a loose strip of decorative wood just below the bottom shelf. *Yes! A secret drawer!* Her pulse zooming into overdrive, she tugged at it. The entire thing

snapped off, and Talia looked at it and groaned. The strip
of wood hid nothing more than the blob of dried glue that
had been used to tack it in place.

Talia glanced over at Rachel, who was leaning one elbow
atop the stack of boxes near the rear entrance—the same
boxes Talia had tripped over two nights earlier. Rachel's
bright blue eyes were fixed on the wall clock. In the next
instant, Rachel swung Turnbull's desk chair around and
pushed it across the floor until it rested right below the clock.

"What are you doing?" Talia said, her voice rising in
pitch. "Do you think there's something in the clock?"

"We'll find out in a minute."

Steadying her combat boot, Rachel hoisted herself onto
the chair. It shifted slightly to the right, and Talia hopped
off the floor and went over to hold the chair in place. "Lord,
you're going to break your neck."

"I saw a clock in Noah's catalog that looks a lot like this
one," Rachel said. "The face is actually a door that swings
open."

"Like a wall safe?"

"Kind of." With her fingertips, Rachel reached up and
began pulling at the edges of the clock, starting at nine
o'clock and moving methodically all around. She'd gotten
as far as two o'clock when the clock front abruptly flew open,
sending Rachel reeling backward. Talia grabbed her, and
they both spilled to the floor in a heap of arms and legs.

Talia let out an *oomph* while Rachel came back with
a more imaginative oath. "Sorry," Rachel said. "Did I
squish you?"

"No, you mashed me," Talia said, "but I'll live if you get
off me."

Rachel rolled sideways and heaved herself upward, then

pulled Talia to her feet. Talia was brushing off the rear of her sweatpants when she noticed a folded square of paper on the floor. She grabbed Rachel's arm. "Rach, that must have been inside the clock!"

With the speed of a rattlesnake, Rachel bent and scooped it up. The single sheet of plain white paper had been folded twice. "There's something in here," she said, unfolding it.

Talia felt ready to leap out of her Keds. "Is it a photo?

"No, it looks like a bunch of newspaper articles," Rachel said. "Copies of them, anyway. Look at this one. 'Student involved in hazing death seeks plea deal.'" She fished through the remaining clips and handed a few to Talia.

The articles, from a newspaper in Monroe County, Georgia, dated back to the fall of 1998. Talia flipped through them and felt her mouth go dry. "Listen to this," she said, reading from a clip dated December 9, 1998. "Susan Benson, daughter of bourbon mogul Claimore Benson, whose involvement in a sorority stunt that left freshman Penny Bachellor dead from alcohol poisoning, has reached a plea deal with the District Attorney's office. 'While we are sorrowful over Penny's tragic and needless death,' Benson's lawyer, Laurence Atkins, said yesterday, 'we are gratified that Susan will be allowed to perform community service in lieu of incarceration.'"

The article went on to recap the tragedy—a sorority hazing stunt gone horribly wrong. But it was the picture next to the article that made Talia gasp. The photo showed a dazed-looking Susan Benson being hustled out of the courthouse by her attorney. She was younger, and her curly hair was pulled back into a prim knot, but there was no mistaking her face.

Susan Benson was Suzy Sato.

16

Rachel backed the Cherokee out of its parking slot and headed down Birch Street. "Refresh my memory. Suzy's the gal who owns the bath shop, right?"

"Right," Talia said, pulling off her ski cap. She tried to process what she'd seen in those articles, but had trouble imagining Suzy Sato taking part in such a thoughtless, deadly act. Not that she knew her all that well, but Suzy had always seemed bubbly and helpful and kind.

"Why do you think Phil hid those articles in the clock?" Rachel said. She flicked a glance at her rearview mirror. "I mean, if all that stuff was in the paper, then it was public knowledge, right?"

"Public knowledge, *if* you know where to look," Talia offered. "And it was over fifteen years ago. Suzy has a new life now. I'm guessing she doesn't want anyone around here to know of her past. I sure wouldn't if I were her."

"You'd never do anything so stupid," Rachel said tightly. "God, what is the matter with people. How can someone . . ." She shook her head.

"I know," Talia agreed. "And I can't imagine what that poor Penny's family has been through. It must haunt them every day of their lives."

Rachel stared straight ahead.

"Rach? You okay?"

"Yes, but I'm pretty sure someone's following us."

A knot of panic rose in Talia's throat. She thought of the creepy guy who'd been watching her earlier. "Then go to the police station. He won't dare follow us there, right?"

"I'm going to try to lose him first."

Rachel drove another three blocks, until they reached the intersection of Pleasant Street. Without signaling, she took a hard right turn, jerking Talia to the left. The car behind them swerved and stayed hot on their tail. In the passenger-side mirror, Talia saw the driver flash his lights—on, off, on, off.

"I guess he wants us to pull over," Rachel said, her voice now laced with alarm.

"Yeah, that is *so* not a good idea," Talia stole another glance at the side mirror. The stalker was practically in Rachel's back end.

Up ahead, the traffic light at Pleasant and Main had just turned green. "Hang on," Rachel said. She swerved at the light and turned right onto Main. The stalker did the same, still flashing his lights.

"This is crazy," Talia said. "Who is this nutcase?" She gripped the strap over the passenger-side window.

And then, with the skill of a NASCAR driver, Rachel jerked the wheel of the Cherokee and screeched right into the now-deserted town parking lot. In the middle of the lot she braked hard, and the Jeep lurched to a stop.

The stalker followed.

"I can't believe it," Rachel said. "He's parking right behind us!"

Within seconds Talia heard a car door slam, and before she could dig her phone out of her pocket, the wild-looking visage of Suzy Sato was gaping at her through the passenger-side window.

"Talia, it's only me. I need to talk to you!"

"Ignore her. I'm calling the police," Rachel said. She flipped the switch on her Bluetooth, and a robotic voice asked who she wanted to call.

Talia gawked at her friend. Why hadn't she done that in the first place?

"Please, Talia, just hear what I have to say," Suzy drawled, her Georgia roots creeping like weeds into her voice.

"Top—" Rachel had started to say, but Talia grabbed her wrist.

"Wait a minute, Rach. I think we should hear what she has to say. Besides, it'll be two against one, right? What can she do to us?"

Rachel snorted. "Shoot us? Stab us?"

Suzy was sobbing now, tears streaming down her face. She tapped on the glass with her tiny fist. "Please, at least roll down the window. I only want to ask you something."

"Oh all right," Rachel grumbled. "She doesn't really look very dangerous. More like a rag doll on the run from a toy factory." She pressed the hang-up button on the Bluetooth.

Talia fumbled for the switch, and then powered down the window about halfway. "Why were you following us?" she blurted, before Suzy could utter a word. "You're lucky we didn't call the police!"

Suzy sucked in a noisy sniffle. "I'm sorry. I didn't mean to scare you. After I left my shop tonight I went to Price Chopper to stock up on groceries. I was on my way home—we only live a few streets behind Birch—when I saw you two sneaking into the back of the lighting store. I'd been trying to find a way to get into Phil's office for weeks. Even before he was . . . you know, killed. I couldn't believe you figured out how to get in!" Her entire body shivered, and her face looked as pale as a mummy's.

Rachel sighed. "She may as well hop in the backseat. I can't stand watching her freeze out there."

"Suzy, get in before you turn into an icicle," Talia said. She powered her window back up.

Rachel clicked the locks open, and Suzy threw herself onto the Cherokee's backseat. Her teeth chattered, and she rubbed her bare hands together. "Thank you. It's nice and warm in here. And again, I'm really sorry if I frightened you. I thought you'd realize it was me and pull over."

"We couldn't see you in the dark," Rachel said sharply. "Why don't you tell us what you want, and make it the short version, please."

Suzy stuck her head into the space between the two front seats. Talia was just turning to look at her when Suzy pulled something out of her coat pocket. Talia jumped.

"Oh for the love of Popeye, it's only my hankie." Suzy waved a scrap of lace in the air and dabbed her eyes with it. "Phil was blackmailing me . . . kind of," she said. "Not for money, but to keep something quiet. That's why I had to sign that stupid petition of his. Do y'all seriously think I cared whether or not that young man opened a comic book store?"

"That's it!" Talia said. "That's what was stuck in my brain. At least twice I heard you say *y'all*. I knew it sounded strange for someone who was supposedly raised in Vermont."

Suzy's jaw dropped. "You checked on me?"

"Sorry, but I checked on everyone," Talia said. "I'm trying to keep Bea from being arrested for murder." She exchanged glances with Rachel. "Suzy," she said quietly, "we know why Phil was blackmailing you. We found the articles in his office about the hazing death you were involved in."

Suzy dropped her head against the backseat and closed her eyes. "I wasn't involved, not the way everyone said I was." Her voice rattled. "Those awful girls . . . they did the same thing to me when I was a freshman pledge. I had to swig down a bottle of cheap burgundy wine in ten minutes or less." She gave out a tortured laugh. "I think I threw up for a week."

"So you knew how it felt." Rachel's voice was brittle. "Is that what Penny had to do? Drink a bottle of cheap wine in ten minutes flat?"

Suzy nodded slowly, her face etched with pain. "They did other things, too—humiliating things. We'd all been through it, survived it. But Penny was a tiny thing, barely weighed a hundred pounds. I told the other sisters to let her be, that there was no way her system could tolerate that much wine. They only laughed and called me vicious names. At one point Penny started shivering—I'm not even sure she was conscious. On the sly, I slipped my quilt over her, the one my grammy had sewn for me when I was a little girl. It was the main reason the judge took pity on me, because I'd demonstrated 'remorse.' "

Listening to Suzy relate the hazing story was making the pup-dogs in Talia's stomach want to relocate to higher ground. "Is that why you moved to Vermont? To escape the publicity?"

"Yes, and because my daddy was so angry and ashamed he couldn't look at me anymore. I finished school at the University of Vermont using the name Suzy, with a Z, Benson. That's where I met my darlin' Ken, and how I became Suzy Sato."

"Every so often your Southern drawl kicks in," Talia said.

In the dimly lit Cherokee, Suzy looked like a ghost. "I worked hard to lose my accent, to sound like a native-born New Englander. But once in a while, I slip."

"What about your husband?" Rachel asked, without a trace of sympathy. "Does he know about it?"

"Of course he does. I could never have given him my hand in marriage without coming clean about everything. You've never met my Ken, but he's the sweetest, gentlest man you'd ever care to know."

"How did Phil find out about it?" Rachel said, her tone noticeably softer. "He must have had to dig hard to dredge up those old newspaper clips."

"That's the kind of thing Phil did," Suzy said hotly. "That was his weapon. He collected information about people, not only about me. When I told him I wouldn't sign his silly petition, he showed up a few days later with all those newspaper copies. I tell you, my heart about sank into my shoes. I've worked hard to establish myself here, to become a respected businesswoman." Tears sprouted on her lower lashes, and she swiped her crumpled hankie over them. "And now Ken and I are trying to have a baby. You can understand why I don't want any of this to be leaked." She leaned forward and gave Talia a pleading look. "I love it here, Talia. I don't want to have to move away. Please, *please* give me those articles you found in Phil's office."

The agony in Suzy's voice made Talia's heart twist. She turned and stared through the windshield for at least a full minute. She was tired of keeping secrets. She'd only wanted to get Bea off the hook, not to hurt anyone else. Besides, Suzy's reasoning was faulty. If someone could find those articles once by digging around online, they could find them again.

Talia reached into the pocket of her sweats and withdrew the folded envelope. "Take it," she said, handing it to Suzy. "But answer one question for me, and truthfully."

"Of course," Suzy said warily, taking the envelope.

"Did you ever have a little girl, Suzy? A little girl with red hair, a bit lighter than yours? A little girl who wears, or wore, orange plaid boots?"

Suzy looked Talia straight in the eye and held up her right hand. "I don't know why you're asking me that question," she said, "but I swear on my sweet grammy's grave that I have never had a child."

17

It was nearly eleven by the time Rachel left Talia's. They'd figured out how to use Jill's tea infuser, and over a pot of strawberry-orange tea they sat in Nana's cozy living room and talked for over an hour. Well, mostly Talia talked and Rachel listened.

Talia filled Rachel in on everything—her run-in with Cliff Colby and his creepy stalker, Jill's bizarre revelations, and Talia's conversation with Misty at the spa. She stopped short of telling her about Bea's offer to sell Lambert's to her. If Talia decided to accept the deal, it would be more fun to surprise Rachel with the news.

Rachel had been unusually quiet, which was definitely out of character. At least twice Talia had caught her staring at the wall, her blue eyes unfocused and her brow creased. Talia didn't press her. If something was up, Rachel would tell her when she felt the time was right.

In the kitchen, the groceries she'd bought at the variety store that morning were still where she'd left them on the counter. She stuck the loaf of wheat bread into Nana's metal breadbox, and then pulled the cat food out of the brown grocery bag. She still hadn't checked the local animal shelter's website to see if anyone reported a lost cat. Would the calico kitty still be prowling the neighborhood? Or had she found her way to back her real home?

Talia opened the door that led to the tiny backyard and turned on the outside light. The scent of burned leaves mingled with the night air, reminding her of how much she loved fall in the Berkshires. In the two side windows of the bungalow adjacent to Nana's, a pair of brightly lit pumpkins beamed from their respective sills—one with a cockeyed grin and one with a scary snarl. The sight made Talia smile, and she called out to the cat in a singsong tone. "Kitty, kitty, are you out there, kitty cat? Would you like something to eat?"

She waited a few minutes and called out again, but the cat still didn't appear. Talia didn't know whether to feel relieved or disappointed. She was just closing the door when a figure popped around the corner and into the yard. Talia gasped and almost did a high jump as a middle-aged woman ambled toward her.

"Oh my gosh, I'm so sorry I startled you," the woman said. She stood about ten feet away, her sandy, shoulder-length hair blowing in the cold breeze. "I knocked on your door earlier this evening but you weren't home. Were you looking for the little cat that's been hanging around?"

"Yes," Talia said, her heart still pounding. "I didn't know if she had a home or not, but I bought her some food today."

The woman stepped toward Talia and offered her hand.

"I'm Vicki Grayson, by the way. My partner and I live three houses down."

"Pleased to meet you, Vicki. I'm Talia." She stepped outside into the frigid night and accepted the woman's handshake.

"That cat used to belong to old Mrs. Sennott," Vicki explained. "She died unexpectedly, and her nasty excuse for a son tossed the poor creature in the street to fend for itself. The cat had never been outside before, so she doesn't know what to do. We've been leaving food for her, but haven't managed to catch her yet. She's an elusive little devil, but she really needs to go to the animal shelter." Vicki's voice was a light sound that made Talia feel at ease.

"I fed her some tuna last night," Talia told her, putting a silent curse on the man who'd so callously abandoned the cat. She hugged her arms to her chest. "She actually crept pretty close to me. I guess she was really hungry."

"Hey, listen, you look like you're freezing," Vicki said. "I just wanted to fill you in about the cat. One of these days, Grace and I will have you over for coffee and cinnamon cake."

Talia smiled wistfully at her. "I'd love to, but I don't think I'll be here that much longer. You probably noticed the FOR SALE sign on the lawn."

"Oh yeah, right," Vicki said. "That's too bad. I can tell you'd have been a nice neighbor. Anyway, it was great meeting you. I'm sure we'll chat again before you move!"

Talia said good night and closed the door, feeling her shoulders droop. How was she ever going to turn her grandmother's house over to strangers? Everywhere she turned she saw Nana.

She couldn't count the times she'd plopped herself in one

of the vinyl kitchen chairs, watching Nana stir a pot of meat sauce over her ancient electric range, her curly gray hair fluffed around her kindly face. Nana would always insist that Talia taste-test the sauce, just in case there was too much of this or too little of that. Naturally, it was always perfect. Next to the stove, the old Zenith radio on the counter would be pumping out big band numbers from the forties. The station was so far away that the songs were more static than music, but Nana didn't seem to notice.

Squashing away a tear, Talia removed two plastic bowls from Nana's cupboard. She filled one with water and the other with a blend of dried and canned cat food, just in case the kitty preferred one over the other. She was setting the bowls down on the front step when she spied a timid feline face peeking at her from behind her Fiat.

"Here you go, sweetie. Eat it while you can," she said in a choked voice. "Pretty soon I'll be looking for a new home, too."

On Sunday morning, Talia awoke with a new resolve. She called the Wrensdale police station and demanded to talk to the chief. He wasn't due in until ten, she was informed. Did she wish to leave a message?

"No thanks," she said, and disconnected. *I'll pay him a surprise visit.*

Rachel's play at the Pines was today, and Talia was eager to see the performance. She also looked forward to seeing her folks, whom she'd been avoiding since Thursday. She loved the daylights out of them, but their concern for her occasionally bordered on the obsessive.

Luckily, the desserts she'd promised to bring were all

taken care of. She'd called Peggy's Bakery early that morning and ordered several dozen assorted cookies and brownie
squares. Talia felt terrible for giving the baker ridiculously
short notice, but she knew Peggy kept a hefty supply of
baked delights in her freezer just for such emergencies.

After gulping down a bowl of soggy Cheerios, she fished
through her closet for something appropriate to wear. She
loved the lilac cowl-neck dress she'd bought when she first
started her job at Scobey & Haight. Not only did it flatter
her petite frame, it made her look a tad taller. Then she
remembered—it was one of Chet's favorites. She gave it a
hard shove to the back of the closet. Instead she chose a pair
of chocolate-brown ankle pants and her bottle-green tunic
sweater. She topped the sweater with her absolute favorite
scarf—the ladybug scarf—wrapping it twice around her
slender neck and securing it with a knot.

The Wrensdale police department, located a block away
from the arcade, was housed in a dark red brick building
that it shared with the public library. Parking was limited,
unless you drove an official car. Talia was sure she'd have
to circle the block a few times to snag one of the precious
spots on Main Street. But then, like a watery mirage shim-
mering in the desert, a prime space appeared. Right in front,
too. *Score!* Talia put on her signal, and was swinging her
Fiat into the space when a car growled past her on the left,
nearly nipping the Fiat's back end.

"Jerk!" Talia said.

The car that nearly hit her roared off down Main Street.
She hopped out of her Fiat just in time to see the vehicle
screech to a jerky stop behind a car at the next traffic light.
Out of nowhere, a patrol car came from behind her, lights
flashing and siren wailing.

Talia laughed. "Now you're in trouble," she said, watching the officer signal to the driver to pull over.

Inside the station, she was met with a wall of Plexiglas that stretched at least twelve feet. Behind the glass, a young officer with a pimply face was sipping black coffee from a foam cup.

"Good morning, ma'am," he greeted her.

"Good morning. I'm here to see Chief Westlake, please." She tried to sound formal, as if she actually had an appointment.

"Name?"

She gave him her name and looked at her watch. It was twenty minutes past ten.

The officer set down his cup, picked up his phone, and punched a single button. "Chief? A *Talia Marby* is here to see you." He pronounced her name slowly, as if she were visiting from a distant planet. After several seconds, the officer hung up. He nodded at the row of molded plastic chairs that rested against the wall behind her. "Have a seat."

Talia sat. She'd promised Rachel she'd be at the Pines by eleven, so she hoped Derek wouldn't make her wait long. Unfortunately, it was a good twenty minutes before he finally sauntered out from behind a locked door. His face looked drawn, weary from lack of sleep, but his blue eyes were sharp as a condor's. He folded his arms over his chest. "What can I do for you, Talia?"

Talia gave him her phoniest smile. "Can we talk for a few minutes? Privately?"

Westlake propped one fist under his sculpted chin. "What about?"

"Oh, for God's sake, Derek, you know what about," she

snapped, and then immediately softened her tone. "I have some information that might be helpful. About Turnbull."

Derek worked his lips into a faint smirk. "Then follow me."

That was way too easy, Talia thought, a thread of unease winding through her. She followed Derek into his office, her black heels clicking against the worn hardwood floor far too loudly for her liking. At the doorway to his office, she stopped short. Sitting erect in a chair opposite Derek's desk was Sergeant Liam O'Donnell from the state police detective unit.

O'Donnell stood abruptly and grasped Talia's hand. "Ms. Marby, we meet again." He gave her a crisp nod and waited until she was seated beside him before lowering himself into his own chair.

"I didn't expect to see you here," Talia said to O'Donnell. She threw Derek a dark look. Was it too late to turn and flee? She'd played right into their trap. Now she was like a helpless fly stuck on a roll of flypaper.

Derek sat in his snazzy-looking swivel chair and leaned forward. "Ms. Marby says she has some information for us," he said to O'Donnell.

"Excellent. I'm anxious to hear it."

Oh goody.

Talia took in a long breath and then launched into her story, starting with Cliff Colby and his admission that he borrowed money from Turnbull, and ending with Kendra's interest in the lighting shop and Turnbull's life insurance policy.

O'Donnell folded his huge hands over his chest. "You haven't told us anything we don't know, Ms. Marby. Is there anything else?"

Talia swallowed. "You . . . knew all that?"

O'Donnell gave her an impatient nod. "We did. This may come as a shock to you, Ms. Marby, but we're quite experienced at interviewing potential suspects. Now, if that's all—"

Talia shifted in her chair, which she was fairly sure had morphed into a block of concrete. "Did you check with the people at the spa to see where Kendra was while Phil was being murdered?"

O'Donnell's eyes flashed. "So it's *Phil* now, is it? How well did you know him, Ms. Marby?"

Talia would've sworn she saw an amused gleam in Derek's eye. "I barely knew him at all," she huffed. "And what I did know, I didn't like. Don't get me wrong, I certainly wouldn't do anything to harm the man. I only meant—"

"We know exactly what you meant, Ms. Marby."

If you call me Ms. Marby one more time, she was tempted to say, *you'll be wearing those polished shoes of yours as earmuffs.*

Oh, who was she kidding? She didn't have an aggressive cell in her body.

Derek finally took pity on her. "Talia," he said gently, "we realize you're trying to help, but you have to trust that we know what we're doing."

"I do, and I appreciate it," Talia said. *Not.* They were treating her like a child, and it was seriously ticking her off. "But I'm willing to bet neither of you has ever indulged in a spa experience. For example, there are times when someone is left alone in a room, lying on a table with cream glopped all over her face. Think how easy it would be for that person to dash out the back entrance, drive to the lighting shop to murder Turnbull, and be back before anyone noticed she was gone."

Not that easy, Talia suddenly realized. Running it through her head that way made her see how silly it sounded.

If only she could tell them about Misty's phone call.

"Or perhaps," O'Donnell said, "she could claim she was having gastrointestinal issues and needed to use the head. Why, she could drag that out for almost an hour, couldn't she?"

Talia felt her face flame. *They already knew.* But how?

"Yes," Talia said quietly. "Yes, she could."

"By the way, Ms. Marby, how did you know about Ms. LaPlante's visit to the spa Wednesday evening?" O'Donnell asked her.

Okay, that one was easy. "Her stepson told me. He stopped by Lambert's for our fish and chips special yesterday, and we had a brief chat. He just happened to mention Kendra's spa visit that night."

"He just happened to mention it?" O'Donnell said.

"Yes." Talia felt her cheeks flush into two ripe tomatoes. Her dignity in shreds, she rose from her chair. "I have one last comment, along with a question. I've known Bea Lambert for nearly twenty years. She's funny, she's quirky, and she's a character and a half. But she is *not*, by any stretch, a killer. I will stake my own life on that."

O'Donnell narrowed his eyes at her. Derek picked at something on his desk blotter. "And your question?" O'Donnell said.

"My question is this: do you have any solid evidence against Bea, or is it all as circumstantial as it appears? I mean, really, whitefish on the knife? Is that what you're hanging your hats on?"

Uh-oh. That did sound pretty incriminating, didn't it? Realizing her mistake, she said, "It's obvious someone set her up to take the blame. No killer with more than five brain cells would use a weapon that would so clearly implicate her, or him, in the crime. You have to see that." She stopped short of pounding her small fist on Derek's desk.

Derek ran a hand over his brush cut, while O'Donnell stood. "Ms. Marby," O'Donnell said, "it seems you have a keen interest in police work, an interest I heartily applaud. I strongly suggest, however, that until such time as you are wearing your own badge, you leave it to the professionals. Have a good day."

Talia left quickly, nearly stumbling over her own heels as she motored out of Derek's office. *Talk about humiliating*, she thought, as she fled to her car.

She jumped inside her Fiat and saw that it was ten past eleven. She texted Rachel. *On my way. Be there in a jif.*

Rachel's reply came instantly. *Faster the better. Brom Bones antsy. Ichabod ready to puke.*

18

The large conference room at the Wrensdale Pines overlooked the rear of the facility, where the carefully tended lawn sloped downhill to the narrow stream forming the property line. In the distance was Mount Greylock, the tallest point in Massachusetts, its summit clear and crisp against the azure sky.

In the mid-1800s, this same view had attracted Herman Melville to the area. He bought a farmhouse in Pittsfield and named it Arrowhead. It was from that house, with its spectacular view of the rolling hills, that he wrote some of his famous works, including *Moby Dick*.

Inside the conference room, chaos reigned. Early on Saturday, Rachel had delivered three huge boxes of props and costumes to the Pines, making one less chore to accomplish on Sunday. Talia's mom, Natalie, had suggested she store them in the conference room for safekeeping. All three boxes were now upended, with kids scrabbling through them in search of their respective accessories. Talia was helping as best she could, but with the decibel level rising and the boxes getting more jumbled every second, she felt as if she'd been dropped into one of those cages full of plastic balls at a kids' amusement center.

"All right, everyone." Rachel clapped her hands over the din. "One at a time, please. No grabbing, no pushing, no—"

"Ms. Ostroski, I can't find my scarf!" A plump little girl with huge brown eyes and a sweet, freckled face tugged urgently on Rachel's arm. "It's pink and has chipmunks on it, and it's my favorite, and now it's gone!"

Rachel knelt before the child, who looked ready to burst into tears. "It can't be gone, Hannah. It probably just got buried in all the other stuff. Come on, I'll help you look for it."

Talia tapped Rachel's shoulder. "Why don't I do that, Ra . . . I mean, Ms. Ostroski," Talia offered. "You've got enough to do."

"Oh, that would be a huge help," Rachel breathed. "Hannah, this is Ms. Marby, and she's going to help you look for the scarf." Rachel winked at Talia. "Thanks," she whispered. "Ichabod and his mom are in one of the visitors' rooms. She's got him calmed down, but I want to make sure everything's still a go."

Ichabod—aka Tyler Crowley—was suffering from a crippling bout of stage fright. Between his mom and Rachel they'd managed to settle his nerves, but from what Talia understood it was touch and go.

After Rachel dashed off, Talia and Hannah methodically went through every prop and accessory in the room. The missing scarf was just that—missing.

Hannah, looking adorable in a smocked peasant dress and white bonnet, folded her chubby arms over her chest. "Someone *stole* it, Ms. Marby. I just know it." Her brown eyes welled with tears.

Talia was at a loss, and then an idea struck her. "I know what we can do, Hannah." She untied the knot of her own scarf. "How about if you wear mine. Do you like ladybugs?"

Hannah nodded vigorously, and Talia arranged her lady-bug scarf around the little girl's neck.

"Oh, thank you, Ms. Marby. It's beautiful!" Hannah raced off to find a mirror, just as Natalie Marby poked her expertly coiffed dark-blond head into the room. "Hey, sweetie, need any help in here?"

Talia picked her way over to her mom and, as she did so, tripped over a plastic horse's head perched on a pole. She couldn't resist a giggle. "What is this, 'The Legend of Sleepy Hollow' or *The Godfather*?"

"That's Gunpowder, Ichabod's horse," her mom said, "or maybe that one's Daredevil. I can't remember which is which."

Talia hugged her mom for about the tenth time since she'd arrived at the Pines. The scent of her mom's Chanel wrapped around her like a warm, familiar blanket. She'd missed her parents more than she realized over the past week. Turn-bull's murder, along with the secrets and the lies and the craziness that followed, had done a number on her psyche. She swallowed and said, "I'm so happy to see you, Mom."

"I'm glad to see you, too," her mom said, tenderness beaming in green eyes only a shade darker than Talia's. She fluffed a few strands of Talia's pixie haircut. "I hate it that you've been staying alone at Nana's since this awful murder. I wish you'd move in with us, at least until there's an arrest."

"I'm not in any danger," Talia assured her. "Phil Turnbull had a lot of enemies, and one of them obviously took a grudge too far."

She conveniently omitted telling her mom about the creepy guy she'd caught watching her, or about any of the other weird encounters she'd had since Phil's unfortunate demise.

"Hey, where's Dad?" Talia asked. "I thought he'd be here by now."

"He should be along any minute," her mom said. "The dryer went on the fritz this morning, and he headed down to the hardware store to see if he could get some parts."

For the next hour or so, Talia helped Rachel set up the facility's dining room, where the play was going to be performed. Several of the parents pitched in, and they managed to get a makeshift stage constructed along one wall. Tables were moved to the back of the room to make way for several rows of chairs, and an area off to one side was cleared for wheelchair occupants. Talia was putting the last leafy touches on a cardboard tree when a towering, round-faced man with a full head of lush white hair entered the room.

"Dad—you made it!"

"Pixie pie!" Peter Marby rushed over to Talia and threw his thick arms around her. "Where have you been? We haven't seen you in a week."

"A week isn't very long, Dad."

He kissed her on both cheeks. "I know, but to us it is." He lowered his voice to avoid being overheard. "Especially with this nasty murder business going on. How's Bea holding up?"

Talia let out a sigh. "She's hanging in there, but it hasn't been easy. It doesn't help that Howie's been laid up for so long.

Hey, want to help me stick a moon in the sky? You seem to be the tallest person here, so you're just the man for the job."

He gave out a belly laugh. "Strangest thing I've ever been asked, but sure, I'll do it."

At three minutes past one, Rachel walked out and stood before the audience. All eyes were glued to her as she read a short introductory passage.

Seated in a folding chair between her mom and dad, Talia leveled a quick glance around the room. On the side of the room nearest the window sat three wheelchair occupants. The remaining chairs had been set up in a semicircle to allow everyone the best view. The audience consisted primarily of the kids' parents and the elderly residents of the Pines. Fortunately the dining room was large enough to seat everyone comfortably.

Talia and her folks had chosen to sit in the back row to give as many visitors as possible an unobstructed view. She grinned when Ichabod strode onto the scene. With his oversized top hat and camel-colored, tuxedo-style jacket, he indeed looked like a scarecrow.

"Spare the rod and spoil the child," Ichabod cried out, his stern gaze floating over the "students" in his mock classroom. His voice was strong, without a trace of the stage fright he'd suffered earlier. From her front-row seat his mom gazed at him, nodding and moving her lips as he recited his lines with the skill of a veteran actor.

Natalie Marby squeezed her daughter's hand. "He's so good!" she whispered.

Talia nodded. She was impressed with the clever job

Rachel had done with the staging. As the scene segued from the classroom to the farmhouse of Baltus Van Tassel, two boys emerged from the shadows and moved silently onto the stage. One carried a tray laden with various waxed fruits and cardboard cakes. He set it down on the table that had been Ichabod's desk in the first scene. The other boy quietly rearranged the chairs to form a parlor of sorts, and then both boys made a fast exit.

Everyone in the audience grinned when Katrina Van Tassel bounded onto the scene. She was thin and even taller than Ichabod, with a wig of sausage curls framing her red-cheeked face. In her long, lacy dress with puffed sleeves, she looked every bit the coquettish daughter of the wealthy Baltus.

Talia smiled when Hannah, as one of the Dutch wives, strolled into the fake parlor. The ladybug scarf looked so sweet on her. With her arm looped through the arm of another "Dutch wife," Hannah pretended to giggle as Ichabod plied the lovely Katrina with his questionable charms.

Talia peeked briefly at her program. In doing so, she caught the eye of a bespectacled man with thick curly hair staring at her from the end of her row. He winked at her and gave her a little wave, then immediately sobered and turned back to the play.

He looks so familiar, she thought. *Who is he?*

The rest of the performance went along almost without a hitch. Brom Bones, Ichabod's rival for the affections of Katrina, tripped over his own horse much the way Talia had earlier. He recovered quickly, and with a dazzling grin persuaded the audience that it was all part of the act. In the final scene, everyone's eyes were on the headless horseman as he galloped across the stage. By the time the grinning pumpkin head rolled across the floor, everyone was clapping and cheering.

Rachel returned, and with a few final words wrapped up the narrative. The audience went into another round of applause. Parents surged toward the stage, hugging and congratulating their kids.

"Hey, that was terrific," Talia told Rachel. She gave her friend a hug. "Very impressive."

Rachel swiped a hand over her forehead as if whisking away perspiration. "Thank heaven, right? Once Tyler got out there, he really kicked himself into gear, didn't he. He was fabulous."

Abby Kingston, the administrator for the Wrensdale Police Department, wended her way over to Rachel with her son, Jacob, in tow. Jacob had been one of the two boys who'd rearranged the set in between scenes. Bright but extremely bashful, he'd told Rachel he wanted a nonspeaking part. He'd been thrilled when she asked if he'd like to be in charge of stage setting. Talia suspected Rachel saw traces of her own brother in Jacob, since she went out of her way to make him feel good about himself.

"Great job all around, Rachel," Abby gushed, smiling down at her son.

Rachel accepted her praise and then hurried off to mingle with other parents. Hannah trotted over to Talia just then. Trailing in her wake was a roundish woman with sparkling brown eyes and a dazzling smile.

"Here, Ms. Marby," Hannah said. She removed the ladybug scarf, rolled it into a ball, and gave it to Talia. "Thank you for letting me use your scarf. It's even prettier than the one I was going to wear."

"Yes, thank you for saving the day," her mom whispered.

"I can't imagine what became of her scarf. She really didn't need to leave it here overnight, but all the other kids left something in the prop box, so she wanted to do the same. You know how kids are."

"I'm glad I could help," Talia said, sliding the scarf around her own neck. Of all her scarves, she favored this one the most. She'd have hated to see anything happen to it.

Food was brought in, including a tray piled with the yummy goodies Talia had picked up at the bakery. One of the attendants rolled a large stainless-steel cart into the room. Small paper cups filled with apple cider lined one side of the cart. On the other side rested a coffee urn, along with cups, sugar, and milk. A pile of Halloween-themed napkins sat fanned out in the middle, along with matching paper plates. Talia grabbed a napkin, along with a cup of cider and a few cookies. She was munching on a raspberry bar when she felt a light tap on her shoulder. She swiveled to see a tall, thirty-something man with rimless glasses and a playful smile beaming at her. He was the same man who'd waved at her during the performance.

"Oh my gosh," Talia said, suddenly recognizing him. "Ryan Collins."

"In the flesh," he said, his voice as deep and distinctive as she remembered. Careful not to spill her cider, he leaned down and gave her a brief hug.

Ryan had been one of Talia's classmates at Wrensdale High. Back then he'd been the quintessential nerd—quiet, unassuming, brilliant. His shoulders were broader now, and the dimple next to his cheek had deepened. The unruly mop of dark curls that used to tumble over his thick glasses was now professionally cut and styled.

"It's great to see you, Ryan," Talia said with a grin. "Was one of your kids in the play?"

He returned her smile. "No, nothing like that. In fact, I'm not even married." Was it Talia's imagination, or did she detect a gleam in his eye when he said that?

"Actually, I'm here with my dad," Ryan explained. "He's a resident here now. He was only fifty-nine when he began to show symptoms of early-onset Alzheimer's. Then his mind got worse quite suddenly, and . . . well, my mother's job takes up most of her time, so she's not in a position to care for him."

"Oh, Ryan, I'm so sorry," Talia said.

"Thanks. He's been here seven months, and he's adjusted pretty well. I work in software design, so luckily I have flexible hours and can visit him when I want. Dad's always been somewhat of an insomniac, so when all the other residents are sound asleep he's usually up late watching something on PBS. So why are you here?" he asked, changing the subject. "I thought I heard from someone that you lived in the Boston area."

Talia nodded. "I did, but then a lot of things changed for me all at once, so I'm back in Wrensdale, at least for a while. Right now I'm working at Lambert's Fish and Chips helping out my old friend Bea."

"Oh heck, wait till I tell Dad that. He loves Lambert's! They've got a great chef here, but she's not big on fried food and Dad really misses his fried haddock. Would you like to meet him? Today's been one of his more lucid days. I think the play brought back memories of his days as a professor of English lit at the community college."

"I'd love to meet him," Talia said. She found Ryan's

chattiness endearing. He seemed so different from the reserved boy he'd been in high school. She followed him to the area near the window where several senior residents were seated.

Ryan leaned over a distinguished-looking man with thinning hair and faded gray eyes. "Dad," he said softly, "I ran into an old friend here—Talia Marby. Talia, this is my dad, Arthur Collins."

Talia moved a step closer. She reached down and took Arthur's hand in hers. "Professor Collins, it's a pleasure to meet you."

At the word *professor*, Arthur's face lit up. "The pleasure is all mine, my dear," he said, squeezing her hand.

"Dad, Talia works at Lambert's Fish and Chips with Bea," Ryan said.

Arthur's expression turned pensive. "Lovely lady, Bea is." He gave Talia a childlike smile. "I miss her cooking."

Ryan looked at his dad through eyes that had suddenly grown damp. "One of these days, Dad, I'll drive you over there and we'll each get a giant order of fish and chips. How does that sound?"

Talia felt her heart twist at the pain in Ryan's voice. How sad it must be for him to watch his dad's mind deteriorate, especially at such an early age. If it had been her own dad . . . well, she couldn't even imagine how terrible she'd feel.

Arthur grinned. "That sounds splendid. Will you be there, too?" he asked Talia.

"You bet I will, Professor Collins."

"Oh, please, my dear, you must call me Arthur."

"Hey, Dad, I'll be right back, okay?" Ryan said. "I just remembered something I wanted to ask Talia."

Arthur frowned at Talia. "Will you come back again to visit me?"

"Of course I will, Arthur. You can count on it. And I'll come back to say good-bye before I leave."

"I hope you don't mind," Ryan said to Talia. They walked over to an area right outside the dining room where they could talk quietly. "I just made the connection between you and the assistant director here. Natalie Marby's your mom, right?"

"She is," Talia said warily. "Why do you ask?"

Ryan gave her a worried look. "My dad has started to misplace things, or lose things, I'm not sure which. Nothing terribly valuable, but when he suddenly notices they're missing he gets very agitated."

"What kinds of things?" Talia asked him.

Ryan lowered his voice. "He had this souvenir letter opener from Shakespeare's birthplace that he bought on a visit there several years ago. My dad is sentimental, and it was quite special to him. He also had a photo of him and Mom when they got married. It was in an oval-shaped silver frame, and he kept it on his dresser. He told me that he woke up one morning and it was gone."

"Did you report it?" Talia asked him.

"Not yet." Ryan winced. "I wasn't sure what to do. I figured Dad had probably tucked them away somewhere, and just forgot where he put them."

"He could have," Talia said slowly. "Have you searched his room?"

Ryan nodded. "Every inch. The reason I'm asking you is . . . well, I wondered, has your mom mentioned any other residents reporting anything stolen?"

"No," Talia said. "Not to me, anyway." She touched his

arm lightly, and an unexpected little blip of electricity surged through her fingers. "Ryan, I think you should talk to her about it. She may have some suggestions or be able to help in some way."

Ryan let out a sigh. "I guess I should."

"I'll ask her about it, too," Talia said. "Maybe together we can figure it out."

Together? What made her say that? What was she thinking?

She felt her cheeks burn with embarrassment, but when she looked into Ryan's face he was smiling, his gray eyes glittering through his stylish rimless glasses.

A young aide wearing a perky gingham blouse maneuvered another cart into the room. This cart had a wheel that squealed loudly, and several people turned at the strident sound. "Sorry," the aide murmured. She parked the cart near the dining room entrance and went about the task of collecting used cups and plates.

Ryan followed Talia back to where Arthur was seated. "Arthur," Talia said, touching his shoulder lightly. "I wanted to say good-bye before I left, but I'll be sure—" She stopped midsentence, stunned. In the short time since they'd left Arthur, he'd shriveled into himself. His chin hugged his chest, and his eyes were squeezed closed. Both arms were tucked between his legs, as if he were preparing for an attack.

His brow creased, Ryan reached down and cupped his father's hand. "I'll be right back, Dad." He touched Talia's elbow, and they moved a few yards away. "He's somewhere else now," Ryan said quietly. "Sometimes he drifts away gradually, but occasionally it's a sudden drop-off from reality. I never know what triggers it."

Talia felt tears poking at her eyelids. "I wish there was something I could do to help."

Ryan smiled at her. "You have helped, more than you realize. Making new friends is important to him. He'll probably start asking me when's the next time you're coming to visit."

Did his voice sound hopeful? Or was Talia only imagining that Ryan wanted to see her again? She tried to sound casual, but she felt her heart doing a tiny jitterbug in her chest. "Well, you promised him fish and chips, so I'm going to hold you to that."

"You got it," Ryan said, cocking a finger at her.

Talia excused herself and went in search of Rachel. She helped her pack up any props that the kids weren't going to take home, and they walked the boxes out to Rachel's Cherokee.

"Hey, listen, Tal," Rachel said with a slight frown. "We have to talk soon, okay? I've got some things to tell you."

"Sure thing. I'm off tomorrow, but I'm driving to Belmont to pick up the rest of my stuff. I don't expect to be back very late, though. Maybe tomorrow night?"

"Maybe," she said. "I'll let you know."

"Are you okay?" Talia asked her.

Rachel laughed. "Lord, yes, I'm fine. I just need to update you on a few things."

Relieved, Talia hugged her friend, and then went in search of her mom. If someone was stealing from Ryan's dad, she wanted to get to the bottom of it.

19

"No," Talia's mom said. She sat erect in her leather desk chair. "No one's reported anything missing. But I'm distressed to hear that Arthur's been having problems. I wish his son had come to me sooner. Was Ryan one of your pals in high school?"

Talia, sitting opposite her mom's desk, plunked her elbows on the edge of the blotter. "We weren't friends, exactly, but we knew and liked each other, at least I think he liked me." She felt her cheeks grow warm. "I don't mean 'like' the way the kids mean it, just that we were friendly acquaintances."

Her mom gave out a soft laugh. "I know what you mean, dear. Ryan certainly is a caring young man." She shook her dark-blond head. "As for Arthur, he has good days and bad. The next time he's having one of his better days, I'll speak to him privately. But I'm also going to make an appointment with Ryan."

"Mom, it was so heartbreaking," Talia said. "One minute Arthur seemed relaxed and content, and the next he just . . . curled up inside himself."

"I'll handle it, honey. Don't worry about it."

Love radiated from her mom's green eyes, and Talia felt herself welling up. "Thanks, Mom," she said hoarsely. "Truth is, I really like Arthur." *Not to mention Ryan.*

Her mom winked at her, and Talia felt as transparent as plastic wrap.

Over a cup of piping hot tea, Talia related the events of her horrible week. She had to edit much of it so as not to alarm her mom, who would immediately tell her dad, who would immediately call out the National Guard to form a protective barrier around her.

"There's one last thing, but you're going to be shocked," Talia said. "Bea and Howie want to retire, and they want me to buy out the restaurant. Take over the whole thing, kit and caboodle."

"What?" Her mom's face lit up. "Oh my, that would be . . . well, I don't know. What do *you* think, honey?"

Talia shrugged. "I'm not sure. The idea intrigues me, and I love Lambert's, but is it right for me?"

"It's true, you've always been happy there," her mom gently pointed out. "Back in the day, when dad and I were going through some tough times, it was your home away from home."

"But I was a kid, Mom. I'm thirty-four now."

"And an excellent businesswoman, *and* a quick learner." Her mom tapped a manicured finger to the desk with each point. "I have every faith that you'd make a success of it. *If that's what you want*," she added, eagerness glowing in her eyes.

Talia gazed up at the ceiling. "Spoken like an unbiased mom." She grinned. "You love the idea, don't you?"

"Well, of course it would be fabulous to have you living here permanently. But it's a decision you have to make on your own. Dad and I would help any way we can, of course. You only need to say the word."

Talia let out a sigh. "I wonder what Nana would think of the idea."

Her mom sat back in her chair, her rose-tinted lips curved into a satisfied smile. "I think you know the answer to that. Come on, I still have work to do so I'll walk you out."

They ambled down the wide hallway, along which hung various framed art prints in peaceful, pastel shades. An elderly woman perched in a wheelchair outside her room brightened when she saw them. Talia smiled and nodded at her. "Hello. How are you?"

"Oh, I'm just peachy keen," the woman said tartly. "My son was supposed to be here twenty minutes ago." She scowled. "Silly fool will be late for his own funeral."

Talia touched the woman's arm lightly and said, "I'm sure he'll be here soon. Have a good visit."

They continued on toward the front lobby. As they approached the entrance to the facility's kitchen, Talia stopped short and took a deep breath. "Ah, is that roast turkey I detect?"

Her mom laughed. "Yes, doesn't it smell luscious? We got a new chef about five months ago and she's been wonderful.

A bit messy and disorganized, but she performs magic with food. I think you know her—Tina Franchette?"

"You're kidding. Tina? Tina the Terrible?"

"I heard that," roared a voice from the kitchen. Out popped a woman dressed in food-stained chef's whites, her frizzy, dishwater-blond hair tucked into a brown hairnet. Hands on her ample hips, she stood and glared at Talia until she couldn't hold the mad face any longer. She reached out and pulled her into a bone-crushing hug. "Look at you, you skinny thing. You haven't gained a pound since high school."

"Tina. It's really you!" Talia squeaked. When she could no longer breathe, she extricated herself and put her hands on Tina's shoulders. "You look . . . fantastic! I had no idea you worked here."

In their school days, Tina had always wanted to be a chef. Even more than she enjoyed food, she loved preparing it for others. During their senior year, she took it upon herself to raise some much-needed cash for the soup kitchen in Pittsfield. She haunted each and every classmate, as well as the teachers, until they dropped coins into her homemade donation can. No one escaped her demand, and with grudging affection she soon became known as Tina the Terrible.

"Yeah, I'm livin' the dream," she said, grinning. "Hey, wanna try my stuffing? I've fine-tuned the recipe, and I think I got it perfect."

"You go ahead, dear. I've got to run," Talia's mom said. "But don't forget what I said about bunking with us for a while, okay? Dad and I would love to have you." She dropped a quick kiss on her daughter's cheek, gave her a fast hug, and hustled back to her office.

"Mom's a worrier," Talia said.

"But a terrific lady," Tina added kindly. "When I first

started working here, some of the equipment was pretty outdated. Your mom put in a requisition for some new appliances and utensils, and it's made my job a whole heck of a lot easier."

The kitchen was a marvel of stainless steel, with unwashed pots and pans covering nearly every surface. A mashed spinach leaf rested on the floor below the wide central work area. Another one was stuck to the bottom of Tina's shoe. On the table itself, a rectangular pan the size of a football field boasted a sea of parsley-dusted whipped potatoes. Next to that was a similar pan packed with fresh-from-the-oven stuffing.

Tina scooted over to a rack of professional-looking knives and whipped out one with a blue handle. She cut a neat square from one end of the pan, plated it, and gave it to Talia with a fork.

Talia carved out a corner and slid it into her mouth. The stuffing was plump and fragrant, with small bits of dried cranberries nestled within its depths. "Oh my gosh, Tina. This is pure ambrosia—the food of the gods." She polished off the rest in record time, much to Tina's delight.

"I'm giving you some to take home," Tina insisted. She pulled a plastic container off a shelf. "And then I'm going to toss your scrawny butt out of here because I've got folks to feed."

Talia held up both hands in mock fear. "I'll go peacefully. Just give me stuffing."

Tina slid a slab of stuffing into the container and sealed it. She gave Talia another bearlike hug. "Come and visit more often, okay?"

"I will," Talia promised. "Maybe you can teach me a thing or two about cooking."

20

By the time she unlocked the door to Nana's bungalow, Talia felt drained. So many thoughts raced through her head. If only she could corral them all and stash them into neat little stalls, she could deal with them one by one. Instead, they butted against one another, vying for attention in her weary brain.

The afternoon had been fun, though. She'd loved watching Rachel's students perform the play. Running into Ryan Collins had been an added bonus.

After changing into her UMass sweats, she ran a vacuum over the living room carpet, dusted the furniture, and swiped disinfectant cloths over the bathroom surfaces. It was a quickie job but it did the trick. A neatnik by nature, she never really made much of a mess.

Talia couldn't help wondering how long it would be before she'd be forced to move out of Nana's house. If she bought out Lambert's, she'd have to use most of her savings as a down payment. Bea and Howie would work out the terms with her, and she knew they'd be more than fair. Still, it was a sizeable investment, and she would have to plan carefully in order to pull it off. She might have to move in with her folks until she could afford a place of her own.

She shuffled into the kitchen in her woolly socks in search of a bite to eat. She'd already tucked the stuffing Tina had given her into the fridge. It would be a tasty treat for her when she returned from Belmont tomorrow, so she resisted its magnetic pull. Hunger nibbling at her, she threw together a peanut butter sandwich and poured herself a glass of chardonnay. Weird combination, but it worked. The wine relaxed her a little.

She was rinsing her dishes in the sink when something on the floor caught her eye. It was a slip of paper that had apparently fallen off the fridge. Talia snatched it up, and with a sinking heart read the message the broker had scribbled.

Good prospect today. Offer coming soon! Any chance you can start clearing out?

Talia groaned. It was exactly what she was afraid of.

The broker hadn't been thrilled when Talia had moved into the bungalow, using it as her temporary home. She was even less pleased that no one had ever removed Nana's furnishings. Now she had a buyer, and she wanted Talia—and all of Nana's things—out.

Talia couldn't blame her. As a former commercial broker, she knew the woman was only doing her job. The timing was bad, but she'd have to deal with it.

Nana's only heirs were Talia's mom and the twins—Talia's aunts, Josie and Jennie Domenica. Once the bungalow was sold, the three sisters would split the proceeds among them.

The twins had lived together for all of their forty-nine years. Neither had ever married, though Talia knew that Aunt Josie, at least, enjoyed her share of romantic flings. Josie was bubbly and outgoing, almost to a fault. Nosy, opinionated, and amazingly artistic, she was the polar opposite of the soft-spoken, brooding Jennie.

The pair had found their niche twelve years ago when they took advantage of Josie's creative flare and started their own greeting card company—Sunday Swizzle. Profits in the first year were dismal, but in year two Jennie used her considerable business savvy to get their line of cards displayed in several major retailers. The aunts now lived in Malibu, and visited Wrensdale only once or twice a year. Talia missed them terribly, but was thrilled with their phenomenal success.

As she'd done the night before, Talia prepared a mixed bowl of cat food and filled a second one with fresh water. She went to the front door and called out to the little cat, who seemed to favor hanging out near her car. Now that she knew the kitty's history, she planned to continue feeding her until she could get her to the shelter.

Or until she herself was forced to move out.

Still in her woolly socks, she turned on the outside light, went out to the front porch, and set both bowls on the step. "Kitty, kitty," she called out.

A brilliant, nearly full moon hung low in the eastern sky. The street was quiet, each of the neighboring bungalows nestled down for the night like eggs tucked into a carton. *What a peaceful place to live*, Talia thought, a feeling of intense sadness welling inside her.

Only a minute or so elapsed before the calico cat emerged from the shadows. Without hesitation, the cat dove into the food bowl. Instead of retreating, Talia stayed where she was, watching quietly from her position near the front door. If she was ever going to capture the kitty and deliver her to the shelter, she would have to persuade the animal to trust her.

The cat scarfed down the food in no time, then took a few delicate sips from the water bowl.

"What's your name, kitty?" Talia said soothingly. "Does anyone know it?"

The cat looked at her with eyes that shone like gold coins. A tiny mewl escaped her—a sound that tore at Talia's heart.

"It's awfully cold out here," Talia singsonged to the creature. "Would you like to come in?" Very slowly, she opened the front door wide and backed her way inside.

The cat lifted one paw and moved toward her. A burst of raucous laughter erupted from a neighboring street, followed by the chatter of young voices. Frightened by the sudden noise, the cat darted under Talia's car.

Disappointed, Talia closed the front door and engaged both locks. She went back into the kitchen and poured herself another glass of wine. She was leaning against the counter, idly twirling her wineglass, when Nana's old Zenith radio caught her eye. No longer resting flush against the wall, the radio was turned slightly to one side.

Had someone been touching it, she wondered, with more than a trace of ire. Although the broker had carte blanche to escort potential buyers through the bungalow, she certainly had no cause to touch any of Nana's belongings.

On impulse, Talia turned on the radio. It burst to life with a loud click. After thirty or so seconds—old radios needed a warm-up—a song blasted out of the speakers. Talia's insides did a cartwheel. The station that came on wasn't the one Nana had always listened to. It was an oldies station, but not the kind that belted out the hits of the forties.

But it wasn't the station, so much as the song, that sent pangs gusting through her. The mournful words from Nana's favorite tune—"Mr. Bojangles"—were streaming from the radio at top volume.

Talia quickly lowered the volume to a more soothing level. She found herself singing along, surprised that she remembered most of the words. She thought about the day, so many years ago, when she'd been driving Nana to the outlet mall to look for a pair of slippers. "Mr. Bojangles" came on the radio, and Nana fell instantly in love with it. The character who inspired the song had reminded Nana of her father back in Italy—a man who often broke into song and dance even during the hardest of times.

A lump rose in Talia's throat. Nearly every reminder of Nana was here, in this adorable little house. And though she'd only been ensconced here for seven weeks or so, the thought of having to move out felt like a sharp jab to the heart.

When the song ended, she turned off the radio. Her gaze floated over the faded Formica counter, where Nana always prepared simple but delectable meals. Talia could almost see her—her hands plunged into a bowl filled with the meat mixture from which she would form her meatballs. She never used a recipe, at least not that Talia had ever seen. She measured her ingredients by the eye, and by the heart. Natalie was coming to dinner? A little more fresh garlic went into the mix. The twins were visiting? Add a link or two of hot sausage to spice things up a bit. And for Talia, the magic ingredient was fresh-grated Parmesan cheese. Nana always made sure to have plenty in the fridge for an unexpected visit from her only granddaughter.

Hmmm, now that she thought about it . . . wouldn't it be interesting to try deep-frying meatballs? She'd watched Nana make them so often, surely she could experiment with the ingredients and concoct her own meatball recipe. Instead of putting all the herbs in the meatballs, she could add some to the batter. Served with a drizzle of spicy marinara sauce, they would probably be a hit!

But she couldn't think about that now, not with Bea still under suspicion. She tucked away the idea in a mental slot for future reference, and headed into the bathroom. Suzy's bath oil had lost its original appeal, so she stepped into the shower.

Her hair, she realized, was in sore need of a trim. The last haircut she'd had was right before she ditched Chet, along with her old life. Since she was going to be in Belmont tomorrow, maybe she should pop into La-Di-Da to see if her stylist, Becky, could squeeze her in for an appointment.

No. Becky was no longer her stylist. That part of her life was over. She'd have to find someone local to cut her hair, and in the meantime she'd add a little more mousse to keep it from tumbling into her eyes.

She'd no sooner tugged on her nightshirt when she heard her cell ringing from Nana's night table. She dashed to pick it up.

"Mom?"

"Hi, honey. Hope you weren't in bed yet."

"Nah. I just hopped out of the shower."

A long sigh issued from her mother. "I had a message from the broker on the machine when I got home," she said. "It sounds like the bungalow might be sold. I know I should be happy, but . . ." Talia's mom sucked in a tiny sob. "I can't imagine not ever being able to visit there again, you know?"

Oh yes, Talia knew. She swallowed. "I know, Mom. The broker left me a note on the fridge. I guess I'll have to think about moving out." And sooner rather than later.

After a momentary silence, her mom said, "I just wish there was something . . ." Talia could picture her mom biting her lip, a telltale sign of the wheels turning in her brain. The thought made her smile, but instantly she sobered.

"I wish there was something, too, but I think we're out of options. Look, don't worry about it, Mom. We'll all pitch in to move Nana's stuff out of here. I'd like to keep a few things for myself, if that's okay with you and the aunts."

Nana's dresser.

The puffy pink chair in the bedroom.

The radio . . .

"Of course, dear," her mom soothed. "You know the girls will give you anything you'd like to keep. But . . . what about you? You've got to live somewhere, too."

"Heck, don't worry about me. Like you said, I can always bunk with you and Dad for a while, right?"

"That's a given," her mom said firmly. Talia heard the smile in her voice.

They bade each other good night, the clock on Nana's night-stand reading 10:23. Talia tried to read, but found she was too agitated to concentrate on the words. Tossing aside her book, she snuggled under the covers and turned off the light. Faces swirled through her head in a kaleidoscope of colors—Jill, Suzy Sato, Arthur Collins . . .

. . . Ryan.

Go away, all of you, and let me sleep!

She would need plenty of rest to face Chet in the morning.

And though she dreaded the drive to Belmont to pick up the rest of her things, it would be a relief to finally get it done.

Fatigue eventually won the battle, and she drifted off. The last thing that fluttered through her mind was a picture of herself in the local paper. Next to the imaginary photo was the official announcement that she was the new proprietor of Lambert's Fish & Chips.

21

Talia was relieved to be off the Mass Pike and away from the clog of traffic that trickled through the center of Belmont. The drive had been nerve-wracking, with trailer trucks whipping past her at a hundred miles an hour. Nearly every bridge, it seemed, had been undergoing construction, sending traffic patterns into a mishmash.

Overnight the sky had turned dreary and gray, the perfect fit for her mood. Rain was predicted for later in the day, but so far it had held off.

She swung her Fiat onto the access road to the Nutberry Village Townhouses. Although she'd lived in the condo complex for the better part of four years, the place never held any real appeal for her. It was Chet who'd picked the townhome. Given the option, Talia would have chosen the quaint, refurbished unit in the old brick schoolhouse they'd looked at when they first started shopping for a place to live.

Not that Nutberry wasn't lovely. Colonial in style, the units were impeccably maintained and formed a U-shape around a central green. Behind the units was a forested area that provided shade during the hotter months. Wildlife abounded—squirrels, birds, chipmunks, even wild turkeys. Every year, during the late fall, she used to toss out nuts for the squirrels to find so they could tuck them away for the winter. Chet thought it was ridiculous to feed wild animals, but she did it nonetheless.

She drove slowly around the U until she reached the building that housed unit forty-two. A sudden case of nerves gripped her. Chet's sporty Acura TL sat in one of the two parking spaces assigned to his—formerly their—rental unit. Even under the overcast sky, the car gleamed like liquid silver.

All at once, Talia wished he weren't going to be here when she removed the last of her things. She still had her key to get in. She could have done this alone quite easily. Plus, she didn't want to face him, didn't want to explain for the hundredth time why their relationship would never have worked.

The spot where Talia used to park was occupied by a blue Honda Odyssey she didn't recognize. Had Chet allowed another unit owner to use their second space, the one where Talia's own vehicle once resided? He knew she was going to be picking up her things today. He couldn't have left that spot open for her?

The thought irritated her as she eased her Fiat along the row of cars. She found an empty slot near the end. With a sigh she locked her purse in her car, jumped out, and headed for the front entrance.

Out of courtesy she rang the bell. She waited a minute

or so and then stuck her key in the lock, frowning when it wouldn't turn. What the—

The door swung open, and there stood Chet. His dark blond hair tousled to perfection, he wore a hunter-green crewneck shirt over beige chinos. "Hey, Tal," he said gently. He leaned toward her and gave her a limp hug.

Talia stood stock-still until he withdrew his arms. He looked uncomfortable, which suited her just fine. "Chet," she said with a crisp nod.

One glance around the formal living room told her that a lot had changed in her absence. The pricy, geometric-design shades Chet had insisted on buying were gone. In their place were heavy, barn red curtains, their rawhide tiebacks hanging from miniature, saddle-shaped hooks.

The glass coffee table still rested in front of the uncomfortable leather-and-chrome sofa, but instead of sporting a slew of magazines, it hosted three antique volumes propped up by a pair of bronze horses. Talia was dying to peek at the titles, but she wouldn't give him the satisfaction. Actually, it wouldn't have surprised her to discover that the books were fakes, like everything else about Chet.

Even the air was different. A woodsy, earthy scent rose from a potpourri bowl that sat on the faux mantel.

She felt like kicking herself for agreeing to pay for half of that awful chrome-and-leather furniture. Too contemporary to be comfortable, it looked like something that belonged on a spaceship. The price had been off the charts, but she'd gone along with it to please Chet. She shook her head at the memory.

Chet closed the door behind her. "I've got some coffee in the kitchen. Can I pour you a cup? Do you need to use the facility?"

The facility. What a pompous boob.

"No, thank you. I stopped on the Mass Pike." Not that she owed him an explanation.

Without warning, a delicate-featured woman with chin-length, curly chestnut hair emerged from around the corner of the master bedroom. In her left hand she clutched an iPad. "Chet, I found that article on— Oh, sorry. I didn't realize she was already here."

She? So Talia was now a mere pronoun?

The woman's face flushed a mottled red as she strode toward Talia on moccasin-covered feet. "Hi, I don't know if you remember me, but I'm Courtney?" She offered up her free hand, which was graced with short, rounded nails. On the ring finger of the hand holding the iPad was an emerald the size of Boston. The rest of her looked like an ad straight out of L.L.Bean's fall catalogue.

And yes, she did recognize the woman. She was the neighbor of the couple who owned the horses where they'd gone riding those few times.

Suddenly, horribly, it all made sense.

The ease with which Chet had accepted her departure.

His eagerness to remove any sign she'd ever lived there.

Ignoring Courtney's outstretched hand, Talia swept past her and stomped toward the same bedroom from which the woman had materialized. Tears pushed at her eyelids, but she was determined to keep them from rolling down her cheeks.

She'd been a chump, a fool. A court jester dancing to the master's tune.

The master, meanwhile, had been finding his recreation elsewhere.

In the doorway of the bedroom, Talia stopped short. Nothing looked the same. The gray-blue comforter Chet had loved so much was gone. In its stead was a fluffy spread the color of apple blossoms, atop which rested a slew of rose-colored pillows edged in lace. A beige fainting sofa with a flowery pattern sat near the window that overlooked the forest. The rest of the room was equally unrecognizable. Nearly everything had been replaced with the kind of feminine accoutrements Chet had always despised.

Hats off to Courtney. The woman works fast.

Bile rose in Talia's throat, but she swallowed it back. The sooner she got out of there, the better.

She moved toward the closet, and then remembered that her own things weren't even in the master bedroom. Chet had needed the entire closet for himself, or so he'd claimed. Talia had been assigned the closet in the smaller bedroom—the room Chet used as his office-away-from-the-office.

She turned to find him standing behind her, a sheepish look on his face. "Hey, um, Talia, I know this all looks really different, but—"

"Actually, I don't care," Talia threw at him. She stormed out of the room and headed for the bedroom that housed her belongings. Chet had moved her clothes toward one end of the rack in the closet, presumably to make it easier for her to grab and remove them. The quilt Nana had lovingly sewn for her before she went off to college sat on the floor, folded neatly into a plastic bag that zipped all the way around. At least he hadn't rolled it into a ball and tossed it on the floor, the way he used to when he claimed it was too hot for a quilt. The real truth was that the quilt was too homespun for him. It clashed with the image he had of himself as an enlightened business executive.

"I'll help you take everything to the car," Chet said in a quiet voice.

"Don't bother," Talia said. She tore an armful of clothing off the rack, not realizing how heavy it all was. She sagged and stumbled sideways a bit.

"You can't get it all to your car by yourself," he said crossly. His face red, he went to the closet in two long strides and pulled her winter jacket and wool blazers off the rack. He secured them all under one arm and then bent his knees and grabbed the handle of the quilt bag.

"Stop!" Talia ordered. She shoved her armful of clothing at him. "You take this. I'll take the quilt."

He glared at her over the mound of clothing, but did as she instructed. Making two trips during which neither of them spoke, they managed to get everything stuffed into the Fiat's backseat. But there was still one thing that belonged to Talia.

"Where's my mahogany candle table?" she said coolly.

Chet let out a breath. "Courtney stored it in the—"

"Courtney has no right to touch my table!"

He held up a hand. "If you'll just listen," he said, in a tone drained of patience. "Courtney wanted to be sure it didn't get scratched during all the renovations, so she covered it with a sheet and placed it at the back of the closet. *Your* closet," he added.

Okay, Talia did recall seeing something with a sheet draped over it at the back of her former closet. She pivoted on one heel and went back inside. Courtney had pulled a vanishing act, which was fine with Talia.

She found her candle table, covered by a striped sheet. She pulled it out of the closet and tossed the sheet on the carpet in a heap.

"Have a nice life," she said to Chet. "I'm sure you and National Velvet will be deliriously happy."

He didn't try to follow her. Fortunately the candle table

didn't weigh a whole lot. Gripping it by its carved mahogany leg, she got it to her car and laid it carefully over the clothing that was piled across the backseat.

A lump lodged in her throat, she drove off. She was only about a mile from Chet's condo when she felt herself breaking down. She swung her Fiat into the parking lot of a chain pharmacy and slammed her gearshift into Park. Tears began flowing like a spring river, gushing over her cheeks. In her glove box she found a stack of napkins from a recent visit to a fast-food joint. She used them to blot her swollen eyes, then tossed them onto the passenger seat.

She thought back to that awful day when she'd explained to Chet why she was leaving. He'd stared at her for a long time, nodding at certain intervals as if on cue. It was almost as if . . .

. . . as if he'd been expecting it.

Like the giant idiot she was, she'd interpreted his stunned silence as grief.

Oh my God, I did it for him, didn't I? I relieved him of the messy task of pulling the plug on our relationship.

Talia sucked in one last, noisy sniffle, and then realized she was hungry. The noon hour had come and gone while she was still loading up her belongings. Since her only breakfast had been apple juice and a bowl of cereal, she needed a bit of sustenance before making the trip back. She went inside the pharmacy, where she bought a bottle of spring water and two packages of peanut butter cups. Armed with hydration and the appropriate fat calories, she started on the highway back to Wrensdale.

The rain that had threatened earlier never materialized. A swatch of sun peeked over the distant rolling hills. Even this late in October, the faded colors of the mountains of the Berkshires made a glorious sight against the gray-blue sky. The closer she got to Wrensdale, the more at peace she felt. In a sense, she'd shed an emotional coat of armor—one she hadn't even realized had been weighing her down.

Talia swung into Nana's driveway at 3:29, filled with a new sense of purpose. She might not have a place to live yet, but the direction in which her life was headed stretched clearly before her.

She was lifting her mahogany candle table out of her backseat when a car pulled in close behind hers. Since the driveway was short, the back end of the luxury vehicle stuck into the road a bit.

Oh no . . . the broker.

"Ah, you're here," the broker bleated, slamming the door of her car. High heels clicking on the blacktop, she eyed the candle table with a curled lip. "You're bringing in more stuff?"

Talia squelched the urge to snap at her, and that's when she saw the young couple emerge from the car. Sweet and petite were the first words that came to mind. Two diminutive towheads, more like brother and sister than a couple, except that one had blue eyes and the other had brown.

"You don't need to worry," Talia said crisply. "My *stuff* and my nana's things will be out of here as soon as they need to be."

Yes, Talia, behave like a spoiled child. That'll really impress them.

"Anyway, these are the Rands," the broker said. "They're about to make a generous offer on your grandmother's house, and I believe your mother is going to accept it."

Talia shook their hands and offered a weak smile, but

her stomach felt like tossing up the peanut butter cups she'd scarfed during the trip back.

They all trooped inside. Talia set the candle table down in the parlor and followed them into the kitchen, where the broker plunked her boat-sized leather tote onto Nana's table. "Quick question," she said to the broker. "Did any of you touch the radio yesterday? It looked as if someone moved it, and the station's been changed." She knew she sounded accusatory, but she was too irritated to care.

The broker looked at her blankly. "Well, it wasn't me, and I'm sure it wasn't the Rands." She spoke as if the couple wasn't standing a foot away.

"No," the male half of the Rands said timidly. "Neither of us touched the radio, although I did admire it from afar," he added. "I love old radios and televisions."

Talia's shoulders sagged. She felt bad for having sounded like such a meanie. "I'm sorry. I didn't mean to be so testy. The radio was probably like that all along and I just didn't notice. Don't worry about it." She offered the duo a half-hearted smile, which they appeared to accept with grace.

"We really do love the bungalow," Mrs. Rand piped in. "We're not planning to have any children, so size-wise it fits our needs to a T."

Talia swallowed back a sob. Strangers were going to be living in Nana's home. The thought was unbearable.

"So, shall we do one more walk-through?" the broker said, her voice more shrill with every word. "Then we can complete the Offer to Purchase and include any items we want the seller to take care of before closing."

Talia felt her hands close into fists. She knew the broker was only doing her job, but the woman was getting way too far under her skin. "I'll just grab something from the fridge and be out of your way," she said.

An idea had struck her, one she'd been tossing around in the car on the way back from Belmont. This was the perfect time to follow through on it.

She snagged the container of Tina's luscious stuffing from the refrigerator and headed to Lambert's.

22

The scent of hot oil, fragrant and inviting, wafted through the dining area of Lambert's. In spite of the lunch hour having long passed, the aroma of fried fish and chips still lingered.

"Talia, luv! What are you doing here on your day off?" Bea toddled out from the kitchen and threw her short arms around her.

Talia set her container of stuffing down on the nearest table and shed her flared jacket. "Oh, it's been a stressful day, so I thought I'd stop by my favorite eatery and hang out with the kitchen crew."

Bea laughed, and then her brow creased into a sad face. "Did you get all your stuff out of the condo?" she asked. "Did Chet try to convince you to come back?"

"No." Talia drew in a calming breath. "Chet has moved

on, and so have I. I won't be seeing him again, and that suits me just fine."

Bea waved a hand in disgust. "Well, he's a barmy idiot, giving up a girl like you. But I'm glad you won't be going back there."

On impulse, Talia hugged her friend. "I have some news. Can we talk for a few?"

Bea's leaf-green eyes lit up. "It's quiet now and Whitnee's on break. Poor girl's having another bad day. Big row with the boyfriend last night, or so I gathered. Anyway, let's you and I have a cup of java and chat."

"Good, because I'd like to discuss it with you privately before she gets back."

Talia grabbed her jacket and the stuffing container, and they went into the kitchen and sat at the tiny table. Bea poured them each a mug of steaming French-roast coffee, adding a packet of raw sugar to her own.

"I've made a decision, Bea." Talia stirred milk into her coffee and took a bracing sip. "I want to accept your offer and take over the eatery. I'm going to miss you and Howie terribly if you move down South, but I promise I will do my best to continue making this restaurant a place to be proud of. This is my second home, and I love it here. I have a lot to learn and I know I'll make mistakes, but I want to do it. I have some savings, and I'll work out the rest with you and Howie."

"Oh, luvvy." Tears filled Bea's eyes. "I was hoping you'd say yes. Howie is going to be so excited when I tell him." She hopped off her chair and gave Talia a squishy hug, along with a noisy kiss on the cheek.

"Oh gosh, I feel terrible about Howie," Talia said after Bea reclaimed her seat. "I'd planned to visit him in the hospital over the weekend, but somehow I never got there."

Bea waved a hand. "Aw, don't worry, Tal. This news will make him so happy he'll probably do an Irish jig across the room, bum knee and all. Of course, you'll have to change the name of the place. You can't call it Lambert's any longer."

"Oh, Bea, I don't know . . ."

"Well, I do. This is going to be your baby now," she said, damp-eyed, "and you need to choose a name."

"We'll see," was all Talia would agree to. "Any news from your lawyer?"

Bea slugged back the last swig of her coffee. "No, nothing new, except that I found out the police searched the Dumpster in the alley the day we stumbled on Turnbull's body. I suppose they were hoping to find a plastic glove with his blood on it, along with my fingerprints."

"Which, of course, they didn't," Talia said.

"No, but my lawyer says I shouldn't be surprised if they ask for a warrant to search my house."

"That's ridiculous," Talia sputtered. "What do they expect to find there?"

Bea shrugged. "Bloody clothing, I suppose."

"But the real killer would've washed the clothes! Or burned them."

"That's true," Bea said. "But supposedly the forensics people have ways to detect blood, even in clothes that were washed." She shook her head. "You know what's really bugging me, Tal? It's the whitefish on the murder weapon. The thought that someone set me up to take the fall crushes me to the core."

The whitefish had been a sticking point in Talia's mind, as well. It seemed too incriminating to be a coincidence. She explained to Bea what she'd learned about Kendra, and how she suspected her of orchestrating Turnbull's early demise.

Bea's eyes widened. "So the witch could've purchased a fancy knife, run it through a slab of haddock, and used it to kill her ex. And all while she was *supposedly* at the spa having tummy troubles!"

Talia sighed. "That's what I'm thinking. But for some reason, the police seem to have let her off the hook."

Bea tapped a finger on the table. "Maybe they're toying with her, letting her think she's free and clear while they build a case against her."

Talia had never thought of that. Was it possible? Did the police play games like that with suspects?

Right now, she had to put it out of her mind. Only so many things were in her control, and police procedure wasn't one of them. Reaching for her container, she explained where she'd gotten the stuffing and proposed her idea to Bea.

"Oh, Tal, that sounds marvelous," Bea said. "I'll get the batter." She turned as Whitnee entered through the dining room. "Oh look, here's our Whitnee now. Hello, luv! Have a good lunch?"

Whitnee shrugged, her carrot-colored red hair pulled back into a tight ponytail. "I didn't really eat anything," she said, moving into the kitchen. Her pale eyebrows dipped toward her nose when she saw Talia standing at the work counter. "What are you doing here? I thought you didn't work Mondays."

Thanks for the warm welcome, Talia was tempted to retort. Instead, she pasted on her sweetest smile. "Hey, Whit. You're just in time."

Whitnee looped her overstuffed book bag over the door hook and draped her coat over it. "In time for what?"

"In time to taste test something. I'd love to have your opinion, and Bea's, too, of course."

"There you go." Bea set the bowl of batter down at Talia's elbow. She turned up the temperature on one of the fryers.

Using a sharp knife, Talia sliced Tina's stuffing into six roughly even squares. "It's been in the fridge all night, so it's still firm," she explained. She swirled the first square through the batter and lowered it into the hot oil. She repeated the procedure with two more squares of stuffing. When the batter reached a golden hue, she raised the basket to drain them.

"Oh my, they, look scrumptious, don't they?" Bea's fingers twitched with enthusiasm.

"Yeah, and they like, smell good, too," Whitnee commented, though a smile never touched her lips.

Talia slid the deep-fried stuffing squares onto a plate, and the three sat at the table. "Careful, now," she cautioned. "They're very hot."

Whitnee immediately plucked one off the plate and bit off a large chunk. "Oh my God," she said around a mouthful of food. "This is, like, amazing. Now I'm glad I didn't eat lunch."

Talia took a careful bite of her own square. The combo of the fried batter and the luscious herbs and cranberries nestled inside the stuffing was like a trip to the heavens on a fluffy cloud of cotton. She chewed slowly, savoring the flavor. Tina *had* to give her this recipe!

Talia glanced around the kitchen. If all went as planned, soon this would be hers. She began picturing the possibilities, ideas diving into her head like mini-parachutes.

What if she devoted a section of the menu to deep-fried desserts? Instantly she thought of peanut butter cups, her absolute favorite snack. What about deep-fried chocolate cake? Drizzled with a light raspberry sauce, it would be positively irresistible! The possibilities were—

"Talia, this is marvelous," Bea cried, disrupting her thoughts. She'd scarfed hers down in about thirty seconds and was eyeing the stuffing container.

Grinning, Talia battered and fried the last three squares and set them on the table.

"Weren't you supposed to, like, see your old boyfriend today?" Whitnee said, snagging another square.

In a brief recap, Talia gave her the highlights of her trip to Belmont.

"Wow," Whitnee said. "Men really are rats, aren't they?"

"Ah, luvvy, they're not all like that," Bea said lightly. "Look at my Howie. Why, he's the dearest man ever walked the planet!"

"Yeah, but he's, like, you know, from the olden days. Guys aren't like that anymore, Bea. At least none of the guys I've met." She scowled at no one in particular.

Talia exchanged glances with Bea. "Is everything okay, Whitnee?"

Whitnee's pale lashes grew damp. "I thought I'd surprise Pug last night and wait for him behind the burger place when he got off from work." She shook her head. "When I pulled around the back of the building, I saw this other car there next to Pug's. Then I saw him and this girl—they were sitting in the front seat of Pug's car, laughing and smoking and . . . and . . . he was playing with her hair." A choked sob escaped her, and she swiped at a lone tear.

"Oh, Whitnee, I'm so sorry," Talia said.

"Did he know you were there?" Bea asked, her kind face creased with concern.

Whitnee sniffled. "I think he might've seen me when I pulled out of the lot. I just . . . I didn't know what to do, so I tore out of there as fast as I could. I cried all the way home. It's a miracle I didn't have an accident."

Bea patted the girl's arm. "Aw, luvvy, he doesn't deserve you, then, does he? You'll meet a nicer boy, one who will appreciate a smart and pretty girl like you."

"That's what my mom said, but I'm not sure I believe it anymore."

"So, things are okay with your mom?" Talia asked.

"Of course," Whitnee said icily. "Why wouldn't they be?"

Oh, I don't know. Maybe because she's a nutcase who threatened to rent out your room to a smelly stranger?

Whitnee scraped her chair back abruptly and stood, leaving her second square of stuffing mostly untouched. She swept past Talia like a cold breeze and headed for the fridge. "We're getting low on slaw, Bea. Do you want me to shred some cabbage?"

"Exactly what I was hoping you'd say." Bea rose and hugged the girl. "Now don't you go fretting over that bloke, luv. He's just another stepping stone on the way to Prince Charming."

Whitnee lifted her thin shoulders in a halfhearted shrug. "Yeah, I guess so."

With a sigh, Talia cleaned up the remains of her experiment. She hated to admit it, but Whitnee's snub had been hurtful. She made a silent vow to never again mention Whitnee's mother. She only hoped she never had to *see* her again.

Talia kissed Bea on the cheek. "I've got a few things I want to check out, but I'll see you early tomorrow. We've got lots to talk about."

"That we do, luv." Bea's face beamed. "That we do."

23

The melodic tinkling of ceramic chimes announced Talia's arrival as she stepped inside Jepson's Pottery. To the right of the entry was the sales counter, upon which sat an old-fashioned cash register. Beyond that and to the left stretched four rows of wooden shelves set at geometrically pleasing angles. Each shelf held a stunning array of pottery pieces arranged by the hues of a rainbow. The air was scented as well, the sharp aroma of incense tickling her nose.

Jim Jepson appeared from around the corner, his gray hair captured in his ever-present ponytail. Splotches of clay dotted his red corduroy shirt, and he wiped his hands on a large cloth as he strode toward her.

"Hey, Talia." His greeting was cordial but slightly under-done, like a biscuit removed from the oven a minute too soon.

"Hi, Jim," Talia said. "Wow, this place is fantastic. I've never actually been in here before."

Jepson gave her a stiff smile, the tension in his eyes unmistakable. Talia thought he might offer her a tour of the shop, but he continued scrubbing the tips of his fingers with the cloth. "So, what can I do you for? Were you looking for anything in particular?" He said it lightly, but it was clear that Talia's visit was an unwelcome intrusion.

"Actually, Jim, I'm here to talk about an unpleasant subject."

Jepson's face tightened into a frown. "Turnbull," he said flatly.

"Yes, Turnbull." Now that she was here, she wasn't exactly sure how to begin. It wasn't as if she could simply ask him if he'd murdered Phil.

With a sigh, Jepson waved a hand to signal that she should follow him. "Why don't you come on back for a few while I work at the wheel? I've got a time-sensitive project, so I've been putting in a lot of extra hours."

Talia followed him past the rows of shelves laden with finished pottery pieces. At the back of the shop he led her into a separate room that was roughly double the size of Nana's kitchen. What she assumed was a potter's wheel sat in the middle of the work area. The wheel itself looked like a flat surface centered inside a large bowl. A blob of wet, taupe-colored clay occupied the center of the wheel.

Jepson tossed his cloth onto an adjacent table that was covered with metal tools. A plastic bowl half-filled with water sat beside them. One tool in particular reminded her of a drill, and looked a tad too sharp for her liking. The image of that awful knife sticking out of Turnbull's neck blew through her mind like a chill wind. She tugged the collar of her flared jacket more closely around her neck.

"Have a seat." He pulled a paint-splattered chair over to one side of the wheel and then dropped onto a stool on the opposite side. "If you don't mind, I'll work while we talk. I've been commissioned to make a full set of plates, cups, and bowls as a wedding gift. The bride and groom want a unique set of pottery dinnerware, something no one else will have."

"What a terrific idea," Talia said, taking the chair he'd offered. She pointed at a grouping of three oversized plates that rested on a long wooden table against the wall. The plates had been painted a glossy sea green and had shallow wells in the center. "Are those the dishes?"

Jepson nodded. "Yup, but I've got a long way to go. I'm making a set of twelve."

"I love the design, especially those slightly raised edges. I imagine they'll help keep the spills to a minimum." She knew she was stalling, trying to figure out how to broach the subject, but she truly was impressed with his work.

"Exactly," Jepson said. He did something with his foot, and the wheel began spinning. "When you're starting a new piece, the first thing you have to do is center the clay. Otherwise you'll lose control from the get-go and have a devil of a time getting it back."

Arms close to his side, Jepson began working the clay. The process fascinated Talia, so much so that she forgot for a moment why she was there.

She watched silently for a few minutes and then said, "Jim, I don't know who killed Phil. I only know that Bea didn't, and she's the one the police seem to be homing in on."

Jepson nodded slowly, but said nothing. He dipped a hand

in the water bowl, and then inserted two fingers into the top of the mound. Before Talia's eyes, the clay morphed into a shape that was either a future mug or pitcher.

"I think all the hoopla over that silly petition might have been blown out of proportion, don't you?" Talia pushed. "I mean, maybe it wasn't about the petition at all. Maybe it was about something else entirely." She wasn't sure she believed that, but she wanted to gauge his reaction.

After a long pause Jepson said, "I don't know what to tell you, Talia. The man had his enemies."

When Talia didn't respond, he stopped the wheel. His pinched face had a defeated look when he said, "Okay, look, I'm going to tell you a little story. When I'm through, maybe you'll understand where I'm coming from."

Talia swallowed. "Okay."

"Once upon a time, there was a young man with lofty ideals. This man envisioned a world where love and peace and equality would crush hatred. A world where everyone would be treated fairly and poverty would be eliminated."

"Utopia," Talia said.

Jepson nodded, and his eyes flared. "In a manner of speaking, yes, but when you're young and idealistic you think all things are possible. Anyway, in college this young man marched for all the right causes—civil rights, equality for women, cessation of war." He gave her a twisted smirk. "He horrified his dour, conservative parents with his antics, but he knew what was right and he fought for it."

Talia knew he was talking about himself, but where was this story headed?

"Then the young man met a girl, a fellow student, who shared his passion for equality and justice. This girl even burned her bra in a campus demonstration one day and got arrested for unlawful gathering." He flashed a smile. "They fell in lust and had a quickie marriage. Seven months later she popped out a boy—a son they named Erik.

"But then something happened to the girl. Her ideals changed. After the baby was born, she moved in with her snooty parents, who agreed to set up a trust fund for little Erik if she would abandon her wicked ways. And her new husband."

"Erik is your son," Talia said quietly.

Jim nodded, and his expression darkened. "A son I hardly ever saw. A son who grew up thinking the world owed him something, that he could hurt people and get away with it because granddaddy would always fix it."

"Jim, that must have been so hard for you."

Jepson blinked. "Fast forward to the mid-nineties. After dropping out of college, roaming the country, and getting in all sorts of trouble, Erik meets a girl and gets her pregnant. Sound familiar?"

Talia winced. "Yes."

"Only Erik doesn't want to be saddled with a kid. So granddaddy shoves a pile of money at the mother. That way Erik can wash his hands of both of them and come out sparkling clean."

"But that baby is your grandchild!" Talia said.

"She's my grandchild, and she was born developmentally challenged," he said. "The mother—her name's Lara—has done a great job caring for her, but it's been tough. Even with granddaddy's dough, the child's special needs were daunting."

"Erik didn't help out at all?"

"No, and there lies the crux of the drama. Erik refused to acknowledge the child, and Lara agreed never to reveal the identity of the father. In return, she receives regular stipends from Erik's granddaddy, so she has no choice but to keep her lips sealed. But let's go back again. Erik straightens out and goes back to school, where he manages to earn a liberal arts degree. At his granddaddy's urging, he moves out of state—Oklahoma, of all places—to a town I'll call Nowheresville. Granddaddy has an old friend there who takes Erik under his wing, gives him a job, sees that he stays on the straight and narrow. Before long, Erik has carved out a little niche for himself. He sets up his own insurance agency and starts making lots of money. I should mention, by the way, that Erik is freakin' good-looking. He took after his mom, not his dad." Jim grinned, revealing one graying front tooth.

Talia smiled on cue.

"So now Erik meets another girl, this time a sweet young thing named Amber. Amber's dad is a former mayor, with lots of political connections. They marry, have two darling babies, and all is rosy in Erik's world. But Erik has bigger dreams. Because of his popularity as a local business leader, he decides to run for state rep. With his father-in-law's connections, and because he's running on a 'family values' platform in a town where flag-waving is almost a blood sport, he's a shoo-in."

Talia shifted in her chair, wishing he would get to the point.

As if he'd read her mind, Jepson said, "Cut to another scene, good ole Wrensdale, Massachusetts. Turnbull tries to pressure me into signing a petition that, in my opinion, is elitist and discriminatory." Jepson's gaze narrowed. "I told him precisely what he could do with his so-called petition. Even gave him some suggestions on how to fold it so it would fit properly."

Talia stifled a smile. She wanted him to get on with the story.

"Three days later, Erik called me in a panic. He'd gotten a call from Turnbull threatening to expose the sins of his youth. Turnbull had dug into my background, found out about Erik and the child he abandoned, and was threatening to disclose it to Erik's opponent. Erik knew he'd lose the election if that happened. He'd be exposed as a liar, not to mention a deadbeat dad."

"So essentially Phil blackmailed you," Talia said. Suzy's words rang in her ears. *That was his weapon. He collected information about people . . .*

"Exactly." Jepson looked away, one foot jiggling nervously. "Erik was so sure no one would ever find out about his past. Turned out it was my fault. Turnbull saw a photo of me with my granddaughter on my Facebook page. She's an adult now, and lives with her mom in Maine. I visit her two or three times a year. Phil connected a few dots, made some phone calls, and tricked Lara into telling him everything."

An uneasy feeling gripped Talia. Clutching her purse tightly, she said, "Was that your son who called the night we were all at the tea shop? I heard a voice yelling at you. He said something like '*you said everything would be okay, that you would take care of it.*'"

Jepson looked away, his eyes glazed. "Yes, that was Erik. And I did take care of it," he added softly. "I did something I was loath to do, but it had to be done. For my son."

Oh dear God, he did murder Phil. So why am I sitting here like a bubblehead, taking his confession?

Talia tried to swallow, but the boulder in her throat wouldn't budge. Her urge to bolt was quashed by the realization that her legs had gone numb. "S . . . so you mean, you . . ."

"Yeah, I signed that lousy frickin' petition. I signed it so Phil would leave Erik alone."

Talia let out the breath she didn't realize she was holding. All at once, the room felt hot, and she had to fight the urge to peel off her jacket. "That's . . . what you meant when you said you'd take care of it?"

"Of course. What did you think I— Oh, wait, I know what you thought." Jepson let out a throaty guffaw. "You thought I killed the SOB, didn't you?"

Talia cringed. "No, honestly, Jim, I didn't really think that. Not until you said . . . I mean—"

"Aw, Talia, you're priceless," he said. "No wonder you were one of my favorite students. You've got guts, girl. You always did." He raised his fist in a show of solidarity. "You keep up the good fight, you hear?"

Talia pushed back her chair and rose. "I will, Jim. I'd better go."

"One last thing." Jepson's voice was sharp. He pointed a clay-mottled finger at her. "In case you're inclined to think poorly of me for violating my principles, keep one thing in mind. In this crazy world where life is fragile and no one is safe, we all protect our own."

Talia scuttled past the shelves of pottery until she reached the exit, those last five words vibrating through her head. By the time she stumbled outside onto the cobblestone plaza, Jim's parting statement seemed to have taken an ominous tilt.

We all protect our own.

The sky was clear—a charcoal canvas scattered with pin-points of light. Talia inhaled a lungful of the crisp air, grateful to be away from that stifling room in the rear of the pottery shop. Even the chill that crept up her arms felt like cool relief.

In the window of the Clock Shop, a faint light was visible. Talia hurried across the plaza, her Keds barely making a sound against the rounded stones beneath her feet. In spite of the posted hours announcing that the shop closed at six— it was now only five twenty—the sign in the window had been turned to CLOSED.

She peered through the leaded glass on the door. A shadow crossed her line of vision, but then vanished off to the left. Was she seeing things, or was Cliff still inside?

Talia felt bad about the way she'd treated him the day she confronted him in his shop. He suffered from the same addiction her dad had once battled, and she knew how all-consuming it was. She, of all people, should have been more empathetic.

An apology was in order. Cliff might reject it, and if he did, that was his privilege. She wanted to offer it anyway.

Truth be told, she had an ulterior motive. Maybe if she offered Cliff a friendly hand, he would open up to her. Even if he had nothing to do with Turnbull's death, it was clear that he had at least one shady associate. A shudder boogied up her spine when she thought about the man who'd approached Cliff in Queenie's. He'd claimed to be Cliff's cousin, but Talia didn't believe that for a second. Whoever he was, he was downright frightening.

A weird feeling suddenly crept over her—a feeling that she wasn't alone. She whirled around, and then laughed at her jumpiness. A trio of teenagers—two girls and a boy— were advancing across the plaza toward Lambert's. One of them spotted her and waved, and she wiggled her fingers in return.

Relieved, Talia turned again and tried the door of Cliff's shop. Just as she felt it give, it slammed shut, the force sending her slightly off balance. The harsh click of a deadbolt rang in her ears.

"Cliff?" she called out. "Is that you?"

She waited for a minute, and then shook her head. Cliff knew it was her and had no intention of letting her enter. No way. No how.

Talia swept her gaze over the plaza. At times like this, when the night was quiet, she found herself envisioning the real sixteenth-century England. In her mind's eye, she saw a horse-drawn cart trek across the arcade, the driver's face haggard from a long day tending his fields. She heard the clip-clop of the horse's hooves moving rhythmically over the cobblestone, the weariness in its gait a sign that he was through for the day, ready for a night's rest.

Shaking away the vision, she crossed Main Street and headed into Queenie's, making a beeline for the pet food section. She snatched up a bag of kitty litter, and on her way to the checkout grabbed a quart of milk and a box of Rice Krispies. The broker would probably flip when she saw that a cat had moved in, but Talia refused to leave the creature in the cold another night. If she could coax her inside, then at least the kitty would have a temporary home. If Talia could find a rental that allowed pets, she might even be able to keep her.

Five minutes later, Talia swung into Nana's driveway. She started to switch off her headlamps when she spied the calico cat. Perched on the front step, the kitty gazed at Talia through big gold eyes. She didn't flinch when Talia got out of her Fiat, or even when Talia closed the car door.

Talia gathered her purse and her purchases, and walked slowly toward the bungalow. "Hey, Bojangles," she cooed. "Are you ready for dinner?"

She hadn't realized until now that she'd named the kitty. The cat darted to the side, but stayed on the porch as Talia slowly climbed the steps. Talia unlocked the door, surprised when the cat skittered inside.

"Success," she whispered.

She set her things down on the sofa while the cat toured her new digs. Bojangles ambled from the coffee table to the sofa to Grandpop's unsightly tweed chair. In one graceful leap, the cat swished onto the chair. She sniffed the fabric and then curled into a circle, keeping her gold-and-black head just high enough to peruse her new habitat.

Talia laughed. "That chair was meant for you, wasn't it? Grandpop loved it, too."

Bojangles opened her mouth and emitted a tiny mewl.

"Okay, I get it. You're hungry."

Talia went to the kitchen and grabbed two bowls from the cabinet. She was pouring kibble into the smaller one when she felt a soft form curling around her leg. Bending low, she stroked Bo's head. "You're so adorable," she said. "How could anyone have tossed you into the street?"

While Bo scarfed her supper, Talia set up a makeshift litter box in the bathroom. The moment the cat swallowed her last gulp, she scooted into the bathroom and availed herself of the facilities.

"You knew exactly what I was doing in here, didn't you?" Talia said. "We'll probably move your box to a better spot, but this will do for now."

Amazed at how comfortable the cat had already made herself, Talia put away the few groceries she'd bought. She was starving, she realized. A whopping order of Lambert's fish and chips would hit the spot right about now. Why hadn't she thought of it when she was out?

On impulse, she removed her cell from her purse and punched in Rachel's speed dial. Maybe she'd be willing to bring over another pizza—Talia's treat, this time.

"Talia?" Rachel's voice seemed faint and distant.

"Hi, Rach. You sound far away. Are you home?"

"Um . . . no, not yet. I'm . . . tied up in a meeting. Can I call you back?"

"Sure," Talia said, releasing a sigh. "Catch you later, then."

A feeling of gloom slid over Talia. She had so much she wanted to tell Rachel—about her trip to Chet's, her news about taking over Lambert's. Not to mention that she had a new cat she might not be able to keep.

Talia thought of calling her mom, but she knew they'd have to talk about Nana's house, and she wasn't up for that. Instead, she made herself a peanut butter and jam sandwich, took a fast shower, and crawled into bed early.

She awoke to the jingle of her cell phone, along with a moist nose tickling her ear. "Hullo?" she muttered, horrified to see from her bedside clock that it was only 5:47. She cupped Bo's silky head.

"Tal, I wanted to catch you before you heard it on the news."

"Rachel?"

"Of course. Who else would call you at this hour? Didn't you tell me that the girl who works for Bea was going out with a guy named Pug?"

"I did? Yeah, maybe, I guess so." Talia's senses went on full alert. "Why, what happened?"

"He's dead," Rachel said. "Someone bashed him over the head behind the burger joint on the Pittsfield-Lenox Road late last night. The paramedics rushed him to the hospital, but he didn't make it."

24

Bea sat at the small table, her coffee untouched and her face ashen. "I can't believe this is happening," she said. "I don't even know what to think anymore."

"I know," Talia said quietly. "I don't, either." She slung her purse and jacket over the hook on the kitchen door.

Bea dabbed her eyes with a crumpled napkin. "Poor Whitnee. The girl had enough stress to start with, what with her classes and that oddball of a mum. And now this . . ." Her words trailed off, and she sipped her coffee, grimacing when she found it cold.

Talia poured herself a cup of coffee, added a touch of milk, and sat down opposite Bea.

"Oh, Tal, you don't think they'll accuse Whitnee of killing him, do you?"

That's precisely what worried Talia, except she carried it a step further. Could Whitnee have had a hand in Pug's death?

Maybe she'd confronted him over seeing another girl? Bashed him over the head in anger and killed him unintentionally?

And why had Rachel known so much about it at five in the morning? Rachel claimed Talia had told her about Whitnee seeing a guy named Pug, but Talia couldn't recall ever mentioning him to her.

"Bea, I honestly don't know. Whitnee obviously won't be coming in today, so you and I have to pull ourselves together, okay?"

"But . . ." Bea sniffled loudly. "What if the coppers come in and ask if we know anything? Oh, I wish Whitnee hadn't told us about finding Pug with that other girl!"

"I know." Talia's voice rattled. "But she did, and if we're asked about it, we simply have to tell the truth."

They spent the next few hours in near silence. Talia gave the floor in the dining area a thorough washing, and then wiped down all the tables and chairs with lime-scented cleaner. Moments before opening time, a hard knock at the entry door made her jump.

The police.

Talia unlocked the door and it flew open, knocking her slightly off kilter.

"Oh God, did you hear what happened?" Whitnee rushed in, her face puffy and her eyes bloodshot. She tossed her book bag onto a table and sobbed for several minutes. Talia tried hugging the girl, but Whitnee pushed her away, tears flowing down her cheeks at an alarming rate.

Bea made her take a few sips of hot coffee. "Aw, Whitnee, why did you even come in? With everything that's happened, I surely don't expect you to work today." She pushed a strand of greasy hair away from Whitnee's face. "You've had a terrible shock, luv, and you need to take care of yourself."

"I . . . couldn't stay home anymore. My mom was, like, driving me nuts, and I know the cops'll want to question me. They'll say . . . they'll think I hurt Pug, and I didn't!" A hoarse sob burst from her. "Plus, I have an exam tomorrow and I've gotta study for it." She swiped the back of her hand over her leaky eyes.

Talia fetched a tissue for her. "I'm sure your professor would let you take a make-up exam. Would you like me to make a call for you?"

Whitnee ignored Talia's offer. "I'll stay here and work, if that's okay, Bea. I can prob'ly, like, squeeze in some study time on my breaks."

Bea bit her lip. "Of course, luv. If that's what you want."

The lunch rush kicked into gear. Whitnee pulled herself together and made it through, even adding a tepid smile to her voice as she took phone orders. At Bea's urging, she managed to swallow a few fries and a helping of mushy peas. But as soon as business quieted, Whitnee burst into another round of tears. "I . . . I think I'd better go," she told Bea. "I can't get Pug out of my head. I wish the cops would just question me and get it over with."

Talia, too, wondered why the police weren't all over her. Wasn't the victim's "significant other" the first one they usually questioned?

Bea made Whitnee promise to call if she needed anything. Whitnee thanked her and left, without so much as a backward glance at Talia.

Taking advantage of the midday lull, Talia took a break and made a fast dash home to check on Bo. The darling little calico was curled up on Grandpop's old chair, looking as comfy as if she'd slept on it all her life. She greeted Talia with a soft purr and a head butt, and then went back to her nap. After ensuring that her new charge had food and fresh water, Talia returned to Lambert's.

Talia was starting to get concerned about Rachel. She'd texted her several times, to no avail. Something was definitely off with her friend. *Yet one more thing to worry about*, she thought, as she and Bea closed up for the night.

They were putting on their coats when Bea noticed Whitnee's book tote hanging on the back of the door. "Ah, the poor girl left her bag here."

"I'll drive it over to her," Talia offered. "Do you have her address?"

While Bea looked up the address, Talia lifted the tote off the hook. It was heavier than she'd realized, and one end slipped off her hand. Two textbooks tumbled to the floor, along with the same glossy magazine on which she'd seen *W + P* inscribed inside a heart. Retrieving the books, Talia stared at the mag in disbelief. She saw now that it was a bridal magazine—a May issue. Had Whitnee been planning a wedding?

Talia stuffed the books and the magazine back inside the tote. Poor Whitnee—she really had been in love with Pug. She'd been planning their wedding and all the while he was flirting, if not worse, with other girls.

Bea located Whitnee's address, and together she and Talia headed for their cars. Anxious to get to the hospital, Bea watched Talia get into her Fiat and then zoomed out of the lot. Talia flipped her a wave and was hooking her seat belt when her passenger-side door abruptly opened. A man jumped inside.

Talia screamed.

"Stop squealing like a girl," Cliff Colby said. "I'm not going to hurt you—I just have to talk to you. Pull out of the lot and hang a left. I'll tell you where to go."

"Why do we have to go anywhere?" Talia gripped the wheel to keep her hands from shaking. "Why can't we talk right here?"

"Because I don't want anyone seeing me with you," he snapped, flicking a look at the passenger-side mirror.

Well, that didn't sound good. She stole at glance at him. Even in the darkness of her car, she saw that his eyes looked wild. No, not wild—terrified.

"What is this, a toy car?" he whined, his knees pressed almost to his chest. "Doesn't this seat go back any farther?"

"Use the side lever," Talia said, getting angry now. "You have a nerve complaining about the seat, you know that? Who invited you to take a ride with me, anyway?"

He jammed the seat back as far as it would go. "Just go," he said. "This'll only take a few minutes. I promise!"

Sure. Like it only took a few minutes to kill Phil Turnbull.

Her heart in her throat, she followed his instructions. Left on Main, right on Baboosic. When she snuck a look at him, his large hands were jiggling in his lap. Did he have a weapon on him? She didn't think so, but she definitely wasn't going to let her guard down.

They followed Baboosic for over a mile. When he ordered her to pull in behind a long-defunct skating rink at the edge of town, her insides cartwheeled. The abandoned parking lot behind the rink was huge, bordered on one side by deep woods.

"Over there, near those pines. I don't want someone spotting this stupid turquoise car. Could you have picked a brighter color?" he griped.

Talia felt like bopping him on his oversized head. Instead, she parked the car but left it running. She considered throwing her door open and making a run for it, but Cliff's legs were so long she'd never get away. Plus, something told her he wasn't actually dangerous. It reminded her of what her dad always told her about the occasional garter snake that wandered into the yard—*it's more afraid of you than you are of it.*

"I have things to do, Cliff," she said. "What do you want?"

Cliff cast a glance in his side-view mirror, then swiveled in his seat and pointed a crooked finger at her. "I want you to *stop* coming into the Clock Shop and to stay away from me. You're a nosy broad, and you've already caused me no end of trouble."

"What did I do?" Talia squealed. "I offered to help you!"

"Yeah, well, your kind of help's gonna get me killed. I got a loan shark on my tail, and he thinks you're an undercover cop."

Talia gawked at him. "A cop! What are you talking about?"

"Don't play dumb. Classy-looking dame like you? You show up out of the blue and start slinging haddock in that fish joint. Then you start haranguing me, following me."

"I did not—"

"He thinks you've been watching him for weeks, and that you and me have some kind of sting operation going. I tried telling him I only met you a few days ago, but he thinks I'm lying."

"That man who was in Queenie's—he's the loan shark, isn't he?"

"Yeah, good guess, Einstein. Here, wait while I pin a gold star on you."

"Cliff," Talia said, furious now, "all I want is to get Bea off the hook for Turnbull's murder. If it helps, I will not even speak to you again or go near your shop."

"Good." He blew out a long, stale, oniony breath. "Now drop me off behind the diner. I left my car there this morning."

"You realize I could report you to the police?" Talia threatened. "And that I probably will," she added with false bravado.

"Go ahead," he said bleakly. "Right about now, jail's the one place I'd feel safe."

25

Talia's heart pounded relentlessly for several minutes before she got it under control. What had Cliff been thinking, nabbing her like that? Clearly he was desperate, both for cash and to escape the clutches of the lowlife who'd been stalking him. But his behavior was inexcusable, and she'd have to consider reporting his actions.

She located Whitnee's house, a sad-looking clapboard affair that begged for a paint job. Whitnee's car was in the dirt driveway. Praying the girl was home alone, Talia climbed the worn front steps and rang the buzzer. She pressed it twice before she saw Whitnee's pale face glowering at her through a side window. Talia held up her book bag.

Seconds later, Whitnee opened the door. "I wondered where I left that," she said, reaching for the tote. She stared inside it for a long moment. Talia had shoved everything back inside with the magazine on top of the books. Did Whitnee notice the contents weren't in the order she'd left them?

"Um, thanks," Whitnee muttered and started to close the door.

"May I come in for a moment?" Talia wondered why Whitnee hadn't even missed the book bag. Hadn't she claimed she had an exam to study for?

Whitnee shrugged, and then took a step back. "I guess," she said dully. "What do you want?"

Talia entered the parlor gingerly. The room was tidy enough, but every surface was jam-packed with bric-a-brac and photos. Seventies-style paneling covered the walls, and the sofa and chairs were the old plush type with stout wooden legs. Retro, but far from chic.

"You seem upset with me, Whitnee," Talia said. "Did I do something to offend you?"

Whitnee flushed pink. "My mom doesn't like you. She was, like, really embarrassed when you threw her out of the restaurant the other day."

Talia couldn't believe what she was hearing. Had Whitnee forgotten the humiliating barbs her mother pinged at her during that awful spat? In front of someone she barely knew? Talia had intervened only to protect Whitnee from further abuse.

"I didn't mean to hurt her feelings," Talia said, "but I was thinking of you. I'm sorry if she felt I was picking on her. Is she home? Maybe I could apologize in person."

Whitnee regarded her through red-rimmed eyes. Talia's heart softened, remembering the $W + P$ etched on the bridal magazine. "No, she works nights."

"Oh. Where does she work?"

Whitnee looked uncomfortable. "She, um, does commercial cleaning. Do you, like, want a soda or anything?"

A soda was the last thing Talia wanted, but it seemed to be Whitnee's way of accepting her apology. "Sure, I'd love one."

Whitnee left the room. Seconds later, Talia heard the sound of a refrigerator door opening and the rattle of ice cubes. While she waited for the soda she knew she'd have to choke down, she wandered toward the bookshelf against the nearest wall. Photos of every size, encased in cheap metal frames, covered the shelves. Curiosity nudging her, she glanced from one picture to the next. It took several seconds before she realized something—every single photo was of Whitnee.

There was a young Whitnee with carroty braids, making faces at the camera.

An unsmiling Whitnee sitting cross-legged on the floor, her straight bangs hanging in her eyes, a fluffy white rabbit wriggling in her small hands.

"Hope you like grape."

"Eep!" Talia jumped and whirled around.

"What's wrong?" Whitnee's pale eyebrows dipped toward her nose in a frown. She handed Talia a paper cup half-filled with a flat purple liquid, a single ice cube floating on top.

Talia patted her chest lightly and accepted the drink. "Sorry, I didn't hear you come up behind me." She sipped from the cup, nearly gagging on the sweetness. "I was just admiring all these photos of you. Is that the bunny you told us about?"

Whitnee's gaze slid to the rabbit photo, and her frown deepened. "Yeah, but I didn't have it long. My stupid brother teased it. He kept poking it with a sharp pencil and, like, wouldn't leave it alone." Her eyes grew distant. "I took it out of its cage to get it away from him, but then the rabbit bit me, kind of hard. Ma was, like, livid when that happened."

"At your brother, you mean?"

"No, at the rabbit," Whitnee said softly.

"It was probably scared," Talia said tightly, incensed that the boy had been allowed to torment a helpless animal.

"Yeah, I suppose." Whitnee looked at her crossly. "Anyway, the next day the rabbit was gone. Ma said it got out of its cage and ran away, but I think she got rid of it."

The room was beginning to feel oppressive, as if the air was being sucked out through a large tube. Talia gulped back the rest of her vile drink, and that's when another photo caught her attention. A photo of a little girl with curly red hair, dressed in a gray snowsuit and orange plaid boots. It wasn't exactly the same as the picture she'd found in Turnbull's showroom, but it was definitely taken at the same time.

Talia pointed at the picture. "Is . . . is that you, Whitnee?" she asked, a tiny elf in her head warning her to leave it alone. "Your hair's so curly."

"Yeah, Ma had given me one of those dopey home perms. She thought it would make me look cuter, but I only ended up looking like a dork." She reached over and absently touched the photo. "Ma was always trying to make me prettier . . ."

Talia looked at Whitnee's pinched face, and a tingling sensation shot up her legs. Hadn't Whitnee said she'd only met Pug a few months ago? Why was she lugging around the May issue of a bridal magazine?

W + P . . .

"You look, like, kind of weird," Whitnee said.

"Oh, sorry." She gave Whitnee her empty cup. "I haven't eaten much today. I think the soda gave me a sugar rush."

"Um, before you go, Talia, can I ask you something?"

"Sure." With an effort to look casual, Talia started toward the door.

Whitnee looked at the floor, and her cheeks flushed pink. "Like, the first time you, you know, *did it* with a guy, did he ask you to marry him?"

Of all the questions Talia anticipated, that one hadn't even made the top fifty. The only man she ever "did it" with had been Chet, but she had no intention of sharing that with Whitnee.

"Whitnee, I don't really feel comfortable talking about that. Why do you want to know?"

Whitnee swallowed. "Well, my mom told me that when a guy, you know, like, takes away your virginity, that he's supposed to ask you to marry him. She said it's, you know, like an unwritten law."

Talia stared at the girl. She was a college student, for pity's sake. Surely she didn't believe that. Could she be that naïve?

"Whitnee, I'm sure that's not true."

Tears hovered on Whitnee's pale lashes. "Never mind. Forget I asked, okay? Look, I know my mom goes kind of overboard about me, but it's because she loves me so much. She's always got my back, you know? No matter what happens, she's always there for me. Without her, I have nothing."

"Whitnee, you don't have to make excuses. I feel the same way about my mom, so I understand perfectly."

Get me out of here.

Whitnee's eyes brightened. "You do?"

"Of course. In fact, she's waiting for me right now, so I'd better dash. Thanks for the soda. Good luck with your exam!"

On legs that felt like pogo sticks, Talia wobbled out to her car. All along, it was right under her nose.

She desperately needed her mom's advice. Maybe she was blowing the bridal magazine out of proportion. Maybe she was only imagining that the *P* penned inside the heart stood for Phil and not for Pug.

But what about the photo? Why had a snapshot of Whit-nee as a child been on the floor in Turnbull's showroom?

Her brain was on overload. She needed her mom to help process it all before she went to the police. Her mother should still be at the Pines, since her promotion to assistant director came with evening hours on Tuesdays and Thursdays.

Talia rang the bell twice. The night nurse smiled brightly as she promenaded toward the front entrance and waved at Talia through the glass. She pressed a button on the wall, and the door opened automatically.

"Hey, Talia! What brings you here so late? You look like you've seen a ghost."

No, just a killer.

"Hi, Nancy. I really need to talk to my mom."

"Oh, of course, dear. She's in a meeting, but I can check to see if she's going to be much longer."

"Thanks, Nance."

"Is everything okay? Your dad's not sick, is he?"

"No, nothing like that. More of a personal crisis."

Nancy nodded and led her to the first floor desk, where a young nurse with pink-tinted hair was sipping tea while she filled out reports. Nancy introduced the woman as Allie and said, "We've had a few crises ourselves today, haven't we, Allie?"

Allie snorted in agreement. "Yeah, it's been quite the banner day. Started when old Mrs. Hartman tossed her cookies, so to speak, on the floor in the dining room after lunch. Poor dear came down with a bad flu bug, I guess. Anyway, her roomie, Gladys, all but tossed her own cookies when she saw all that, you know, *vomit* splattered on the floor. Next thing we know, Gladys screams and drops to the floor in a dead faint, right in that puddle of pu—"

"All right, all right! Enough with the graphic descriptions!" Nancy waved a hand at Allie and then plopped herself onto a chair in front of a free monitor. "Even worse, while all that was going on, Mr. Lunford managed to escape wearing nothing but a johnny and a pair of red socks. Got as far as the corner of Amherst and Pine before Livvy at the florist shop nabbed him and called the police."

"Welcome to the zoo," Allie said with a chuckle.

Nancy shot the nurse a look. "Don't you start," she chided. "Bad enough we have to hear that kind of talk from the maintenance staff. Anyway," she told Talia, "your mom's in a meeting with Mr. Lunford's daughter and son-in-law. They went nuts when they found out what happened, and drove straight over from New York." She reached for the phone. "I'll find out if she's going to be much longer."

"That's okay; don't interrupt her." An idea had popped into Talia's head. "I know it's after visiting hours, but while I wait for Mom, could I say a quick hello to Arthur Collins?"

"Professor Collins? Well, sure, I think he'd like that.

You'll have to take the elevator to the second floor, then take a left and another left to the end of the hall. He's in room nineteen. He usually leaves his door open a smidge until he tucks in for the night." She reached for the phone. "I'll let the nurse on that floor know you're coming."

"Thanks," Talia said. "I'll only stay a few minutes."

Following Nancy's directions, she headed to the second floor. The desk nurse acknowledged her with a quick wave, and Talia did the same. The hallway was eerily quiet, broken only by the sound of an occasional moan, or voices drifting from a television. She passed a janitorial cart full of cleaning supplies that was parked near an emergency exit, a spaghetti mop sticking up from one of its side slots. At the back of her brain a memory teased her, but it hovered just out of reach.

Talia hustled down the hall until she reached room nineteen. The door was partway open. Occasional flashes of color from the television told her Arthur was still up.

"Arthur?" She knocked lightly and peeked inside. "It's Talia Marby. May I come in for a minute?"

Arthur stiffened. "Do I know you?"

Dressed in a flannel robe and tan slippers, Arthur sat hunched in a wing-back chair beside his twin bed. On his opposite side, a water carafe capped with an upturned drinking glass rested on a polished piecrust table, along with a volume of sonnets by Shakespeare. Behind his chair was a tall bookcase crammed with hardcover volumes. From the top of his oak bureau, a bust of the Bard himself surveyed the room with pensive eyes. Had Arthur brought it from Shakespeare's birthplace along with the letter opener that went missing?

Talia went over and stood beside him. "I met you on Sunday, Arthur. I'm Talia, Ryan's friend from high school."

Arthur's shoulders sagged, as if with relief. "Talia, my dear, thank heaven you came."

Talia remembered Ryan's concerns about his dad misplacing things. It tore at her to see the mind of this brilliant man fading behind the veil of a debilitating disease. "Arthur, do you need help? Is there something I can do?"

He pursed his lips in deep thought, and then his gray eyes brightened. "Did you bring my fish and chips?"

Talia smiled and squeezed his hand. "No, the restaurant is closed for the night. But I will soon. I promise. I just wanted to say a quick hello. I'm going to leave and let you rest now."

From the hallway, the sound of a squeaky wheel grew nearer and nearer. Arthur's ears perked. He gave out a tortured whimper and cowered into his chair.

The cart drew closer, and then Talia heard another, tauntingly familiar sound.

Swish. Swish.

The scrape of polyester-clad thighs, rubbing against each other with every step.

"Don't leave me," Arthur begged. "That's the bad lady."

And in that instant, the memory came to her.

Time to go clean the zoo.

Connie Parker's words.

Crazy Connie Parker, fixated on her daughter to the point of obsession.

No wonder Whitnee had been so evasive about her mother's job—she didn't want Talia to know she worked at the Pines.

The morning after Phil's murder, Whitnee had shown up for work in clothes that were stained and rumpled. She'd blamed it on her mother having left work sick the night before and not having done the laundry. The truth now dawned. Connie left work "sick" so she could confront Phil. Had she planned to kill him? Or was she only going to give him an ultimatum?

Talia looked around the room, scanning the area near the bed. Shouldn't Arthur have a call button? She yanked her purse off her shoulder. "You're right, Arthur, she's badder than you know, but she's not going to hurt anyone again." Her hands shook as she dug around for her cell phone, which had somehow migrated to the center of the Earth. Before she could curl her fingers around it, the door flew fully open, slamming the rubber door stopper.

Connie barged into the room, dragging her janitorial cart behind her. With one foot she pushed the door shut. "Nosy bee-yotch. I heard what you called me."

Her mouth dry with terror, Talia stepped in front of Arthur. "You have no right to come in here, Mrs. Parker. Please leave."

Connie reached for her mop handle. "I bet you think you're real smart. I talked to my girl a little while ago. She told me about you comin' to our house, actin' like you're some kind of detective. You think you got it all figured out, don't you?"

"I don't know what you're talking about," Talia said, hating the tremor in her voice. "I—"

Wielding the mop like a baseball bat, Connie slammed the handle into Talia's left leg. Talia yelped, and her purse flew from her shoulder as she toppled to the floor. Pain soared up her leg like a rocket of white heat.

"You think I was gonna let that piece of crap in the lamp store get away with what he did to my girl?" Connie spat out.

Pain seared Talia's shin, and her eyes watered. "Is

that why you killed him? Because he had an affair with Whitnee?"

"My girl was *pure* before she met him! He did the dirty deed with her and then dumped her like a piece of trash. Now she's just used goods. No decent man will ever want her."

Talia struggled to twist her body into a sitting position, her shin throbbing. "Mrs. Parker, that's simply not true."

"That's simply not true," Connie mimicked. "Why do you think she had to go out with the likes of Pug Terranova? I told Whitnee when a man ruins a girl, he marries her. That's the way it works. Period."

So with starry visions of wedded bliss and a deranged mother for an advisor, Whitnee bought a bridal magazine and started planning the nuptials. So what if her intended wasn't in on the plan? A minor detail, right?

Biting her lip against the pain, Talia inched backward a smidge. If she could get to Arthur's table, she might be able to reach his carafe and use it as a weapon.

Distract her. Keep her talking.

"But how . . . when did Whitnee meet Phil? She never mentioned him, except to say that he dissed her."

Connie's upper lip curled. "Not that it's your business, but she met him last spring. He saw her walkin' to her car after work one night—she was parked behind his store. He started flirtin' with her, tellin' her how he'd been admirin' her from afar. All he wanted was to get into her pants, but my poor, gullible girl fell for it, like a fish swallowin' a worm. I didn't find out about any of it till she came cryin' to me that he dumped her. For him it was nothin' but a fling, but my Whitnee thought she was in love. When she told me what he did"—Connie's eyes darkened with rage—"I told her that scumball had better be plannin' to marry her, after what he robbed her of."

Stifling a cry of pain, Talia moved a millimeter closer to the table. "Is . . . is that why Whitnee bought the bridal magazine? Because you told her he had to marry her?"

"Yeah, but when she told him what I said about marryin' a girl you ruined, he laughed in her face."

The throbbing in Talia's shin was growing worse. "Why did you wait so long to kill him?"

Connie pointed the mop handle at her. "I was givin' him a chance to do the right thing. Whitnee kept hintin' like they were gettin' back together. I figured she started seein' Pug just to make Phil jealous. But last week, when she told me how Phil insulted her and called her a ditz, I knew she was only foolin' herself. It was time to make him pay."

"Where did you get the knife?"

"That slob of a cook who works here must've dropped it. It was the day she cooked that disgustin' cod. I remember, because the kitchen still reeked from it. I found the knife stuck halfway under the stove when I was washing the floor." Connie cackled. "Her loss, my gain."

Talia glanced up at Arthur, who looked almost catatonic. It she could keep Connie talking, maybe Nancy would realize Talia had been gone too long and send someone looking for her. "How did you get into Phil's shop?"

"Oh, that was easy. Whitnee told me he left his office every night at seven sharp, through the rear door. She used to park her car next to his and wait for him. So I pretended I was sick and left work early, then I waited outside his door. Sure enough, he trotted out the back door at two minutes past seven. I shoved him right back inside, the little wimp.

I gave him a chance, though. Even showed him my girl's picture when she was a darlin' little thing, so he'd see how sweet she was and change his mind and marry her. Know what he said?" Her eyes hardened. "He said she was just another slutty flirt, like all girls, and he only gave her what she wanted."

Bad move, Phil.

"But he underestimated your motherly devotion, didn't he?" Talia scooched, ever so slightly, toward the piecrust table.

Connie tossed her head back and laughed. "Did he ever! He tried to escape through the store, but I showed him my knife and turned him right back around. Afterward, I unlocked the front door so the cops would think the killer got in that way." She tapped a forefinger to her temple. "People think I'm dumb because I clean for a livin', but I outsmarted 'em all."

"Yes, you did," Talia agreed. She edged a few inches closer to Arthur's table. "You must be awfully strong to have overpowered a young guy like Pug."

"Pffft." Connie waved a pudgy hand. "I'm strong as a bull, but that one was easy. He was sittin' in his car with some bimbo, smokin' God only knows what. But I was crouched behind it, waitin'. After the bimbo left Pug got out, and I smashed him from behind with a big rock I found in the woods behind the strip mall. And you know what? I'm sick of explainin' all this to you. It's time I got rid of you, and I got a good idea for that, too."

Connie reached into the yellow nylon bag attached to the bottom of her cart and began rummaging through the contents. Ignoring the pain shooting through her leg, Talia dragged herself a few inches closer to the piecrust table.

When Connie straightened, her chunky fingers were wrapped around the handle of a silver letter opener. "I'm gonna stab you with this and blame it on the daffy doodle over there. His fingerprints are already on it."

"So are yours."

"Of course they are!" Connie chortled insanely, and her thick jowls jiggled. "That's because I found it stickin' out of your neck and tried to save you by pullin' it out!"

Gripped by sheer terror, Talia said, "Leave Arthur out of this, Connie. He never did anything to you."

Connie's eyes bulged with cold fury. "Oh, yeah?" She reached into the nylon bag again and whipped out yet another photo of Whitnee in the orange plaid boots. "Him and me, we got talkin' one night, and I told him all about my girl. I showed him this picture, and know what he said? He said my girl was funny-lookin'. *Funny-lookin'!* That's why I started stealin' his stuff, to pay him back for being so nasty." She tossed the photo at Arthur. It landed on his thigh, and he flinched.

"The police won't be fooled, Connie." Talia moved her fingers slowly toward the base of the piecrust table. "How will you explain the bruise on my leg?"

"Shut up!" With a demonic grin, Connie twisted the letter opener.

It was now or nevermore. Talia shot her arm up and grabbed at the carafe, but she wasn't quite close enough to grasp it. The carafe toppled and shattered, spilling water over the floor.

Arthur's eyes widened. In the next instant he sprang off his chair, one shaky finger pointing at the puddle spreading over the floor. "Water, water, everywhere, and all the boards did shrink!"

Connie gawked at him in surprise. "What the—"

His eyes aglow with the passion of the poem, Arthur advanced toward Connie. He was taller than Talia realized, and made an imposing figure. "Water, water, everywhere, nor any drop to drink!"

Talia used the distraction to her advantage. She lunged for Arthur's chair and hauled herself onto her good leg, her shin pulsing with pain. She hopped over to Arthur's bureau and reached for the bust.

Connie's eyes flickered in confusion. She shifted her gaze between Arthur and Talia, as if trying to gauge who was the bigger threat. She jabbed the letter opener wildly at Arthur, stuttering backward until she rear-ended her own cart. "Get away from me, you crazy coot!" She kicked him in the knee with the bottom of her shoe.

Arthur buckled but didn't stop. He thrust his arm past Connie and snagged a spray bottle from the cart. "Yea, slimy things did crawl with legs upon the slimy sea!" He squeezed the handle fiercely, squirting a shower of lemon-scented liquid into her startled face.

Connie shrieked with rage. She still held on to the letter opener while she dug at her eyes with the thick fingers of her other hand. "I'll kill you!"

Talia seized the bust off the bureau and fast-hobbled over to Connie. Using every bit of strength she could rally, she swung it into the side of the woman's head. Connie's eyes crossed like a cartoon character's, and she crumpled to the floor in an ungainly heap. A thin river of blood trickled toward her ear.

With a choked sob, Talia dropped the bust onto Connie's cart. She stumbled toward Arthur. "Are you okay, Arthur?"

He looked at her blankly and then stared at the spray bottle in his hand, his eyes clouded with bewilderment.

Talia took the bottle from him and tossed it to the floor. "Come on, Arthur, let's sit down. I need to call for help. Could you get my purse for me?"

The throbbing in her shin had subsided to a burning ache. Arthur gripped her waist and helped her limp over to his chair. He fetched her purse, and she used her cell to call the front desk, instructing Nancy to call 911.

Arthur bent to retrieve the photo of Whitnee that had fallen near his chair. He pointed at it. "Funny-looking," he said, with a childlike giggle. "These boots are funny-looking."

26

Howie Lambert reached for his wife's hand, his smile stretching from one large ear to the other. "Ah, look at her, Bea. She's always been a natural at this, hasn't she?"

"That she has, luv." Bea squeezed her husband's hand, and then moved his wheelchair back a smidge so as not to block Talia's path.

"Oh, you two are biased and you know it," Talia scolded, loving every word they said. She removed two meatballs—which she'd dredged first in a Parmesan batter of her own design—from the deep fryer. She set one on a plate for each of them, along with a plastic fork. From a small saucepan on the stove, she ladled up a spoonful of marinara sauce and dribbled it over each of the servings. "Don't gobble, now," she cautioned. "These are sizzling hot."

Ignoring her warning, Howie jabbed his fork into his meatball. "Never too hot for me," he boomed and plopped the entire thing into his mouth. He grinned broadly after he swallowed. "Talia, these are going to be a hit."

Favoring her right leg slightly, Talia moved over to the work counter to be sure everything was ready for Ryan and Arthur's early lunch. They'd promised to come by around eleven fifteen. The thought of seeing Ryan again sent a pleasing little zing through her, though it was Arthur to whom she owed her life. Ryan had texted her an hour ago that Arthur had skipped his breakfast so he'd have plenty of room for an extra helping of fish and chips.

Bea speared her meatball. "I can't help feeling bad for Whitnee. Poor luv, growing up with that daft mum."

"I know, Bea. I feel the same." Talia covered the bowl of Bea's freshly prepared slaw with plastic wrap and slid it into the fridge. "I really wanted her to stay on, but the publicity over her mother's arrest was more than she could face."

Whitnee had long been aware of her mother's obsession with her, she later told the police, but never realized it had turned deadly. The day Whitnee bawled to her mother about Phil's rudeness to her, something inside Connie snapped. She'd waited months for Phil to propose marriage to Whitnee, but after the incident at Lambert's she saw it was never going to be. With her little girl "ruined," the perpetrator had to pay.

Interviews with neighbors had revealed similar—and disturbing—vendettas. It seemed Connie sought revenge for every minor infraction, even going so far as to flatten the bicycle tires of a little boy who accidentally kicked his soccer ball into her scraggly yard.

"Well, at least Whitnee's switching her major to fine arts," Bea said, shaking her head. "All along, it was her mum who coerced her into taking those business classes. Poor girl hated them, but didn't want to disappoint that awful woman." She nibbled a corner of her meatball. "Oh, luvvy, these are marvelous!"

Talia smiled, thrilled that her meatball concoction was, so far, a success. Over the past few days, she'd experimented with a few other "deep-frieds," and was itching to try them out on Ryan and Arthur.

And she was more than grateful that Connie Parker had survived her clash with the bust of Shakespeare, although the woman did suffer a severe concussion. The cleaning fluid Arthur had squirted into her eyes was nontoxic and caused no permanent damage. On Friday morning, sporting a thick bandage and a hard scowl, Connie was indicted for the murders of Phil Turnbull and Brandon "Pug" Terranova.

The door opened and Talia swiveled around, prepared to bestow a dazzling smile on Ryan and Arthur. When she saw who entered, her lips flatlined. "K . . . Kendra," Talia stammered. "What are you doing here?"

Kendra LaPlante tossed back her blond curls and laughed. "Well, isn't that a fine greeting." She tugged off her black leather gloves and stalked over to the counter. "By the way, kudos on nailing Phil's killer, Talia. From all accounts, you were quite the heroine. Or do they say hero these days?"

"Thanks, but I only reacted. Arthur Collins is the real hero."

"Not the way I heard it." Kendra slid her hand into her Coach clutch. "Interesting tidbit for you. It seems a young woman telephoned Always You a few nights after Phil was murdered, pretending to be my assistant."

"I . . ." Talia sputtered.

"This *impersonator*," Kendra barreled on, an amused

twinkle in her eye, "was trying to find out my whereabouts on the night Phil's life was so brutally snuffed."

"Huh, how about that," Talia muttered, admiring the shine on the blue-and-white tiled floor.

"The truth is," Kendra said in a low voice, "I ditched my massage that evening to sneak into the spa's office. My goal was to copy their client records onto a flash drive—a little industrial spying, if you catch my meaning. Well, it seems a little bird tipped off the police that I'd gone missing during my massage, which prompted the spa to view their surveillance films."

A little bird . . .

"You can imagine the fetching picture I made for the hidden camera, attired as I was in my spa towel and unmade-up face."

"Kendra, I . . . don't know what to say."

"Luckily, the spa agreed not to press charges, as long as I never set foot in there again." Kendra gave out a tinkling laugh.

"Wow. That's, um . . ." Talia had no response that wouldn't make her come off like a Nancy Drew wannabe, so she crossed her arms over her blue Lambert's apron and zipped her lips.

"The truth? You actually did me a huge favor. As long as Phil's murder remained unsolved, the life insurance company was balking at paying out. I am pleased to report that I received a check from them yesterday morning, for the full amount of the policy."

"Oh. Well, then . . . congratulations, I guess."

Kendra withdrew two gold-engraved lavender cards from her bag and presented them to Talia. "One for you and one for Bea. When my spa opens next fall—fingers crossed—I'd like to invite each of you to enjoy an all-day luxury treatment, on me."

Bea scuttled around Howie's wheelchair and went over to claim her ticket. "Why, what a lovely gesture," she gushed. "Thank you!"

"Yes, this is very generous of you," Talia agreed. "So, is Aaron going to open the comic book store now?"

"No, and I no longer care." With a curl of one cherry-tinted lip she slipped her gloves back on. "He wants to *draw* comic books, instead. Can you believe such idiocy? Oh, and I'll be selling the lighting shop to the highest bidder, so if you know anyone . . ."

Talia and Bea shook their heads, and with a flip of her hand Kendra was gone.

"She's a strange one," Bea said, and the door opened again.

"Hey, everyone. Did you save any fish and chips for us?"

Talia's insides did a tiny jig at the sound of Ryan's voice. He entered with his arm looped through Arthur's, and for the first time Talia saw the strong resemblance between the two. Strong jaw, slender build, kindness beaming from intelligent gray eyes.

Hugs were exchanged all around, and Talia led them to the table she'd set for them.

"You look wonderful, Talia," Arthur said. His gray eyes were sharp and focused, and Talia knew he was having a good day. "How's the leg?"

"Well, I have a bruise the size of Rhode Island, but at least I didn't break any bones. Connie Parker has one heck of a batting arm."

She was a thief, as well, the police later discovered.

Along with the silver frame and letter opener she'd pilfered from Arthur, a number of other stolen items were found stashed in her cart, including Hannah's pink scarf.

Arthur tensed at the mention of Connie's name, and Talia instantly changed the subject. "Before I serve your fish and chips, would you like to sample some new menu items?"

"I'm game." Ryan's warm gaze lingered on Talia's face, and she felt an odd tingle in her chest.

"Will Bea and Howie be joining us?" Arthur asked.

"No. Very soon we'll be busy with the lunch crowd, so they're going to hold down the fort, so to speak."

Talia was grateful Bea had forced her to stay home the past three days to rest from her ordeal at the Pines. She used the downtime to concoct some new recipes and came up with a few that she thought were keepers.

Over the next half hour, Talia treated her special guests to a selection of deep-fried delights—mini hot dogs dribbled with tangy mustard sauce, dill pickle spears with honey-mustard dip—and, of course, her yummy deep-fried meat-balls. Tina had given her some tips on creating the sauces, but the meatball recipe was her own. All those years she'd watched Nana prepare them had stuck with her. *Thank you, Nana.*

Customers began streaming in for lunch and for takeout orders. Bea and Howie swung right back into their old routine and handled it all with ease. Howie didn't allow his wheelchair to hamper him one iota.

Talia was glad she'd tucked her guests away at a corner table where they could enjoy some privacy. The other diners seemed to glean that a celebration was taking place, and sent head nods and waves in their direction. In spite of all the deep-fried goodies Talia's mother would have claimed "ruined their appetites," Ryan and Arthur each put away a massive helping of fish and chips, along with heaps of mushy peas and slaw.

"That was unbelievable." Ryan grinned and pushed aside his plate. "I don't think I'll be able to eat again for at least a week."

Arthur beamed. "I've never enjoyed such delicious fish and chips." He turned to Talia, his voice cracking with emotion. "Bless you, my dear, for having us as your guests. This has been one of my finest days ever."

Talia leaned down and hugged Arthur, then excused herself for a moment. She returned with a flat package wrapped in hunter-green tissue paper. "Arthur, this is for you," she said, presenting it to him.

Arthur stared at it in surprise, and then peeled the wrapping off a slender volume. "Oh my. 'The Rime of the Ancient Mariner.'"

Talia was proud of her find. She'd scoured the Internet to locate the perfect edition, and this one had wonderful illustrations. "I'm glad you like it, Arthur."

Arthur turned the pages gently, and his eyes brimmed with tears. "I can't imagine a more perfect gift," he said. "Thank you, Talia."

Talia could still hear Arthur, brilliant and fearless, flinging the lines from the poem at a bewildered Connie Parker. She smiled, and Ryan winked at her. With his dark curls, rimless glasses, and inquisitive gray gaze, he made quite the pleasing picture.

Ryan caught her staring at him, and she felt heat rush into her cheeks. She thought over the events of the past few days.

A killer had been caught—that was a biggie.

Suzy had popped in to see Bea late on Friday. Talia was sorry she'd missed her, especially since Suzy had delivered some exciting news. By next summer she'd be towing a baby girl in her wake, and she and her husband were ecstatic.

Jill had undergone a startling change. With the weight of her personal albatross lifted from her shoulders, she realized she didn't want to lose Gerry. The two were planning a month-long European vacation together. Talia hoped it would help them heal. Jill had been vastly relieved when the police quietly returned her bracelet to her. With the killer identified, they no longer needed it as evidence.

Talia had chosen not to report Cliff's actions to the police. She'd recruited her dad to talk to him privately, and Cliff agreed to seek help. The loan shark had vanished, at least for now, but Talia suspected he'd be back. Her dad persuaded Cliff to work with the police if the man ever turned up again.

Ryan leaned forward and touched his dad's arm. "What do you say, Dad, shall we give these nice people a break and head back to the Pines?"

Arthur's face fell, but he nodded his assent. "Yes. It wouldn't be fair to wear out our welcome, would it?"

"Ryan," Talia said. "I've asked my mom and dad to stop by Lambert's after closing time this evening for some cider and snacks. I have an announcement to make, and it involves Bea and Howie. I'd love it if you and Arthur could join us."

She'd also texted Rachel an invitation, but hadn't heard from her yet. Her best friend was still avoiding her, and Talia didn't know why.

Arthur's face lit up. "Can we, Ryan?"

Ryan laughed. "Are you sure we won't be in the way?"

"You won't be in the way."

"Then it's a date," Ryan said. "I mean, you know . . ."

Talia smiled. "See you at seven."

Talia originally planned to make the announcement wearing a grease-stained Lambert's apron and her favorite pair of Keds. Looking around, however, she was grateful she'd opted for the denim-blue textured sweater she'd bought three months ago before she left her job in Boston. The paisley infinity scarf Nana had given her two Christmases ago, along with her aquamarine earrings, complemented it perfectly.

Talia's gaze skimmed the faces of the group gathered before her.

Mom and Dad, holding hands beneath the table, their expressions a combination of curiosity and concern.

Bea and Howie, their bubbly smiles dancing on their faces in anticipation of Talia's announcement.

And her new friends, Arthur and Ryan, who she hoped would continue to be a part of her life.

Rachel still hadn't called or texted her. Talia didn't know if she was more hurt by the snub or angry at Rachel's insensitivity, but she refused to allow it to tarnish her plans for the evening.

"I don't want to keep you in suspense any longer," Talia said, rising from her seat. "Mom, Dad, I know you've probably guessed why we're here, but this makes it official." She held aloft her steaming mug of hot mulled cider. "You are looking at the future proprietor of Lambert's Fish and Chips."

Cries of joy rose from the table. Her mom and dad rushed

over to hug her while Ryan pumped his fist and Arthur clapped his applause.

"When will it happen?" her mom pressed. "Will you still call it Lambert's? Who's going to work for you? How—"

Talia laughed. "One thing at a time, Mom. December first is the official takeover date, but we'll be scrambling to get ready for the transfer of ownership during the whole month of November. As for the name . . ."

"I told her she needs to give it a whole new name," Bea insisted. "Especially if she's going to be serving all those lovely new creations!"

"So I'm up for suggestions," Talia said. "I haven't done any hiring yet, but that's in the works."

"Bea . . . Howie, what will you two do?" Talia's dad asked.

Bea giggled like a teenager. "We're going to spend the winter in Myrtle Beach," she said. "After that, who knows? If we like what we find, we might just settle there for good."

Talia stared at the pair. "But . . . I thought that was your retirement dream!"

"Oh, it was," Howie said. "But the thought of leaving the Berkshires . . ." He shrugged. "We'll take it one step at a time."

Talia knew she was being selfish, but part of her—a huge part—hoped they hated it there and came back. She looked over at her folks and smiled. "Mom, Dad, is it okay if I bunk with you for a while? Until I find an apartment I can swing on my own?"

Her mother and father looked at each other for an uncomfortably long moment. Then Talia's mom said, "No."

Bea rose from her chair "Whaaa . . . ?"

"I can't?" Talia squeaked.

"That's correct," Natalie Marby said, sounding more like a school principal than a loving mom. "Two days ago, I received an offer on your Nana's house." She sniffed. "A generous one, I might add. I immediately called the twins, and we all came to the same conclusion." She reached over and took her daughter's hand. "Talia, we turned down the offer. We want you to have the house."

Talia felt her heart leap. "But, Mom, even with today's rates I can't afford a mortgage on my own."

"Maybe not, but you can afford the deal we're offering. The girls and I are going to take back a zero-interest mortgage. Your Aunt Jennie did the math, and she believes you can make it work. More important, your nana's bungalow will stay in the family, as it should."

"Oh, Mom. You know you still have to pay the broker's commission, right?"

Her mom smiled. "We do, but we explained the circumstances and she's agreed to lower her commission to three percent. We'll shave the savings off the sale price."

Hugs were exchanged all around, and Talia caught Ryan grinning at her. A loud bang at the entrance made them all turn around, and the door flew open.

"Sorry we're late," Rachel said, striding over to their table. Behind her was a sheepish-looking Derek Westlake, looking handsome in a navy pullover and bun-hugging jeans. He nodded at everyone, blushing when he caught Talia's stare.

"You? And *Derek*?" Talia said. "But—"

"Sorry I couldn't tell you before, Tal." Rachel's smile was apologetic. "With Bea under suspicion and Derek involved in the case, I had to lie low for a bit."

A memory jolted Talia. The night Suzy was following them, Rachel had started to call the police. She'd flicked on her Bluetooth and said the word *top* before she disconnected. She'd been calling Derek directly. She'd obviously given his number the voice code Top Cop!

Rachel must have been the "little bird" who told Derek what Talia had learned about Kendra and her massage. No wonder that detective had acted so smug!

BFF code, indeed.

A mischievous gleam in her eye, Rachel conveyed a silent message to Talia: *No worries, what happened in Turnbull's office stays in Turnbull's office.*

Talia grinned. There was so much she wanted to ask her friend, but there'd be time for that later. For now, enjoying the company of the people she cared for most was all that mattered.

Derek moved toward Bea. "For the record, Bea, I never thought you killed Turnbull. But the whitefish on the knife threw us all, big time."

Bea waved a hand at him. "No hard feelings, copper."

Derek laughed, and he and Rachel pulled up chairs and helped themselves to hot mulled cider. Talia left everyone chattering and laughing and headed into the kitchen. Peggy at the bakery had given her a loaf of chunky apple-cinnamon bread, and Talia had sliced a slab of it into triangular-shaped wedges. One at a time, she swirled each wedge into the sweet batter she'd prepared and lowered them into the fryer. When they were crisp and golden she drained them, dusted them with powdered sugar, and placed them on a serving platter. Noses twitched with anticipated pleasure as she delivered them to her guests.

"I have something I want you all to try," Talia said. "If you like them, I might start offering them as a seasonal item."

A sea of hands reached into the platter, and it was soon clear from the moans of pleasure that everyone loved the fried apple-cinnamon bread wedges.

"I've got enough batter for one more wedge," Talia said, when the platter was empty. "Anyone?"

All but Ryan declined. "Sure," he said. "Go ahead and fry me a sliver."

"Fry me a sliver," Talia repeated slowly. "I like it!" In her mind's eye, she pictured the new sign, hanging in front of the eatery.

When everyone was through and they rose to leave, Talia's mom pulled her aside. "Honey, this came in the mail for you today." She winced. "I didn't know what was inside, and I didn't want to spoil your evening by giving it to you sooner."

Mystified, Talia took the legal-sized envelope from her mom. The return address was Chet's. Heart pounding, she opened it. Inside was a sheet of paper folded around a check.

Hey, Talia. Here's a check for your half of the furniture. Courtney hated it, so I sold it to my boss, who wanted it for his kid's new condo on the wharf. Wishing you the best, now and always. Chet.

The check was generous, more than half what she'd contributed to the cost of the furniture. It was almost enough to make a down payment on the bungalow.

Talia kissed her mother's perfumed cheek. "Don't worry, Mom, it's good news. Now why don't you and Dad come home with me and I'll introduce you to my new cat."

RECIPES

BEA'S COLESLAW

½ head of green cabbage, shredded
½ head of red cabbage, shredded
2 medium carrots, shredded
1 large shallot, diced
½ cup mayonnaise
¼ cup sour cream
1 tsp. white sugar
1 tbs. chipotle paste
2 tsp. salt
Finely ground black pepper (to taste, about ¼ tsp.)

Using a box grater or food processor, shred the cabbage and place it into a colander. Sprinkle the salt over the cabbage and combine, then place a plate over the cabbage and weight it with a large can of tomatoes or something of similar weight. Place the colander into a bowl and refrigerate for an hour. This will allow the excess water to drain.

In the meantime, prepare the dressing, whisking together the diced shallot, mayonnaise, sour cream, white sugar, chipotle paste, and ground black pepper.

Drain and rinse cabbage and dry thoroughly with paper towels. Combine cabbage and carrots. Add the dressing a little at a time until you've reach your desired consistency. Chill before serving.

~Serves 8 to 10~

TALIA'S DEEP-FRIED PICKLE SPEARS WITH HONEY-MUSTARD SAUCE

Ingredients for pickles:
   Vegetable oil for frying
   ½ cup all-purpose flour
   2 eggs, beaten
   ½ cup cornmeal
   ½ tsp. of cayenne pepper
   Pinch of salt
   16-oz. jar kosher spear pickles, or deli pickles (quartered)

In a heavy pot or Dutch oven, heat 2 inches of oil to 350° (test with a candy thermometer). Place flour in one bowl, beaten eggs in another bowl, and cornmeal in a third bowl. Blend the salt and cayenne pepper into the cornmeal.

Dip the pickles first in the flour, shaking off the excess; dip into the beaten egg, then dredge in the cornmeal mixture to coat. Once the pickles are coated, fry them in small batches for about 30 seconds or until golden brown. Using a slotted spoon, transfer fried pickles to a plate lined with paper towels to drain. Serve while hot with the honey-mustard dipping sauce.

To prepare the honey-mustard sauce, stir together the following ingredients:

¼ cup Dijon mustard
¼ cup mayonnaise
2 tbs. honey
¼ tsp. lemon juice
Pinch of black pepper